Neither the Time
Nor the Place

Jack Schultz

Neither the Time Nor the Place is a work of fiction. Names, characters, and incidents are used in a fictitious context. As noted under Comments and Acknowledgments, however, a few characters have been adapted from real-life and two incidents have factual bases

Copyright © 2004 by Jack Schultz

All rights reserved, including the right to reproduce this book or portions thereof in any form. For information contact Millstone Publishing; 66 Chaplin St; Chaplin, CT 06235-2302

ISBN: 0-9664159-2-2

First printing December 2004

Cover illustration by Karen Castaldi

Cover design by Oxford Colour

Editor: Roberta J. Buland

Printed in the United States of America

Individual orders of this book and author signed copies may be obtained by sending a check for $13.00 to Millstone Publishing; 66 Chaplin St.; Chaplin, CT 06235. Connecticut residents please add $ .78 for sales tax. Millstone Publishing will cover the cost of shipping.

Discounts are available for purchase of more than one copy. For details call 860-455-9062; fax 860-455-0574 or write to the above address.

1

We spent most of the afternoon cross-country skiing in the Yale Forest behind Annette's place. Since she was familiar with the trails and was the better skier, she took the lead. I had to stop occasionally to catch my breath and wipe the sweat from my forehead—and watch Annette as her lithe body and rhythmic movements increased the distance between us. By late afternoon, we emerged from the shadows of the tall, open pines into a scattering of birch saplings at the edge of a field where the sinking sun was now low enough to produce a glare from the bright snow. We were on our way home—less than a mile from Annette's house—when she suddenly stopped. "You hear that, Paul? It sounded like a gunshot. The hunting season's over, isn't it?"

"Yes, by at least a month. Did it come from your property?"

"I don't know," Annette said, "it could've come from Lynn's. They own the land next to Aunt Lettie's." During a brief rest, she had explained that the property had belonged to her Aunt Lettie and Uncle Matt. He was older than she and had died ten years ago; Aunt Lettie died last year at the age of 82. Annette said that three years ago she left her failed marriage and moved in with her elderly aunt to help her during her final years. She paused a moment before mentioning her *failed marriage* like she did not know what to call it or did not know whether to tell me about it.

Annette dug in her ski poles and started off again. As we left the Yale property, the trail followed a collapsed stone wall. Annette stopped and, gesturing with her ski pole called back to me, "That's the Lynn's field over there. This property includes the woods on this side of the wall and about half of that field. If you look carefully you can see the wire fence marking the boundary out in the field; Nathan leaves the gate open in the winter so the deer can go back and forth without having to jump the fence."

After a few hundred yards, Annette stopped again. When I caught up to her, she said, "Look at this, Paul," pointing at deer tracks from the open field that crossed the wall and trailed off into the woods. It looked like the animal had dragged itself over the wall but had paused long enough to leave patches of blood on the stones and snow. She started to follow the track while I rested and divided my attention between watching her and visually following the deer path back from where it had crossed the field. Some distance beyond, where the track disappeared in the fading twilight, a small house was visible. I assumed it was the Lynn's home.

I turned my attention back to Annette, who even after breaking trail over fresh snow for several hours was still gliding effortlessly following the deer track. I was glad she had volunteered to take the lead during our hike; from that position, she could not see how much I struggled to keep up with her. My cross-country skiing would best be described as a lot of pushing and shoving for each small gain forward. Along with this lack of skill my hip was starting to hurt. Although the one the army had installed for me toward the end of the Vietnam War was supposed to be state of the art, it certainly was not as good as the original. "Keep it well exercised," the therapist told me; "walk and cross-country ski." As I rested, I puzzled over how Annette, who is so slight, is still able to deliver such powerful thrusts and maintain such stamina. When I first met her, I thought of her as fragile. I was obviously wrong.

Annette's plan for the afternoon, which we had by now nearly completed, was to ski up one side of her 40 acres, make a large circle through the Yale Forest, return down the other side of the property and arrive back at the house before dark. Reflecting on the forest we traveled through today, I was reminded of why I moved to this largely unsettled corner of northeastern Connecticut. Its solitude had appealed to me; it was what I had sought after living in two large cities and experiencing the burnout of that frenzied pace. What I had not anticipated was falling for Annette even before I really knew her and before she began to reveal the complexities of her life and inner self. In fact, I had not thought about having a close relationship for many years, not after being burned so badly by the last one.

As I watched Annette following the deer track, I wondered why she had invited me on this excursion; we hardly knew each other at the time. Once a week she had passed through the newsroom to drop off her article on gardening. She always said, "Hi Paul," as she went by my desk. The first time she came in, she was wearing wire-rimmed glasses; a full, ankle-length skirt; and a blouse with long puffy sleeves. I thought she was a flower child left over from the 1960s. Later, I learned she worked at Old Sturbridge Village in Massachusetts and did not always change out of her work clothes before stopping at the news office. Her job in the historic village was as an interpreter of nineteenth-century life and crafts.

The story of how I happened to be following Annette through the woods had its beginning in the *Chronicle* parking lot. I was getting into my car to go on an assignment when Annette pulled into the space next to me. She disembarked from her aging Subaru, faded yellow with one gray fender. The conversation went something like this, "Paul, does that rack on your car roof mean you're a skier?" A slight smile at the corner of her lips imparted an impish quality to the question.

I was not prepared for the rush of blood I felt. I laughed, a little embarrassed, and said, "I have some cross-country skis but they travel better on the car than on my feet. I've only been on them three times."

"The real question is, were you better at it the third time than the first?" Her grin broadened and I could see that her face had a serene, almost radiant quality to it.

"You know, Annette, I'm glad you brought that up; I believe I was better the third time out. This gives me new hope. How about you, you ever try it?" I said jabbing my thumb in the direction of the ski rack.

"You mean being strapped to a ski rack on top of a car?" she laughed and swirled her long skirt slightly in an intriguing manner.

Before I could respond, she said, "There are ski trails in back of where I live. They hook up with miles of trails in the Yale Forest and adjacent state land. I explore them a little at a time hoping to build enough stamina and familiarity with the trails to take a real hike some day without getting lost. You want to try them some time?"

Was Annette asking me for a date? Was I really ready to spend time in the company of a woman I had already discovered could so easily stir my emotions? I found myself agreeing and arranging a time to go skiing with her before my hesitant mind could engage my negative question. Immediately, I was flooded with the anticipation of getting to know her. After all, I chided myself; I have had very few nineteenth-century interpreters in my life. So, here I was, exhausted and gasping for air while Annette glided along searching for the wounded deer. She had gone a couple of hundred feet when she yelled excitedly, "Here it is, Paul."

When I joined her, she was standing next to the deer gently poking at it with a ski pole. "It looks dead," she said. The young buck, a spike horn, had fallen, and apparently, in an effort to regain its footing, churned up a mixture of blood and snow around it before it died.

"So, what do we do now?" Annette asked.

"It's on your land, isn't it? Apples from your neighbor's tree that fall on your side of the fence belong to you, so I guess you could take it home and eat it."

I thought I was teasing her but she said, "Do you know how to dress one of these things and turn it into steak?"

I was surprised Annette was not squeamish about the dead animal. Also, she did not seem bothered that someone had shot and wounded a deer out of season or that it came over on her land and died. I could not decide if she was joking about lugging the deer home and eating it, or if she was seriously considering it. When I did not answer immediately, she pulled off her yellow ski hat and looked at me, her face radiant with the excitement of the adventure; her blue eyes sparkled while her long, light-brown hair was teased by the breeze. I found it hard to believe that Annette is 39—but that is what she had told me. I began to explain how limited my butchering skills are, but stopped when I heard a tractor coming toward us from across the field.

Annette said, "That has to be Mr. Lynn. His wife, Harriet, has frequently told me his tractor is his legs."

"Mr. Lynn can't walk?"

"He can walk but he's 84 years old. He injured one leg in an industrial accident over 30 years ago when a hot, acid cleaning solution spilled on his leg. Apparently gangrene set in. Recently I took him and his wife to the V. A. Hospital for his annual physical exam. I had driven him there several times before. On this last visit, while we were walking down the hallway, we encountered a doctor who was coming toward us. Mr. Lynn walked up to him, put his hand on the doctor's arm and asked in his raspy, cigar hacking voice, 'You 'member me? I'm Nathan Lynn. See that leg?' he said, giving it a slap. 'That's the leg you wanted to cut off 30 years ago. I wouldn't let you and you can see I'm still walking on it.' Mr. Lynn was clearly pleased with how much smarter he was than the doctor."

When I laughed, Annette said, "Self-righteous is Mr. Lynn's middle name."

"How did the doctor respond?"

"He was polite; he quietly said, 'Congratulations,' and went on. I'm sure he didn't remember Mr. Lynn from so long ago."

"What will Mr. Lynn do about the deer? He won't be able to drive his tractor over the wall to get to it."

"I don't know," Annette said, "Let's duck behind these hemlocks and see what he does." She was still excited about our adventure. It was exciting to be near Annette; her enthusiasm and zest for life were contagious.

Mr. Lynn stopped at the wall, shut off the engine and climbed to the ground, favoring his bad leg. Then, he pulled a rifle out from next to the seat of the tractor and limped over to the wall. He paused briefly to study our ski tracks on the other side. I whispered to Annette, "Maybe we should forget about the venison, he's got us out gunned."

"Let's wait 'till he finds the deer so we can see how he deals with it," she said.

By the time Mr. Lynn limped along the deer tracks to where the deer lay, my feet were starting to get cold; but Annette did not look like she was ready to leave yet.

Mr. Lynn studied our departing ski tracks and, then apparently convinced that whoever made the tracks was no longer around, he took a short piece of rope from his mackinaw pocket and tied it around the deer's neck. With the rope over his shoulder, he leaned forward pulling the load, one hand on the rope, the other holding his rifle. The deer barely moved. After he had struggled for several minutes and progressed less than eight feet, Annette said, "Let's help him." Without waiting for me to respond, she swished off.

Nathan did not hear her approach until she was quite close. When he looked up, he smiled and seemed a little embarrassed. I suppose being caught on someone else's property with a freshly killed deer out of season would be cause for embarrassment. "Oh, it's you, thought so when I saw ski tracks all over the place."

Annette cheerfully said, "Hi, Mr. Lynn, I see you got one."

"Yes, you know, hard winter like this, these deer come up from the woods—eat my fruit trees and anything else they can find to chew on. Too many damn deer now that people don't hunt much anymore. 'Course, those I shoot don't go to waste. Venison along with what Harriet freezes and cans from the garden pretty much gets us through the winter." He obviously took great pride in his lifestyle and would have continued; but I had joined Annette before the conversation started and Annette was waiting for Mr. Lynn to stop talking so she could introduce me to him. Finally, he slowed down to remove a piece of cigar that must have been lodged in his teeth. She said, "Mr. Lynn, I'd like you to meet my friend, Paul Hurst."

I was surprised that Nathan walked the 15 feet or so over to where I was planted in my skis so we could shake hands. His hand was so cold, lean and bony that I wondered how he was able to produce such a firm grip. In fact, now that he was up close, I could see that everything about him was lean: his face, his wrists and the rack of bones that supported his mackinaw all seemed to have remarkably little flesh covering them. The deer weighed more than he did. Nathan studied me carefully, and then repeated my name, "Paul Hurst," he said. "You're the paper man aren't you?"

"Yes, I'm a reporter for the *Chronicle*."

"I noticed your name on that article last week 'bout that ruckus up at Trish's involving Todd Bowen."

Annette quickly asked, "Mr. Lynn, can we give you a hand with the deer?"

Initially, I assumed Annette's interruption was out of concern that Nathan's comment might expand into a lengthy conversation; but later I wondered if she was specifically heading off discussion of Todd Bowen. Maybe she knows something about this rascal she would rather I did not find out.

"You know I don't need help getting my deer home," he said. After a brief pause he continued. "But it's almost dark. I wouldn't want to get stuck in a low spot I couldn't see 'cause of poor light and have to walk home without my tractor."

I was sorry Annette had volunteered to help Mr. Lynn with his illegal activity, especially with all the evidence spelled out so clearly in the snow. But Annette felt the need to help him, and I could not think of a tactful way to avoid it. She was already unfastening her spring binders, so I joined her. We took the rope and pulled the deer back to the wall, lifted it over and deposited it in the bucket of Mr. Lynn's tractor. The old man had trailed along behind providing us with a steady flow of advice even though we were too far ahead of him to hear what he was saying.

While we waited for Mr. Lynn to catch up, Annette apologized for getting me into the situation. She explained that for the past two years she had been worried that the Lynns would not survive the winter. They used to drive to South Carolina in November and stay the winter in a house trailer parked in the backyard of Mrs. Lynn's sister. For the last two seasons, though, when fall arrived they loaded the car and got ready to go, but for various reasons delayed their departure until the snow came. Then they were reluctant to risk the drive. "Would you believe," Annette said, "that, at the age of 82, he was still driving from Connecticut to South Carolina without stopping overnight?"

I shook my head in disbelief and asked if they took turns driving.

"Mrs. Lynn doesn't drive; she says that once Nathan gets started it's easier to keep going than it is to stop overnight. I'd guess they parked and napped in the car. Whatever they did it was probably to save money. Mr. Lynn is quite thrifty. They are both remarkably skilled at living on very little. I'm sure they would never accept financial help from the outside."

The old man climbed over the wall and stood breathing heavily for a moment before walking over to look at the deer in the bucket. When he saw it, he shook his head up and down, apparently satisfied although his strong, independent nature did not easily express gratitude. "Guess I can take it from here," he said. We watched him return his rifle to its place next to the seat of the tractor and climb up. Before he started the engine he looked squarely at me and said, "That article you wrote about the happenings up at Four Corners, there's a heck of a lot more to that story than you wrote." Before I could respond, he started the engine. After backing away from the wall, he waved and turned the tractor toward home.

We watched until it looked like he was moving along all right then went back for our skis. While we attached our spring binders, Annette was quiet. I hoped I had not done anything to displease her but I didn't know her well enough to read her moods. Finally, I asked if she was worried about finding our way back in the dark.

"No," she replied, "I've been over this trail quite a few times; I don't think I'll have any trouble. Anyway it's not far and we still have a little light. If I seem worried, I suppose it's because talking with Nathan sets me fretting about Mrs. Lynn. She's such a fine, gentle person, I'm afraid that at 79 she's become too frail to continue the harsh life he insists they lead. She was a schoolteacher and is clearly the intelligent one; but he's strong-minded. She always defers to him."

Annette led us back to the trail. From then on all I heard was the swish of our skis until we reached her yard where we were greeted by a persistent "Baa, Baa."

Annette called out in a lilting, motherly voice, "OK, babies, I'm coming, soon's I can." While she removed her skis, she casually commented, "I have a pot of beans in the oven; why don't you get out of your ski boots and join me? We'll have to feed the sheep first, though."

Annette disappeared into the house and immediately the yard was flooded with light. Before I had my shoes tied, she was standing next to my car wearing a pair of pull-on boots. We walked toward the baaing sounds, which were coming from a small barn 100 feet behind the house. Inside were two woolly sheep that ran up to the railing separating them from the area where firewood, hay, grain and tools were stored. Annette introduced me to her eight-year-old twins, Lily and Ebony. Then she poured grain into their feeders and tossed in some hay. On the way back to the house she said, "The sheep were one of Aunt Lettie's projects. She was a weaver for many years. By the time I arrived, her health had deteriorated to a point where she was ready to turn the project over to me–sheep, spinning wheel, loom and all."

"How did you know what to do with all of that? I would think it would take years to learn even the rudiments of those skills." I tried to picture Annette draped in her long skirts spinning and weaving.

"The rudiments one can pick up fairly fast but to become anything close to a master weaver takes time. I have a ways to go on that. As for keeping sheep alive, they let you know if you're not doing it right. I had spent most summers with Aunt Lettie when I was a schoolgirl. She let me participate in her projects; I was surprised at how much I remembered from those early days."

"Is spinning and weaving what you're in charge of at Sturbridge?"

"I don't feel like I'm in charge of anything in my life, but spinning and weaving are crafts I demonstrate at the

Village." Her tone caught me by surprise. I wondered what she meant about not being in charge of her life, but she seemed reticent about opening up to me.

We hung our coats on wooden pegs in the entryway near where Annette earlier had parked her skis and boots. The aroma of baked beans greeted us as we entered the kitchen. It was a strange house; the outside was early 1900s Victorian with faded yellow wood siding and a hexagonal turret; but the inside, for the most part, was fairly modern. I must have been gawking, because when I looked at Annette, she was smiling and waiting for me to absorb it all. I told her, "I can't decide if this is an old house that's been updated a century or two, or a new house that's been built to look old."

"Maybe if you have a beer it will help you figure it out." She removed two dark bottles from a modern refrigerator and poured the amber liquid into hand crafted pottery mugs.

"These are nice. Did you make them?"

"Yes, they are OK, but pottery isn't my strong suit. Sometimes I fill in for the regular interpreter when he's off. He's really good but I don't think he'll stay much longer. His wife is going to have a baby, and without her salary, Elmer is going to have to get a better paying job."

I wondered how Annette could support this huge house with the same kind of job that Elmer's family could not live on. As I sipped, I watched her rejuvenate the fire in a fireplace large enough for a person to stand in. It was beautiful, but it looked out of place in the modern kitchen with its vinyl floor, electric stove, refrigerator and dishwasher. The bricks of the fireplace were small and irregular; they must have been made by hand many years ago. "You stole that from work," I teased.

"The fireplace? Sturbridge Village doesn't have any as old and large as this. It was rescued from an early 1700s colonial that was being demolished." She was obviously still entertained by my reaction to the house and was providing limited information, only enough to sustain my curiosity. The only things in the kitchen that complemented the fireplace were a large antique loom and a spinning wheel.

The fire had caught nicely, and its warmth along with the beer revived my tired muscles. As Annette talked about the spinning wheel, the flickering light from the fire reflected off her face giving her a soft glow. She was so lovely I had to suppress an urge to grab her and hold her to me. I thought my arousal must show, but then I decided not since next Annette led me off into the adjacent room, the dining room. Like the kitchen, it was larger than what was typically seen in Victorian homes. One corner of the room was drawn out into a circle—well, actually a hexagon with four windows. It served as a small greenhouse for a variety of plants. I asked Annette, "Is this the lower part of that turret-like structure I saw from the road?"

"Yes, it is a turret. It extends from ground level up to slightly above the roofline; it has a cone-shaped roof of its own. On the second floor, it forms one corner of Aunt Lettie's bedroom. Uncle Matt had a window seat built for her. She used to sit for hours in the sun thinking about the old days. In her later years, the past became more important to her than the present. She especially enjoyed thinking about old boyfriends. She was a very attractive woman and apparently enjoyed the attention of men when she was young."

"I would imagine that could have bothered Uncle Matt."

"Oh, yes. He apparently was quite jealous; she told me she had to be careful not to be flirtatious with other men after they were married—or at least not in his company. It must have been difficult for her, though; flirting was such a large part of her. She said Uncle Matt was proud to have a beautiful blonde wife, one that other men couldn't help staring at; but he felt as possessive about her as he did his Cadillac—he wouldn't let anyone else near that either."

"So you don't think she ever cheated on him?"

"No, at least I would be surprised if she had. I think Aunt Lettie's rich memories were developed before she married Uncle Matt. She never admitted it, but I think she had an intimate relationship with a man who later married her best friend shortly after she married Uncle Matt. I was old enough to be aware that even in Aunt Lettie's later years, when she entered a room, there were men who seemed to forget about their wives; he was one of them. She spoke fondly of him in her later years along with several others that occupied her mind while there in her sunny corner."

I asked Annette if Uncle Matt had built her this elegant house to keep her from wandering. She said, "Sort of, but it's a little more complicated than that. I had the impression he bought her whatever she wanted—anything to make her happy, especially if it had a tendency to keep her home. He didn't seem to want her socializing in his absence. It wasn't as though she was held captive; but as an older man, he preferred to have his young wife spending her time weaving and making pasta by hand than shopping or consorting with who knows. That big fireplace in the kitchen was a gift to buy her off after she discovered a pack of condoms in Uncle Matt's Cadillac. He tried to tell her he had loaned the car to a friend, Joe Esposito, but she knew better than that. In one of her recurring tantrums, she took a knife and slashed up the leather upholstery in his car. She kicked him out of her bedroom and barely spoke to him for a long time. Aunt Lettie told me she was so upset about it she didn't do much of anything except read to try to keep her mind off what happened. One day Uncle Matt told her, 'There will be some workmen coming in a few days; I want you to go to Ohio and spend some time with Erma. I'll let you know when to come back.' Erma was my mother; I was less than a year old at the time. That is when the fireplace was built. She had wanted an early American fireplace when the house was initially built, but Uncle Matt talked her out of it—not appropriate for a Victorian house, he argued. She had given in that time around, not because Uncle Matt was any authority on architecture, but because she knew he was anxious to get out of Boston and didn't want to lose any time redrafting plans for the house."

"With their rocky relationship, wasn't it a surprise that Uncle Matt trusted her to come back from Ohio?"

"Aunt Lettie and Uncle Matt were raised Catholic. He knew that, if she became balky about returning, my sanctimonious mother would insist that she 'get her ass' back to Connecticut. In fact, Aunt Lettie said that when she whined about Uncle Matt's infidelity, my mother told her, 'You married a shyster lawyer. What did you expect? That's the way they are. They marry beautiful blonde women for showpieces; and afterward, they think it's still their God given right to romp with as many women as they please. But, don't you ever look at another man,' Mom told her, 'or you'll get the tar beat out of you.' Anyway, after a couple of months, Uncle Matt called and Aunt Lettie returned home. I think she was quite ready; she gave me the impression that she had had enough of my mother's advice."

"Does your mother still give you advice?"

"I'm sure she would if we were still in contact."

I did not know if that meant her mother was dead or that they had had a falling out and no longer communicated with each other. Rather than volunteer an explanation, Annette returned to her story. She said, "When Uncle Matt picked Aunt Lettie up at the airport, she knew immediately he was pleased about something. She pestered him all the way home from the airport trying to find out what it was; but he wouldn't tell her. Well, if you have ever been inside an original Victorian house, that's what this was originally like, made up of many small rooms. You can imagine Aunt Lettie's surprise when she walked in and found that the entire downstairs had been renovated with these spacious rooms, which included a modern kitchen and a fireplace from the eighteenth-century."

When Annette and I returned to the kitchen, she stoked the fire and then said, "I have to let this burn down a little and develop more hot coals before we cook on it."

"What happened to the beans you promised me?"

"This fire is for hot dogs. The beans are already cooked," she said pointing at the small, black steel door in the brick wall of the fireplace. "They're in there." Then she pulled a bowl of dip from the refrigerator and set out some chips. "This will hold us," she said.

When the fire was ready, Annette took a package of hot dogs from the refrigerator and handed me two wrought-iron forks that had been hanging from a hook on the fireplace wall. I took the hint and began testing my cooking skills in the fireplace. It was no different from broiling hot dogs over an open fire, which I had done many times before, except that now I was distracted by my compulsion to look at Annette. She was so beautiful I suppose I kept looking at her to reassure myself it was true. Why had I not paid more attention to her when she walked by my desk in the newsroom? Am I such a nerd that I am too buried in my work to notice a lovely woman passing by even when she says, "Hi Paul"? No, definitely not. She hides her attractiveness when she travels in the outer world and today turned it on just for me. I was a little embarrassed when she caught me looking at her but she did not seem to mind—at least she didn't tell me to pay attention to my cooking even though I had held one of the hot dogs in the flame long enough to have it turn black and split full length.

2

By the end of dinner, our conversation had become superficial. I traced back to where it began to lag and realized that it was when I tried to explain Nathan's criticism of my Todd Bowen article. I told Annette my editor had cropped it down to one-fourth of its original size and that important things had been lost. But, instead of asking what was lost she just nodded and changed the subject. I had a feeling she did not want to discuss Todd Bowen and was trying to bury him under layers of small talk. I have never been good at superficial conversation, so I could not contribute much to it. Mostly she was telling me about visitors she had met while working at the Village—none of them interesting enough to rise above what was occupying my mind. By the time we were sipping coffee, she gave up and said, "This isn't the direction I had hoped our evening would take."

I did not know what she had been hoping for; I was, in fact, surprised that she had any plans beyond our afternoon of skiing. When I realized she was waiting for me to respond to her comment, I stopped peeling the label off my empty beer bottle and thought more carefully about what she had said. I realized then that our conversation would have been more interesting if I had not left most of it up to her. But, I still wondered what she and Mr. Lynn knew about Todd Bowen. Finally I summoned the nerve to ask her.

Initially, Annette frowned; but then she broke into a smile and said, "You think I've run out of chitchat and now I'm ready to talk, huh? Well, you were not saying anything, so I was just trying to fill in the dead airspace. But as far as Todd is concerned, what is it you're so anxious to find out?"

"Well, for one thing I'm curious about what his neighbors think of him."

"Curious, huh? That's a mild word; it's more like you abandoned me, and except for brief periods, went back to your reporter job."

Her words "abandoned me" were interesting. I wanted to think about them; but right now I was anxious to move ahead on Todd Bowen, so I said, "Annette, I apologize; I can not get Mr. Lynn's comment about Todd Bowen off my mind. But I'm more interested in what you know about Bowen than what Mr. Lynn knows."

"I didn't tell you I know him," Annette declared with indignation. I recoiled a bit, hoping this was not going to put a sour end to what might be developing between us.

Trying to keep the conversation light I said, "Oh, somehow I had the impression you did. Do you know how Mr. Lynn knows him?"

"I have two reasons for not telling you. For one thing, the Lynns are very private—old New England. They would be upset, no, angry if they saw comments they had made to me appear in your paper." I could tell by the rising pitch in Annette's voice that the reporter in me was still killing any romance that I was hoping for. I should have changed the subject. Instead, I said, "Mr. Lynn didn't mind letting me know what he thought of Todd when we were out there in the woods."

"No, but I'm sure he would have regarded that a private conversation. He would be furious if you treated it otherwise."

"And, what is the other reason you won't talk to me about Todd? You said there were two."

"Because I wouldn't want you quoting me in the newspaper over something I told you about Harriet, Nathan and Todd."

"Isn't that the same reason?"

"Yeah, I guess so."

"But not quite, is it? You personally know something about Todd that isn't connected to Mr. and Mrs. Lynn."

She looked at me without answering. I could not tell if she was trying to decide whether to trust me, or if she was about to tell me to go home. I did not want to go home yet, so I said, "Mr. Lynn would've been right, you know. I wouldn't have published something I learned from him in a private conversation without his permission. If you feel you have to be wary of everything you say to me because of my job, you're always going to be uncomfortable around me. All I can do is assure you that whatever you tell me I won't print unless you tell me I can."

"I've never really known a reporter before, I mean not really. I haven't talked much with the other reporters at the *Chronicle* except for a little bit with Beth, but those reporters I see on television, seem pretty aggressive and ruthless."

"Yeah, sometimes it was like that when I worked at the *Cleveland Plain Dealer* and then later for the *Boston Globe*. When you're in competition with reporters from all over the country, being well mannered doesn't usually pay.

It's different, though, working for small town newspapers like the *Chronicle* where the national and international news comes primarily from a wire service and in-house reporters deal primarily with local matters. Since our news comes mainly from tips or contributions provided by people in the community, we have to be careful not to alienate the source."

"How come you left the city and settled here in the wilderness?"

I laughed. I suppose I felt a little silly telling Annette what happened. It seemed like such a personal thing; but after I started it seemed to go all right. I told her that after completing a lengthy and complicated feature article with my editor, Art Richter, we stopped off at a local bar to celebrate. I told Annette, "A few drinks into our little party Art made a comment I thought was so funny I could hardly stop laughing. When I settled down, he said, 'You know Paul, we've worked together for over a year and this is the first time I have heard you laugh out loud, sure, maybe a polite chuckle once in awhile but never a belly shaking guffaw. When you're working on something, which is most of the time, you become so intense and oblivious to your surroundings it's a wonder you're able to find your way home at night.'"

Annette nodded thoughtfully and asked, "Had you realized you were that way?"

"I suppose so, but I didn't concern myself over it until Art mentioned it. Then it occurred to me that if other people saw me that way, too, maybe I should pay more attention to who I am. What I found was that as long as I was in a high intensity job that's how I behaved; so I quit the *Globe* and took up a calmer existence that would give me time to reflect on my own life, write a book, ski and fall for a beautiful woman."

"C'mon, Paul. If your referring to me as the beautiful woman, all I can say is I'm glad you're easily satisfied—but writing a book? Really! How much do you have done?"

"Practically nothing. By the time I had enough material assembled to start putting my first book together, several publications covering the same subject came out; so I shelved mine. I've barely started the new one."

"So, what you're telling me then, is that since you left the city, you have settled down and have really become the nice person I thought you were?"

"Yes, at least I had hoped I was becoming a nice person; but now that my interest in Todd Bowen has come up, you're making me feel unsure of myself. I want you to know, though, I really am trying to be a nice guy."

"OK then," she smiled. "I'll be back in a minute." She opened a door and disappeared behind it. It sounded like she went down to the basement. Maybe Annette was not planning to dismiss me after all. When she returned she was holding a bottle of brandy. "I've never tasted brandy," she said. "Uncle Matt left half a case of it down there; he used to serve it to his business associates from Boston. They would sit here before the fire smoking cigars and sipping this stuff like it was a special gift from God. Aunt Lettie didn't allow cigar smoking in other parts of the house. In this room, smoke is drawn up the fireplace chimney. Uncle Matt's been gone for 10 years. Do you think this stuff's still good?" she asked, handing me the bottle.

"It could be since the bottle hasn't been opened and it was stored in the cool of a basement. Are you sure I'm important enough for something this grand?"

"Oh, I think you'll squeak by now that you've assured me you're trying to be a nice guy. Uncle Matt's friends were important to him; but I wasn't impressed with them." Then she added with a short laugh, "Of course, I was pretty young at that time, maybe 10 to14. On the other hand, my youthful interpretation wasn't that far off; two of his regular guests were later sent to prison on charges of racketeering along with other crimes that often go with it."

"We better drink the brandy before they finish serving their time and come back for it."

"It may not be a laughing matter. But, I really don't know that much about Uncle Matt's friends or business associates. He rarely talked with Aunt Lettie about them and he certainly didn't tell me anything. You open the bottle, Paul, and I'll get Uncle Matt's brandy glasses."

As I drank, it became evident that whatever else there was about Annette's uncle, he had good taste in liquor. Annette seemed more like herself now, open and warm. Before long she said, "OK, Paul, about Todd Bowen. When you and I were in the woods with Mr. Lynn, I interrupted him before he started one of his long rambling stories about Todd and his escapades. Had he continued, he might have told you what Todd was like but at greater length than you would have cared to hear while freezing in the woods. I've heard his collection of Todd Bowen stories several times; Todd isn't the kind of guy to go unnoticed in *the quiet corner* of Connecticut. Mrs. Lynn is afraid of him. I don't know how much you want me to talk about Todd's background; you may already know quite a bit about him. I didn't read your article in the *Chronicle*." She laughed with embarrassment, then added, "I don't subscribe to a newspaper."

"That's O.K., just tell me everything you can remember. I really don't know that much about him. Besides I enjoy hearing you talk."

"That's pure flattery, Paul. For a while I wondered if you were listening to me at all. Anyway, Todd is a single guy around 40 years old. He lives alone in a small apartment above his parents' garage, about 10 miles northeast of the Lynns. Mr. Lynn spends a lot of time on the screened-in porch of their little house; he told me he sees Todd go by now and then. Sometimes he stops to chat. Mr. Lynn said on one occasion when Todd stopped, he smelled like a brewery. Mr. Lynn knew right off that his visitor wanted something more than just talk; it didn't take Todd long to ask if he could borrow $20. When Mr. Lynn tells the story, he raises his voice at this point like he's yelling at Todd. He says, 'You're asking me for money? You—young and able-bodied—asking an 84 year old man for money. You been drinkin', haven't you? And now you're out of beer and come here lookin' to borrow money so you can buy more beer. You've had enough. You get on outta here. Go home and sober up and get a job.'"

"That's pretty heavy stuff, Annette, for an elderly man with so little beef to back it up."

"Yes, it is. Apparently, Mrs. Lynn was in the kitchen at the time listening to their exchange. She never liked Todd, so she hadn't joined them on the porch; but the door to the kitchen was open. She heard it all. She told me about it later, and said she worried that Nathan's outspokenness might bring them trouble. Most people who know Nathan don't take him seriously; but Todd swore at him, called him a 'crazy old son-of-a-bitch' and told him 'he'll get his one day.' The Lynns live only about 30 feet from a main road, along a stretch where no other houses are in sight; their sight; their lives are wide open to foul play. The nearest neighbor, Dr. Malak, an M.D. who practices in Springfield, lives more than half a mile away. Mr. Lynn doesn't hold him in high regard and gives the impression he'd never call him for help. I feel the Lynns are quite vulnerable; I worry a lot about Mrs. Lynn's situation."

I asked Annette if she didn't worry about Mr. Lynn, too. She said, "Well, yes, of course; but since he is so in charge of their lives, my concern for him is in a different category. Besides, it's difficult to feel sympathy for a man who is perpetually self-righteous, negative and insulting."

The brandy had freed Annette's spirit. She was now tossing off her answers lightly without measuring her words. Maybe it was time to risk the question that was gnawing at me, "You ever go out with Todd?"

"You turd," she whispered softly. "How'd you know that? I didn't even tell you I knew him. Why didn't you at least ask me that first?"

"Because it wouldn't have jarred you into calling me a turd. I certainly didn't want to miss that. Besides, the question I asked stunned you into blurting out the truth before you could think up a lie."

"Lie! Why should I lie? You know, you're not only what I just called you, you're a lot of other things, too." She stood up and took a playful jab at my shoulder; I blocked it, stood up and drew her to me. We embraced for a moment; and when she looked up, I kissed her. It was nice and lasted until she felt me becoming aroused then she broke away and said, "I think it would be safer at this time for us to go back to talking about Todd."

"I've lost interest in Todd."

"Yes, I thought so; but maybe you could force yourself to listen? Give me a moment, though, to calm down." She sat back in her chair and took a sip from her glass. It was exciting to see her sexually stimulated. She was so innocently lovely yet sensuous that I could hardly restrain myself; but I knew there would be no point in pursuing my romantic interests further at this time so I sat down and tried to cool off, too.

"OK. Now, about Todd. Once, when I was visiting the Lynns, Todd stopped by. This was before the incident of Todd wanting to borrow money from Mr. Lynn and before the event you reported in the newspaper. Mrs. Lynn introduced me to him as Lettie and Matt Hyde's niece. We sat and chatted for about 20 minutes, most of it consisting of Mr. Lynn complaining about the awful mess the government was making of the country. I could feel Todd's eyes on me as Nathan talked; so, when I got up to leave, I wasn't surprised to hear him announce that he had to be going, too. Just as we reached our cars at the edge of the road, he called over and said, 'Hey, Annette let's swing by Little Eddy's for a beer on the way home.'"

Annette explained that Little Eddy's is a small, local restaurant where you can buy a meal and a drink. "It's kind of a friendly joint," she said. "Anyway, I followed Todd's car to Little Eddy's where we took a booth and ordered a couple of beers and a bag of chips. Todd was pleasant and well-mannered. Our conversation started out with him asking me how I happened to know the Lynns. I explained that the property I live on adjoins the Lynn's in the back."

"Would Todd know how to navigate that tangle of roads off Route 71 to get to your property?"

"I don't know? He told me he was born not far from here, in the house up at Four Corners where his mother and stepfather now live but that he hasn't lived in the area for over 20 years, not until recently. He said that when his mother married Herb Trish eight years ago, her new husband just moved in with her. She owned the house and it was all paid for. Todd said that the Lynns and other local folks often talked to him about neighbors as though he knows them. So, when Mrs. Lynn introduced me to him as Lettie and Matt Hyde's niece, Todd told me that at first he didn't pay any attention to it, but then, half-way through his second beer for some reason the name Matt Hyde started to seem familiar to him. For the rest of the time we were at Little Eddy's, Todd was bothered that he couldn't remember what the name Hyde meant to him."

I asked Annette if Todd tried to jog his memory by asking her questions about her aunt and uncle and she said, "I guess that's what he was doing. First of all, he wanted to know where Lettie and Matt's house is. I reminded him that I already told him the property butts onto the back of the Lynn's land. Next he wanted to know who lives in it now. I told him it doesn't matter because my aunt and uncle are both dead. But, he kept pressing me until I told him I live there as sort of a caretaker." Then she looked concerned and said, "Paul, you think I'm stupid for telling him that, don't you?"

"Todd's questions and your answers were reasonable for two people getting acquainted. It's just that bad guys don't always look and act bad; and after all, he appeared to be a friend of the Lynns."

"Well, I guess he wasn't really. The next time I visited the Lynns, they warned me not to become too friendly with him, that he was just released from prison a year ago after serving less than five years of his sentence for voluntary manslaughter. They said they didn't feel they could say anything to me about him while he was sitting there. By the time they told me, it was already too late."

"When you told him you live in the house as a caretaker, did you tell him you live alone in the house?"

Annette said, "I don't know. I may have. As the conversation continued and we both became comfortable with each other, Todd revealed tidbits about himself he probably wishes he hadn't. I was into my second beer and he was nearly finished with his third—that's when he told me he had served time at Walpole. He said he was released a little over a year ago and lived in Massachusetts for awhile before he came to live in Connecticut. Paul, did you know he had been in prison in Walpole, Massachusetts?"

"Yes that was brought up at the recent hearing over the altercation he had with his stepfather. The police record indicated that Todd earlier had had a fight with one of his guests during a party and shot him."

Annette said, "Todd told me they were both drunk and got into a fight. When it was over, the guy was dead. Todd claimed it was an accident and that the court treated him unfairly. I'm not sure where this happened but it wasn't around here. It was when Todd was in college."

"The crime and trial were probably in Massachusetts, since Todd served time in a Massachusetts prison, Walpole, like you said—the same prison where the famous Joe Esposito served his last days."

"Joe Esposito! He was one of the men who visited Uncle Matt! He was one of Uncle Matt's business associates, one of the two I told you about who was sent to prison. Mr. Esposito was younger than the other men who visited my uncle. He would have been the right age to be Todd's old cell mate who died in prison."

"I don't understand what you're saying, Annette. Did you just make a leap to consider that Esposito was Todd's cell mate and the name Hyde was familiar to Todd because his cell mate, Joe Esposito, had mentioned him?"

"Paul, is that really so far-fetched?"

"Maybe not; but how did you get there so fast?"

"It wasn't a long leap for me with Matt Hyde being my uncle. Besides I've spent more time than you trying to figure out why Todd was interested in me. Already at Little Eddy's I suspected Todd's reason for asking me out for beer had to do with Matt Hyde being my uncle."

"You don't think it was because Todd found you attractive?"

"I did at first. He was pretty flirtatious, you know, attentive, solicitous. I thought it was odd, though, how willing he was to tell me about his cell mate, how Joe told him a lot of stories about the old days and bragged about how he was going to be rich when he got out of prison. It had to do with a stash of money. Todd said he tried to get Joe to tell him more about it, but he wouldn't."

"Did the questions Todd asked you about your uncle make you think he was trying to confirm the Esposito-Hyde connection?"

"I don't think so, at least I couldn't tell from the questions Todd asked. They were more personal, like how many children did Uncle Matt have and did he have a previous wife before Aunt Lettie. I didn't pay much attention to it at the time and thought of it as conversational babble until you brought up Esposito. When Todd was telling me about his cell mate, he said that Joe talked a lot about what a big man he used to be and all the money he had; but that Joe was careful not to give any clues about where this money was. Todd said most of the other cons didn't listen to Joe's mumblings; they thought he was wacko. Todd told me, though, that he always listened carefully to Joe and paid particular attention to names and places he mentioned."

"And you think one of the names Joe mumbled to Todd was Matt Hyde and you now suspect that this stash of money is why Todd took an interest in you and where you live?"

"Yes. Don't you?"

"Maybe, but it seems like a stretch. Esposito is a pretty common name. This may not be the same Esposito that visited Uncle Matt. Besides Todd didn't tell you his cell mate's last name was Esposito, did he?"

"No."

"Todd probably just made up this money story to impress you."

"Yeah, I bet—all part of Todd's charm," she said with a slight laugh.

I could not tell what Annette was thinking, whether she was concerned Todd might appear at her door looking for hidden mob money, or if he appealed to her in some wild way and she was flattered by his interest in her. I have never understood why women are sometimes attracted to bad boys. When I asked Annette what else Todd had to say about the Hyde connection, she shrugged and said, "Nothing. As a matter of fact, based on the way our beer date ended, I thought it bothered him that he told me anything about his being in prison or about his cell mate and hidden riches. He became quiet, sat their swirling the beer remaining in his glass. Then he abruptly announced that he had to go. He would have left me sitting there if I hadn't moved quickly so it would look like we left together."

Now that the subject of Todd was on the table, I had a lot of things I wanted to ask Annette, but she looked tired. Also, when I considered where our conversation had taken us, it was more like an interrogation than a pleasant date. We were left at such a long distance from our earlier romantic surge that I realized returning to it would be unlikely tonight. I thanked her for the splendid afternoon and evening and moved toward the door.

She followed me and said with a smile, "I bet you think I'm tired?"

"I think we both are, but it was really fun. Could we do it again some time?" I asked.

"Yes, I'd like that but I can't promise Mr. Lynn will provide a sideshow for us. The rest of it I can arrange."

I told her I found Nathan interesting but that he was a distraction we could do without. I kissed her good night soaking up as much warmth from her body as she would allow before I stepped out into the cold.

3

I live 20 minutes from Annette's. As I drove home, I barely noticed the road; my mind was filled with things she said, her pretty smile, and how much I cared for her. But, at one point the acerbic taste of Todd Bowen seeped into my mouth and my mind returned to the question of his elderly cell mate. Was there any likelihood he was Joe Esposito? No sooner would I convince myself it could not have been Uncle Matt's old friend than my mind would reflect back to an article I had read about Esposito some years ago while I was still working for the *Boston Globe*. It was a review article prompted by his move to the state prison at Walpole from a federal prison somewhere in the Mid-West. As my concern for Annette's safety mounted, I wished I knew more about what she was dealing with, as well as, how she was coping with it. I reminded myself that Annette had not flatly declared that Todd's pot of gold fantasy had no basis, nor did she tell me it had nothing to do with Uncle Matt. Why had she been so tight-lipped about this issue?

I was anxious to see Annette again but I was not able to reach her by phone. I assumed she was at work during the day. I did not want leave a message on her answering machine asking her to call me back because my evenings were taken up with school board meetings in the surrounding towns. It was budget time, an intense period for the local schools. Polarized opinions and ill-considered comments of parents, teachers and board members all made lively news. Often the meetings ended at a late hour and I had to work into the early morning hours to have my column ready for the afternoon paper the next day. I hoped to see Annette when she turned in her weekly garden column but I was on an assignment the afternoon she dropped it off. Finally, I decided to leave a phone message to let her know how much I enjoyed our time together and that I wanted to see her again.

The following week, Todd's cell mate story was still nagging me. I set aside the things I was working on to search old microfilms from the *Boston Globe* for the article I had read to see if Todd Bowen and Joe Esposito were indeed at Walpole at the same time. It did not take me long to establish that my concern for Annette could have a real basis. I had copied the article and as I finished reading it Annette showed up with her garden column. Her hair was swept up in a bun. In combination with her dated clothes she looked like she had just stepped out of a time machine. When she saw me, her face lit up with a radiant glow that immediately ignited my feelings of passion and affection. It was not the time to show her the Esposito article.

"I missed you when I was in last week," she said with a grin, "but I got the message you left. I looked up the word 'hankering' in the dictionary to be sure I knew what it meant before I expose myself to you again."

"I've never looked it up," I said. "It was an emotional choice. How does your dictionary define it?"

"It says that 'hankering' is a strong or persistent desire. That sounds good to me, Paul, but what exactly did your have in mind?"

"I guess you will just have to 'expose yourself' to me again, if you're going to find out."

"Oh, God. I did say that, didn't I?"

At the next desk, I could see Beth Turbot out of the corner of my eye trying to pinch back a smile so we would not know that she was eavesdropping. Beth is a fellow reporter, tall, 64 years old with fuzzy red hair. She is outspoken and likes to manage things, so I knew it would not be long before she joined our conversation. When Beth could not hold back any longer, imitating disgust she said, "Gees, guys, one date and you're already looking for a motel."

When we stopped laughing I said to Beth, "You know Annette, don't you?"

She said, "I thought I did but I guess not. Anyway, I hope you two have a great time. I'm going to leave now so you two can define this contract in greater detail."

I shook my head as she left. "We better settle this before she comes back and wants to go with us. I don't have any appointments tomorrow and no meetings to attend tomorrow evening."

"That's good, Paul; I'll get someone to sub for me. To begin with, I want to take you over to meet Mrs. Lynn. After that we can do whatever you want to." I noticed I had a tendency to interpret comments, such as her last remark, more optimistically than she may have intended.

In the early afternoon Annette and I left for the Lynn's. I was anxious to hear what Mr. Lynn had to say about Todd. I hoped it would help me assess whether he represents as serious a threat to Annette as I imagined.

The Lynn's house was unconventional. It had no recognizable design and appeared to be constructed of whatever building materials were available at the time—free or at bargain prices. The outside was covered with sheets of composition board, a pressed sawdust material designed for indoor use. Most of the house had been painted apple green a long time ago; now the paint was faded and worn thin. The quarter of the house that was not green was battleship gray. A white, clapboard one-car garage attached to the house opened east toward the road. The construction looked like the garage was the original building and the house was an outgrowth from it. The sun porch at the front of the house faced a large garden area to the south. Mr. Lynn's tractor was parked in the yard not far from the entrance to the house.

 I stepped out of the car into a sharp wind that spoiled an otherwise beautiful day. Before I could get around the car to open Annette's door, she was outside calling, "Hi, Mrs. Lynn." I did not see her at first because I was looking for her in the direction of the house; instead, she was carrying a bucket of water up the gentle slope from the lake—actually a 10-acre pond—75 feet west of the house. She wore only a sweater over the top of a thin dress. The wind pressed her clothes against her, revealing a body frame with even less flesh on it than Mr. Lynn's, which I thought was already testing the minimal limit of what is necessary to sustain life. Her soft gray hair was covered with a hair net, and her feet carried an oversized pair of buckle-on goulashes that looked like the same pair Mr. Lynn had worn when he was deer hunting.

 Mrs. Lynn teetered along a narrow path through the deep snow—not a shoveled path but one formed by successive trips to the lake. She reached the entrance to the house at the same time we did, breathing heavily, but smiling as she put the bucket down in the small shoveled area at the foot of the steps. When Annette introduced me to her, Mrs. Lynn said, "I'm so pleased that Annette brought you around, Paul; I've wanted to meet you ever since Mr. Lynn told me what a fine young man Annette had found in the woods." Then she pointed at the bucket of water and laughingly explained, "Our pump quit working during the cold snap a couple weeks ago. Mr. Lynn chopped a hole in the ice so we could get to the water. I guess we're lucky the lake didn't dry up." I thought she was also lucky they lived in a remote area where pollution was probably minimal.

I picked up the bucket, and we followed her up the steps to the porch where Mr. Lynn, clinching a cigar butt between his teeth, was holding the door open. His red suspenders against his gray shirt and skin were in stark contrast but without them he could not have kept his pants up—he had no hips or butt. The porch, which Annette had described earlier as screened in, was now outfitted with storm windows. With the afternoon sun shining in, it was pleasantly warm, but smelled of wood and cigar smoke.

Mrs. Lynn said, "If you notice the porch smells a little smoky, it comes from the stove in the kitchen. We leave the door open between the porch and the kitchen on sunny days so the house can soak up as much heat as possible and we don't have to burn as much wood."

Mr. Lynn explained, "I cleaned all the nooks and crannies inside the stove—took the stovepipe down and cleaned that last summer. Guess I'll have to get up on the roof and run something down the chimney. Been so much snow on the roof since the stove started misbehaving that I can't get up there." His high-pitched, raspy voice had an unsettling quality. Mrs. Lynn seemed genuinely nice and had an old schoolteacher charm.

I asked Mr. Lynn if they had another source of heat, and he said, "Yes, we've got an oil furnace in the woodshed but that uses the same chimney. We don't use the furnace much anyway. Two weeks ago Gladys Talcott loaned Mrs. Lynn an electric heater. She told Mrs. Lynn to take it with her wherever she goes so I don't soak up all the heat."

Mrs. Lynn said good-naturedly, "No need for me to worry about that, Mr. Lynn doesn't let me turn it on very often; he says it uses too much electricity. But, I have to admit that he lets me use it on cold nights or at times when the stove is so smoky we have to open a window."

He turned to me with a knowing smile and said, "You ever go out and look at the electric meter when one of those heaters is plugged in? That little wheel inside the glass is spinning so fast it's a wonder it doesn't lift the house off its posts. The stove doesn't smoke too badly once it gets going; the problem is when you start it up, it takes awhile to get the chimney hot enough to produce a good updraft—course by then, the house is full of smoke."

Mrs. Lynn stood up, and walked toward the kitchen saying, "Come in here, Mr. Hurst; I'll show you the culprit." It seemed strange to me to have an older person call me "Mr." I asked her to call me, "Paul."

"OK, Paul, there it is," she said pointing with pride at the wood range. It was beautiful, composed mostly of blackened steel with a small amount of blue and white enamel trim. "You see here," she said, raising one of the four round lids on the cooking surface, "that's how big the fire box is. It holds enough wood to last for six hours. I do all the cooking on it. When it's working properly, it produces all the heat and hot water we need. When it's not working properly, we realize how dependent we are on it."

I asked her how many rooms they heat and she said, "Just this room and the bedroom. We don't heat the woodshed, that's at ground level. As long as we keep the outside door closed, nothing freezes in there. Most winters we go to South Carolina. We have a house trailer in my sister's backyard. Before we go, Mr. Lynn drains the water pipes so they won't freeze. As far as the chimney is concerned, I don't believe Mr. Lynn has cleaned it for several years. I don't remember exactly; but I'm pretty sure it wasn't this fall. We were too busy packing to go to South Carolina at the time he would normally clean it. Then, when the snow came early, we were busy unpacking and preparing to spend the winter here."

When we returned to the porch, Mr. Lynn was pointing out the window telling Annette something about the pine trees across the road. He turned and asked me if Mrs. Lynn had talked my ear off. "That stove is her pet; when it gets sick, she keeps cleaning and polishing it like that's going to make it all better." He was sitting in a padded rocking chair; with his cigar stub and the two fingers holding it, he gestured to the worn overstuffed chair next to him for me to sit down. Mrs. Lynn and Annette settled into the two ladder-back kitchen chairs that Annette had carried in from the next room.

"Mr. Lynn, how will you get up on the roof to clean the chimney," I asked.

"I use a ladder to get on the shed roof, then crawl on my hands and knees up the main roof to the chimney. Last time I used the ladder, though, it seemed like it was heavier than it used to be. I've been thinking about having Mrs. Lynn raise me up to the shed roof in the bucket of my tractor," he teased. "She's never run the tractor; but she used to be a schoolteacher, so I guess she could learn."

"School teachers teach," Mrs. Lynn said. "That doesn't say anything about what they can learn. Besides, I only taught one through six, which didn't include tractor driving." Annette had already told me that Mrs. Lynn had been a schoolteacher, which explained how well-spoken she and Mr. Lynn both were. She continued, "I told Annette some time ago that I taught for nearly 30 years in a one-room country school. You've probably never seen one of those; most of them are gone now."

"Sturbridge Village has a one-room schoolhouse." If you ever become nostalgic, Mrs. Lynn, I could arrange for you to teach a class once in awhile."

"It sounds like fun, Annette; but I believe I'm going to be busy for the next couple of years with my tractor lessons."

It was interesting to hear the Lynns banter with each other. I was sure Mr. Lynn did not expect the little woman to operate his tractor. Maybe he was hoping I would offer to help him; but I did not have a sense yet about his version of country protocol so I didn't volunteer outright; instead, I asked if I could come and watch him clean the chimney. Mr. Lynn formed a slight smile and said, "It might be a good idea so you'll know how to clean your chimney in case it starts smoking." I did not divulge that I do not heat with wood, but I said I would watch the weather and when it looks like the snow would be gone from his roof, I would visit him. Mr. Lynn nodded without offering resistance.

I was becoming fidgety, though, over the smoke and chimney talk. I wanted to move the conversation in the direction of how the community felt about Todd, but Mr. Lynn was selecting the topics. He said: "When you came back from the kitchen, Paul, I was telling Annette about that land over across the road. I farmed that piece most of my life. As a matter of fact, up there on the hill is where Mrs. Lynn and I used to live; but one spring when we came back from South Carolina, the house was gone—burned to the ground. So, we moved into the garage on this side of the road. I gradually added to it as time and materials became available. That was during World War II. Building materials were hard to find in those days—too expensive anyway; but I was able to get my hands on some good secondhand stuff."

"What caused the fire?" Annette said.

"We had burned some cardboard and paper in the fireplace when we were cleaning up to leave," Mrs. Lynn said. "Some pieces of wood may have been left with hot embers that were fanned into a flame by wind coming down the chimney. Sparks may have been blown out of the fireplace onto the wooden floor."

Mr. Lynn looked annoyed with her and said with certainty, "The fire was out when we left and I had closed the flue, so wind couldn't have come down the chimney. I don't know why she tells that story. Vandals set the fire. The neighbors said the house burned early in the evening of the day we left. They were just waiting for us to be gone. The neighbors said that by the time the fire truck arrived it was too late."

"I suppose that's what happened," Mrs. Lynn agreed. "Anyway, no one knew how to contact us, so it was quite a surprise to come home and find the house gone. That's when we moved into the garage and gradually added on to it until we had enough house so we could give the garage back to the car."

Although Annette had told me a lot about Todd, I was still interested in the Lynn's perspective of him, especially now that I knew he was focused on Annette and that he knows where she lives. So, as soon as an opportunity arose to change the subject, I said, "Mr. Lynn, when we met out in the woods, we didn't have time to talk much; but I remember you mentioned Todd Bowen. I've been wondering how you and the neighbors feel about him."

"He lives up at Four Corners, you know, above a garage that's attached to the house his mother and stepfather live in. People around there say he's a nice guy but he can get pretty mean when he's been drinking. You never know what he'll do."

"Four Corners is about five miles from here, isn't it?"

Mrs. Lynn replied with amusement, "Yes but we have an ambassador from there; Gladys Talcott, you know, the electric heater lady. She visits about once a week to deliver the news from Four Corners. The antics of Todd Bowen are a large part of her conversation; she seems quite fascinated by him."

Mr. Lynn said, "After high school Bowen went off to a small college in western Massachusetts. I guess college is where he learned to drink—probably about all he learned. While he was in college he threw a big, drunken party, got into a fight and killed one of his guests. He spent five years in prison for it. When he got out, he lived with a local woman up there in Massachusetts for about a year but she took a job in another state. Todd didn't have any place to go so he returned home to live with his mother who meanwhile had married Herbert Trish."

Mrs. Lynn interrupted, "We don't know either Margo or Herb Trish. Gladys told us, though, that Herb wasn't happy about having 'Margo's jailbird son' living with them; finally Herb agreed to let Todd finish that one-room apartment above the garage. It's got an outside stairway, so Herb doesn't have to endure Todd going through the house to get to it. I gather Todd has some carpentry skills. He helps local contractors when they need extras, but he's too unreliable to hold a regular job."

"Todd has stopped here a few times," Mrs. Lynn said. "He knew we were friends with Gladys so I guess he felt free to drop in, too. Mostly he's pleasant enough. Annette met him." Annette nodded in agreement and Mrs. Lynn continued, "According to Gladys, as soon as he moved to Connecticut, he made new friends and resumed his drinking. Gladys said that one night he had a few of his buddies over. They became so drunk and rowdy that Herb went up and asked them to leave. Todd and his friends called Herb some nasty names and told him he was the one who had to leave since he wasn't invited to the party. Herb called the police, who came out to quiet them down; but when a couple of the guys mouthed off, the police gathered up all four and put them in jail overnight. Todd came home the next day and found all his clothes and other things stuffed into his Bronco; the door to the apartment was boarded up and Herb had gone off to work."

"I gather Todd didn't just go away," I said.

"No," Mrs. Lynn said, "Gladys didn't say much about the hassle Margo and Herb had over her son. But Todd had his tools in the back of his car; so he took out a wrecking bar, pried the boards off and moved back in."

Mr. Lynn said, "Gladys told us some time ago that not only did Margo own the house, but when she married Herb, she helped him with some of his debts. She had settlement money from something. I'd guess at times like this she reminded him about how much he owed her."

Mrs. Lynn nodded and said, "Gladys told us Margo probably reminds him everyday."

When there was a pause, Annette stood up and said, "We'd better be moving along, Paul."

Mrs. Lynn said, "Oh, just a minute." She went into the kitchen where I heard her open and close the refrigerator.

When she returned she was carrying a package. "We thought you might like some of the venison you so kindly helped Mr. Lynn with. Do you like venison, Paul?"

"I've never eaten it but I'm anxious to try it."

Annette said, "'I guess you know, Mrs. Lynn, how much I like it."

Mrs. Lynn nodded and said, "There are two packages there, one is frozen but the other isn't, so you could have it for dinner tonight if you want to."

We thanked her and departed for the car.

4

As we drove away from the Lynn's, Annette said, "Paul, when you and Mrs. Lynn returned from the kitchen, do you remember that Mr. Lynn was talking about the ages of various stands of pine trees across the road?" I nodded and she continued, "That wasn't casual talk, you know. Indirectly he was telling me that my half of the field did not get mowed last year and brush has started to come up. He's afraid I'll let it grow back to forest. A couple years ago he was less subtle about it. I had acquired 100 small pines from the state and planted them along the fence between his property and my aunt's. I had hoped it would help define the boundary for Mr. Lynn who has trouble adjusting to the fact that he no longer owns the whole field. Every time I check on them, a few more were missing. It looked like the trees had been cut off with a knife. On one occasion when I was visiting the Lynns, he said, 'Say, did you notice those little trees you planted along the fence? It looks like beavers or something cut nearly half of them off at the base.' Paul, it would have been easier for him to pull them up, but then he wouldn't be able to blame the beavers. Besides, those trees were a long way from where the beavers live. Aggravated as I was about it, Mr. Lynn apparently wasn't satisfied with his rate of progress; either that or he got tired of squatting down to cut them off. At any rate, he mowed the whole field with his tractor and that was the end of my trees."

"What did you say to him?"

"I didn't say anything. I'm sure he expected me to thank him for mowing the field. I just stopped going over there; I had been visiting Harriet about once a week. After about six weeks of not seeing either of them, I went out in the field to close the gate and make repairs on the fence so I could graze the sheep there. I had been working about an hour when I saw Harriet coming across the field toward me. She greeted me in her usual cheery manner then said, 'Nathan thought you might enjoy these fish. He took them out of his trap this morning. We think bullheads are the best tasting fish in the pond.' I presumed it was a peace offering."

"From Harriet or Nathan?"

"I wondered that, too. My guess is that Harriet didn't know why I stopped visiting and kept asking Nathan what he thought until he confessed. The fish she gave me were cleaned and in an empty milk carton. Harriet and Nathan probably decided the offering would be better received if she presented it. And that was certainly true. I never could have refused her; but if Nathan had given them to me, he probably would have been wearing them home on his shirt."

"I don't think so."

"No, but it makes me feel better about myself to think otherwise."

It was dusk when we left the Lynns so I put on the headlights. As we approached Annette's house another vehicle pulled on to the road and turned in our direction. I asked Annette if it had not come out of her driveway. She said, "Yes." As it went by, she added, "That looks like

Todd's Bronco." I started to ask if he had become accustomed to dropping in but then realized that was none of my business. The strong feelings I had developed for Annette did not give me the right to feel possessive or protective of her either. After all, this was only our second date and it was more than two weeks since I had last seen her. If Todd is interested in her, for whatever reason, he probably has not been idle. By now we were in the yard and the sheep were calling to be fed.

Annette said, "You take the venison in and get a fire going in the fireplace while I attend to those starving animals." The backdoor was unlocked, which struck me as a careless way for a single woman to live. As I opened the door, the yard light shined on a small note stuffed into a crack in the door. I left it there for Annette and went into the house where it was uncomfortably cold. Annette must have turned the heat down; but since she did not tell me to turn it up, I did not bother to look for the thermostat. I rebuilt the fire from a remaining nest of hot embers. Then, I went back to the car for the six-pack I had stashed in the trunk just in case I was invited to stay for dinner, which I sort of assumed had already happened; but now, in view of the note, maybe I should not have been so presumptive. "Does that son of a bitch have the hots for Annette, or is he up to something?" I muttered.

Annette joined me as I was returning to the house. She saw the note, scanned it quickly and said it was from Todd. All he had to say is, "Hi."

I thought it said more than that, like "I know where you live; I'll be back later." But then, maybe he had been here before when Annette was home so she already knew he had found the place. But, she did not react with alarm to either the note or his car pulling out of her driveway.

When Annette started to take off her jacket, I suggested she might want to leave it on until the house warms up. "Naw," she said, 'this bulky sweater will be enough. I'm used to a little cold."

"Don't you have a central heating system?"

"Yes, but I keep the thermostat low. When I'm home, I spend most of my time in the kitchen; the fireplace is all I need."

The spinning wheel was close to the fireplace and a loom was not much further away, "Now I understand why you have so much wood in the barn. Do you save a lot of money by burning wood and freezing your buns?"

"Yes, with the thermostat set on 55 degrees, it doesn't take much oil to heat the house. Hill Dillard, who lives up the road, runs a sawmill. From time to time, he brings me a truckload of slabs in return for the logs I let him cut out of the woods in back."

Annette went to the cupboard for beer mugs; and since she still seemed entertained by my questions about her lifestyle, I continued to pry. I reminded her that she had not commented on whether the saving was worth the effort and discomfort. What I was really interested in is how she managed the cost of running this large property. I wondered if she was being frugal to get by or if living this way is just an extension of her life at Sturbridge Village—complete with cooking in the fireplace. She set the mugs on the table. I poured the beer not knowing if she was trying to decide what to say or if she was reluctant to answer me.

Finally, Annette said, "I guess I can tell you about that but it's complicated. Let me set some potatoes to bake first—drink your beer." She washed and forked the potatoes, and put them on a rack near the fire. As I watched her, I thought about how we baked potatoes on an open fire when we were children. We used to toss them right into the fire, leave them a few minutes until the skins were black, peel the burnt crust away and eat what was left; the center was usually raw. Annette's process of cooking them slow and all the way through would allow her time to answer a lot of questions. As I watched her graceful movements and the way her jeans tightened against her shapely thighs as she squatted before the fire, my interest in the questions I had asked faded.

Annette returned to the table, took a sip of beer and said, "OK, Paul, before I tell you about the financial operation of this property, I have to tell you a little more about my aunt and uncle. To begin with Aunt Lettie loved this house—far more than she loved Uncle Matt. My guess is she would have divorced him immediately after finding out about his infidelity; but she was afraid the court might not award her the house, so she put up with his philandering. After she ejected him from her bedroom, Aunt Lettie said she blocked her feelings about him from her mind; and it wasn't until after he died that she became aware of just how much she truly hated him.

"In the last years of Aunt Lettie's life and that was during the time I was living with her, she struggled to find a way to keep her beloved property intact after she died."

I thought about the way people sometimes do this, but I never fully understood it. Before I could ask Annette about it she said, "It wasn't because Aunt Lettie believed she deserved a monument for her less than exemplary life. It was because she didn't want to die knowing that her home would be hacked up into apartments or be allowed to deteriorate. She wanted to be sure that this house—the only trace of her life in this world—would remain after she was gone.

"Aunt Lettie, of course, wouldn't have anything to do with Uncle Matt's kin after he died, so all of her potential heirs were on her side of the family, none of which were interested in moving to Connecticut. If they inherited part or all of Aunt Lettie's property, they would want to turn it into cash as soon as they could. She had me talk with the Nature Conservancy, Joshua's Trust, the Audubon Society and others but none of them would assure Aunt Lettie that they would maintain the house, so in the end the responsibility of fulfilling her wish became mine."

"Congratulations!" I did not know what else to say. Based on her aunt's interests, I assumed there were onerous conditions attached to this grand gift.

"Thanks," Annette said, "The rent's free but I don't think I can afford it—to tell the truth, though, I haven't really sat down to figure it all out."

"But, if you can't afford it, what options do you have? Could you sell the house and run?"

"Not without a heavy conscience; since to set Aunt Lettie's mind at ease, I promised to honor her wishes."

"Maybe you should look for Joe Esposito's stashed money. Maybe it's here and maybe that's why Todd has taken such an interest in you."

"For my money?" she laughed. "You don't think it's because he has a passion for me?"

I didn't want to respond to either question but she remained focused on me, apparently amused by my struggle.

Finally, she said, "Paul, you are such a serious man but now it's time for you to cook the steaks." She rearranged the coals and placed a grate over them. Then she handed me one if the venison packages from the refrigerator. When I looked at her, she gave no indication that she planned to talk about Esposito's loot or what Todd's interests were in her.

While I fumbled with the meat, Annette handed me various tools to help and added small bits of advice when disaster seemed imminent. She also prepared a salad, set the table and otherwise occupied herself in ways that precluded my directing the conversation. After we settled down to eat, Annette said with a smile, "You must be very good at your job."

"What do you mean?"

"I'm talking about the way you pry into my life without revealing anything about your own."

"It's just that your life is interesting and mine is boring. Besides," I said, fumbling for words, "I care about you. To be honest it even goes beyond just caring."

"Uh huh," she said with a smile but did not indicate what her response meant. I wondered if she was accepting what I said at face value, or if she was back to inferring that my interest in her was only to gather information about Todd—or maybe she could see how aroused I had become and the "Uh huh" was a cynical measure of the depth of my caring.

Without dealing with the "Uh huh" or what I said about caring, she asked, "Paul, have you ever been in a foreign country? Were you in the service? Do you have a professional job with a reasonable salary?"

I shrugged and said, "Yes."

"Yes to all of them? Then why are you serving me this 'boring life' rubbish? These are all large and exciting things I have never experienced."

Not knowing how to respond, I said, "I don't know that they were more exciting than your experiences."

"Oh, sure, I bet you think demonstrating weaving to children and caring for an old aunt are more exciting than your boring life, but try me on a few tales from your past," she said, "and let me judge whether or not you have had an interesting life."

"OK. Where would you like to have me begin?" I said in a carefree tone, trying to infer that my life is an open book; but at the same time, hoping she would not ask about several things I would be uncomfortable answering.

"OK," she said, "Why aren't you married?"

"That wasn't on your original list of questions. Is it the thing you're most interested in?"

"Not necessarily. It just happens to be on my mind now. I'll get around to the other things eventually. And, if you really do care about me, like you said, you won't limit me to one question."

"OK, Annette, your first question picks up three of the others along the way. The reason Emily and I broke our engagement was because I was drafted into the Army and sent to Vietnam. At first we wrote to each other regularly. Then her letters became less frequent. Instead of writing, she sent me news clippings about student demonstrations and anti-war riots. One of the articles had her name in it as one of the demonstrators arrested. She was very proud of her activities. She also sent me editorials on the atrocities we invaders had committed in Vietnam as well as the political reasons why we should pack up and come home—as though soldiers had a choice."

"How did you respond?"

"I wrote what I thought were nice little stories about the Vietnamese people and my friendships with some of the men and their families, as well as our efforts to help the villagers with their food supply, sanitation and housing. I lived close to the villages and traveled with Vietnamese troops as an advisor."

"Did you see a lot of combat?"

"Not much." Annette was waiting for me to continue. I helped myself to some more salad, hoping she would pick up the conversation, but she did not. Finally, I told her, "Combat over there was kind of an impersonal thing. You're out on patrol with, say, 20 guys and you hear some guns go off. The forest is so dense you rarely see who's shooting at you, so you kind of listen to what they've got—automatic weapons, mortars or whatever, and you try to figure out how many of them there are. If it seems like you're out-gunned, you withdraw. If you think you've got more muscle than they have, you fire back to let them know and they withdraw.

"Anyway, when I got home, Emily and I talked a couple of times. She gave me my ring back and went off with one of the longhaired guys she had been protesting with."

"Yeah, I can see why you don't like to talk about that part of your life. The way you glossed over it tells me it was very upsetting for you. Do you know the back of your neck is red?"

"Yes, I can feel it getting warm. It always happens when I try to talk about the war. It also feels like the hair on the back of my neck is standing up. Is it?"

She walked around behind me to look; and when I leaned my head forward slightly she said, "I don't know; I can't tell." Then, she kissed the back of my neck and hugged me, nestling her head next to mine. When she withdrew, she said, "Thanks," then gathered dishes to take to the sink. I moved to get up and help, but she said, "You stay put. You cooked the steak—and just right, too, I might add. Guess what we're having for dessert?"

"The rest of Uncle Matt's brandy—or did you finish it?"

"I think there's a little left." When she brought the bottle out, it was obvious that Uncle Matt's friends had not stopped for a sip during the two weeks since Annette and I had last sampled it; and also to my relief, neither had Todd had any. She poured me an ample amount, but a considerably smaller splash for herself. Then she sat down and raising her glass toward me said, "Here's to our friendship, Paul, may it one day grow strong enough for us to trust each other with our inner souls."

I said, "Yes, to trusting souls." We clinked our glasses together and smiled warmly at each other; but the back of my neck began to heat up again as old images flashed in my mind. I tried to force my attention back to the table and to Annette, who was looking at me as though she were reading my mind. She rose from her chair and walked to my side of the table. I stood up and she took me in her arms and held me for a long time. When she withdrew, her cheeks were smeared with my wet tears. I felt like a sentimental old fool in the arms of this beautiful girl. I had to remind myself that she wasn't that much younger than I; she just looked and seemed younger.

While I was regaining my composure, Annette changed the subject. With a subtle smile she said, "Aren't you going to ask me if I've been dating Todd during the two weeks you've been neglecting me?"

She knew I was jealous of Todd and was teasing me. I asked, "How come you wanted me to talk about myself? You're already inside my head and know what I'm thinking most of the time."

"Come on, Paul, people can't read minds, besides the corners and tunnels in yours are too dark to read. Your concern that I might succumb to Todd's handsome charm, though, is right out there on the surface where it provides me with a warm measure of how much you care about me. What I'm about to tell you, though, isn't to fuel that as much as it is to inform you of what he has been up to."

I was embarrassed that she could read me so easily. She probably knew how much I loved her better than I did. And she also knew how concerned I was about Todd's role in her life so I said, "Yeah, you better tell me before I break out in a rash."

"OK. Todd showed up at my door a day or two after you were here last time. He said he had something interesting to tell me and wanted to come in. I wouldn't let him in and told him to just go ahead and tell me. He said, 'This is important. Something we should talk about. I can't just tell you like this.' We went back and forth until finally I agreed to meet him at Little Eddie's.

"Todd said he'd drive, that we don't need to take both cars. I told him, 'Forget it; the last time we were at Little Eddie's, you left me so abruptly I hardly had time to say goodbye. I was lucky I had my own transportation.'"

I said, "I suppose by now he had an elaborate explanation for his fast exit?"

"I'll say he did! He told me the reason he rushed off was because, while we were talking, it finally came to him why the name Matt Hyde was familiar to him when Nathan introduced us. He said he dashed off to confirm what he suspected before saying anything to me about it. Now he wants to share the interesting news with me. I can't say I wasn't curious. That's the real reason I followed him out to Little Eddie's, not his charm. Once we were settled in a booth behind mugs of beer, I said 'OK, so what's this about? It better be good.'"

"Was it?"

Annette shrugged and said, "The way he was looking at his discovery made him feel good, but it didn't do anything for me. What he said was that he's my Uncle Matt's illegitimate son."

She paused to give me a chance to respond. I tightened my lips and nodded several times trying to assess the implications of what she had revealed. Then I poured more brandy into her empty glass and said, "So now Todd thinks he owns the farm?"

"More than that, he was so overwhelmed by his good fortune of being Matt Hyde's illegitimate son that he offered to extend his joy to me. He said that he plans to take over the property and move in as soon as his ownership is legalized but that I don't have to worry about finding another place; I can continue to live here as long as I like. His enthusiasm continued to grow as he drank. The highpoint came when he said, 'What the hell, after we get to know each other, we may even become kissing cousins and share a bed.'"

I didn't have to tell Annette how angry I was; she knew. She reached across the table and patted my hand to calm me down then said, "I stayed to hear Todd out so I'd know what I was dealing with."

Once I had simmered down enough to speak without yelling, I asked, "Were you really that cool? I mean to just sit and listen to his crap without reacting."

"Not really. I don't know how I appeared to him, but I was quit upset. Immediately after he told me Uncle Matt was his father, the resemblance became so clear I couldn't deny it. What helped to contain me, though, is my belief that the terms of ownership of Aunt Lettie's property preclude his contesting her will even if he can prove he's a blood relative."

"What caused Todd to think he was Uncle Matt's son?"

"Todd's birth certificate lists Matt Hyde as his father."

"Did he show it to you?"

"Yes. Todd said he thought I might not believe him so he brought it with him. He said he had to sneak it out of his mother's strong box while she was out shopping. The only time he had seen it before was when he was eight years old and snooping in her stuff. She had caught him at it and that's when she bought a strong box to keep her papers in. He said one of the other interesting documents in the box was that Matt Hyde was the previous owner of his mother's house—the one Todd was born in and where his mother now lives with Herb Trish. Six months before Todd was born Uncle Matt signed the house over to Margo Bowen, Todd's mother. So, what do you make of that, Paul?"

"My guess is that Uncle Matt set Margo up in the house as his mistress but retained ownership. When Margo became pregnant, she put pressure on Uncle Matt for a more secure arrangement for herself and her baby."

"That's what I suggested to Todd; he agreed it was possible but that he really didn't know. He said it would be difficult to ask his mother about it since she told him when he was still little that his father was killed in the war and she didn't want to talk about it; she didn't say which war. What's more she wouldn't take it kindly to know that he had found the key to her strong box and had been snooping in her business. Can you guess, Paul, where he found the key?"

"In her jewelry box."

"Yes, the first place he looked."

"Annette, this is an interesting story. Why did you wait all afternoon and most of the evening to tell me?"

"I wasn't going to tell you at all, even after you saw Todd pull out of my driveway and found his note in the door. I guess the brandy loosened me up."

"You weren't going to tell me because you were enjoying how jealous I was and you wanted to perpetuate it?"

"How about I was afraid you'd threaten him with violence? You're joking now," she said, "but you were pretty mad when I told you what he said—and it isn't over yet. The note he left in the door only said, 'Hi'; but the fact is he doesn't have any reservation about showing up unannounced. He'll be back, Paul, and we both have to keep our heads about this until it works its way out. I assure you it will go away."

I promised to be patient, even though I wasn't sure I could. If Annette had explained how this issue would work its way out, it might have helped; but she did not show any inclination to tell me. In spite of Todd's charming façade, he is not a patient man either; and since he has a history of violence, he is not likely to retreat from idle threats.

5

When most of the snow had melted, Annette arranged for us to go out to the Lynn's so I could help Mr. Lynn clean his chimney.

The barn door was open when I arrived at Annette's, so I went over to see if she was inside. "Hi Paul," she called to me, as I stepped through the open door. "You're just in time; I'm looking for something; I think that's it on the top shelf." She was pointing at a one-foot square box. "I can't quite reach it". That was an understatement. I'm five-ten and I could hardly reach it; Annette, is five feet, four inches tall.

When I had the mystery box in my hands, I could see by the label that the contents "guaranteed satisfaction for discriminating chimney sweeps." Annette said, "I thought we should bring this. My guess is that Mr. Lynn will want to drag the brushy top of an old Christmas tree through the flue like his ancestors did. This wire brush works better and it isn't nearly as messy." Inside the box was a square wire brush to which one screwed together a succession of poles depending on the height of the chimney. Annette had already found the extension poles, so as soon as she said good-bye to the sheep, who seemed fascinated by what we were doing, we left.

Mr. Lynn was near the front of the house working at

his chopping block. We left the chimney brush in the car and joined him. Annette had been right. With a hatchet, he was trimming the top of a hemlock to a size that would go down the chimney. "I thought you'd a come last week; snow's been off the roof for some time." He sounded testy. Before I could explain that I had been too busy at work to get away, Mrs. Lynn was at the door waving and calling to us cheerfully. Annette joined her on the porch, leaving me to work it out with Mr. Lynn.

"I don't suppose you know what this is," he said.

I didn't answer him; instead I went back to the car and got Annette's chimney brush hoping to substitute it for his primitive creation. When I returned, I said, "Let's try this first; if it doesn't work we can try yours."

"I've heard about those," he said. His tone inferred that he was not impressed with what he had heard, but he did not elaborate. "I'll show you where the ladder is."

The shed contained an abundant collection of things, including the freezer Mrs. Lynn had spoken of earlier, an ancient washing machine with wringers and the water pump, now disconnected from the plumbing and lying on a sheet of plywood on the dirt floor. Mr. Lynn pointed at it and said, "I'm still trying to figure out whether the pump is shot or if the intake line from the well is frozen. You know anything about pumps?"

I told him I did not, which was not completely true; but then, when I thought about Mrs. Lynn carrying the water bucket up from the lake, I said, "Maybe a little. I'll look at it when we finish with the chimney." A wooden ladder was hanging on the wall. I asked, "Is that the one we're going to use?"

"Yes, but be careful, it's heavier than you'd think."

Actually, it was fairly light—it seemed too rickety for

my 185 pounds. Having offended him about his chimney brush, I decided not to express concern about his ladder for fear his next choice would be to lift me to the roof in the bucket of his tractor. I attached a couple of lengths of the handle to the wire brush; and as I carried it up the wobbling ladder, I wondered why I was risking my wellbeing on this project. It was because of Annette, I reminded myself. My feelings for her were so strong that I wanted to be part of her life, even if it meant climbing an old, rickety ladder.

The slope of the roof over the shed was gentle enough so I could walk upright to the main part of the house; there the roof became so steep I was afraid I would slide off. My tendency would have been to crawl up on my hands and knees; but my pride would not let Mr. Lynn see me do that, so I leaned forward and dashed for the peak. Once I had a hold of the chimney, my comfort level returned to a point where I could work.

As I ran the brush down the flue, I could hear chunks of creosote clattering down. At several points along the way they must have clumped together and blocked the hole. I had to jab the rod up and down several times to loosen the clod, no wonder the smoke circulated through the house rather than go up the chimney. Not until I finished and was on the way down did I realize Mr. Lynn had been giving me detailed instructions throughout the process. The last one he issued was for me to hand him the pole and brush so I would not have to carry it down the ladder. That sounded like a good idea; it freed both of my hands so I could hold the ladder together—at least, that is what I felt I was doing.

Mr. Lynn was almost smiling when I reached the ground, so what I did up there must have concurred with what he was telling me to do. After I had the ladder back in the shed, I asked him where all that stuff went that I pushed down the chimney. He showed me a little metal door at the base of the chimney and said he would clean it out later. His interest already had turned to the pump; drawing my attention to it presumably was a vote of confidence after I had successfully cleaned the chimney.

I asked Mr. Lynn if they were still hauling water from the lake. When he said they were, I took a bucket and went to the lake for water. The lake was still covered with ice but it was melting rapidly. The small hole Mr. Lynn had made during the winter was now about 15 feet in diameter. When I returned with the water, Mr. Lynn had several lengths of plastic pipe laid out. I took a short length of it, slid one end over the intake pipe of the pump and put the other end in the bucket. Mr. Lynn plugged the electrical cord into the outlet; the pump belched a couple of times then spewed out a steady stream of water.

Mr. Lynn nodded and said, "Guess the pump is OK. The line to the well must be frozen or split."

"Yes," I agreed. "It looks like the ground is still too frozen, though, for us to dig it up, so I guess Mrs. Lynn isn't going to have water in the kitchen for a while." The pipe was barely underground at the point it left the dirt floor of the shed to the outside. Although the daily temperatures went above freezing, it would still be a while before the ground thawed enough to dig up the pipe. I put the pump back where it belonged and ran a length of pipe overland to the well. A few seconds after I primed the pump and plugged it in, excited voices sounded from the kitchen. The faucet at the kitchen sink had been left open; Mrs. Lynn and Annette were surprised by the sudden gush of water.

Mr. Lynn and I joined the women in the kitchen. Annette patted me on the shoulder while Mrs. Lynn expressed her gratitude. I felt good about what I had done; it was a better feeling than the negative thoughts that had run through my mind earlier as I had made my way toward the chimney. Mr. Lynn built a fire in Mrs. Lynn's stove while I washed my blackened hands at the kitchen sink. Mrs. Lynn excused herself and went into the bedroom, which I presumed had a bathroom. She soon returned smiling to the sound of flushing water; shortly after, I heard the pump in the shed click on and run. Both sounds are good signs of a civilized rural home.

I went over to the stove and held my hands up to enjoy the heat that was starting to build. It was a pleasant thing to have in the kitchen—captivating, with its crackling wood and the little flecks of flame showing between the joints in the steel plates. Smiling at the childlike pleasure I was taking from Mrs. Lynn's stove, Annette said, "Don't get too comfortable, Paul, we have a reservation for dinner tonight at Little Eddy's and it's time to go."

As we drove to the restaurant, our conversation reflected the warm glow we both felt over the way Mrs. Lynn had responded to the restoration of her water supply and stove. Most days and nights were still cold enough to have a fire. Annette sat close to me as I drove, which she had not done before; I enjoyed the feel of her body against me. "Where did you learn about water pumps?" she asked.

"As a kid I worked as a plumber's helper; and then in Vietnam, one of the things we were supposed to do was to help the people stabilize their food supply. I got some water pumps from the Army Corps of Engineers, so during the dry season the people could pump water from the river to their gardens and fields. We even used the pumps to supply water to a fish pond we made to raise fish in."

"I didn't know our soldiers did that kind of thing over there. I doubt if many people back home knew that."

"No, most people were overwhelmed by the killings they heard about. Victory was measured in terms the body count. Every day, you know, it was so many of them and so many of us." I stopped myself from saying any more on that subject. I could already hear the strain and change of pitch in my voice.

The restaurant was a friendly place as Annette had described it. Booths lined the walls; wooden tables and chairs occupied the rest of the space, except for a small area left clear so one or two couples could dance to jukebox music. Tammy Wynett was singing *Stand by Your Man* when we arrived. The tops of the tables were bare wood with the initials of previous patrons carved on them. Annette selected a booth as far away from the juke box as she could find. "It's hard to talk when you're too close to the music," she said.

As soon as we were settled, Annette asked me to guard her purse while she went to the ladies' room. I asked if she wanted me to order her a drink while she was gone. "Beer," she said. When Annette went to the restroom, I surveyed the other people in the place. It was not very crowded, three other booths were occupied, as well as two tables; half a dozen men were at the bar. The patrons were a mix of younger and older people. The waitress, a plump middle-aged extrovert was telling some people several booths away about a couple that comes in every once in awhile. "He's large," she said, "always orders two complete steak dinners for himself. When I deliver their order, he whips out this big hunting knife, wipes it across his pants to make sure it's clean; and then proceeds to cut off big chunks of meat, which he delivers to his mouth on the end of the knife." Her audience thought it was hilarious and tried to guess who he was, but the waitress said, "Can't tell you, wouldn't be professional." Still laughing she moved on to our booth, "You heard that, huh?" she said, jerking her thumb toward the booth she had come from, still laughing. "Can I get you guys a couple of beers, Hon?"

Her name tag said Melba, so I said, "Yes, Melba, two drafts, please, one for me and one for my friend."

Annette was back before the beers arrived. She asked, "Wouldn't they sell you beer?"

"I think they are being poured now. Is that Little Eddy manning the spigot?" Annette confirmed that the six foot-four, 350-pound man at the bar was Little Eddy.

"Don't you have to go?" Annette said.

"No. I went behind a bush while we were at Lynn's."

"I never get used to the fact that men can do that."

Just then Melba arrived with our beers and told us what the specials are. At her recommendation, I ordered the meatloaf dinner; Annette ordered chicken. Before she left, Melba leaned over and whispered to Annette, "I like him better than your other boyfriend."

Annette smiled at Melba and said, "Especially now, huh?"

"Oh, you are so right," Melba called back over her shoulder as she walked off. Melba must have seen the newspaper article about Todd and his friends. I did not think Annette wanted to talk about Todd tonight, so I asked, "Did you really make a reservation for us?"

"No. I just said that because it was getting late and I didn't want Mrs. Lynn to feel she should provide dinner for us. After that I thought, it really wasn't such a bad idea since you said you have never been to Little Eddy's. Also it would be closer to the truth if we did follow through."

"Have you told any other lies you want to confess at this time?" I teased.

"As a matter of fact, yes," she said looking directly at me. When she saw my response, she smiled, took a sip of beer and said, "And that lie is another reason I wanted to come here tonight. I wanted to explain that something I told you earlier really wasn't a lie; I just misled you and thought it would be easier to talk about it if we weren't at my place fooling around cooking or otherwise fooling around."

"You sure know how to get a guy's attention."

"That's good," she smiled, "because what I want to tell you isn't trivial. In fact, Aunt Lettie was the only one who knew about this."

"I'm honored you've chosen to tell me."

"A while ago when we were talking about whether you would publish things people told you in private and you said you wouldn't, and assured me that you really are a good person. Well, I saw today that you are a good person, and even though I sense you're holding back a ton of stuff from me about yourself, I'm going to go ahead and tell you something very personal that really bothers me deeply.

6

Annette had a faint smile on her face as she introduced her "dark secret." I thought she might be leading me on; but as she progressed with her story, I realized she was simply feeling relieved over the decision to talk about a matter that had troubled her for a long time.

"Paul, when I told you I had been married, I didn't really lie to you; but I know I gave you a false impression."

"OK." I nodded and waited.

"I used to live in a convent; I was a nun for 23 years."

When I recovered from that announcement, I said, "So, when you told me you were married, it wasn't to a man; it was to God. Ring and all?"

"Yes."

"I never would have guessed—except for the way you freeze up when I become overly amorous. But there really isn't anything so terrible about your having been a nun; it isn't something you have to hide along with the rest of life's dark secrets."

"That confession wasn't my terrible secret—just background material—but I don't usually tell people I was a nun because they immediately treat me differently." Annette hesitated; I could not tell if she was uncertain about what to say next or if she was still deciding whether to continue. Neither, it turned out; when she spoke, she asked, "Do you want me just to blurt out what I did or should I tell you the sequence of events that led up to my fall from grace?"

"I want to hear all the details—how you happened to become a nun, why you quit and why you're so bothered about it—everything."

"OK. But if it sounds like I'm rambling, remember that all roads lead to Rome." I nodded and she continued. "The reason I don't subscribe to a newspaper is because I have dyslexia. It isn't that I can't read, it's just that it's too much of a struggle for me to enjoy it. I make better use of my time getting my news from television."

"What about your garden column in the *Chronicle*?"

"I do that to challenge my dyslexia, so I don't back-slide, sort of like exercising, You know, once you get in shape you have to keep at it or lose what you've gained. Writing the garden column forces me to read a little and write a little. The length of the assignment is just right and it imposes a deadline. I won't tell you, though, how many hours it takes to produce those few inches of column. I do it on a small computer Uncle Matt left behind. It's primitive but it beats the struggle I would have with a typewriter. Before I learned to use the computer, I used to wear out the paper with an eraser trying to arrange the letters into words. You would not have been able to make sense out of my early drafts."

"The finished copy reads well."

"Thanks, but like I say, it's not without a lot of work. Anyway, my reading and writing disability is part of the reason I entered a convent. My grades in school were pretty poor. I did OK in math and art, and in parts of courses that involved discussions—as long as I didn't have to read too much—but courses like English, geography, economics, civics and history killed me."

"Yet, you have a fine vocabulary and good grammar."

"I suppose struggling to read and write helps me to remember what I learn better than if it came easily. Anyway my mother, who was a strict Catholic, insisted that I attend a parochial school. Most of my teachers had a rigid, no nonsense policy; dyslexia was no excuse for poor performance. Although a few nuns were sympathetic, I felt the others thought I was just dumb. My grades, of course, weren't good enough for me to consider college. The alternatives, as my mother saw them, were for me to marry young, face life with a low paying job, or go into a convent."

"Did she have a preference?"

"Marriage was the lowest on her list. My father worked for a carnival that toured small towns—north in the summer and south in the winter. When the carnival was in town, my mother got pregnant. Sometimes he sent her money but it wasn't anything she could depend on. Once the house was filled with kids, he didn't visit us anymore and the checks stopped coming."

"How old were you when you last saw him?"

Annette shrugged and said, "I don't know; his withdrawal was kind of gradual; besides he didn't have enough significance on our lives for me to pay attention to his comings and goings. I'd guess I was 11 or 12. I was the oldest, next came my three sisters then my brother who was probably two when Pa failed to return. Mom hadn't encouraged us to get to know our father. When he did visit, he said the usual things adults say to kids like, 'My, how big you're getting. How's school? You're so pretty I bet you have a lot of boy friends." After spending an evening or two with us, he'd look up old friends, and then, he'd come in late smelling of beer. Mom and I were usually the only ones still up. He'd tell me about his travels and about things that happened at the carnival; that part of him was interesting but his stories were filled with colorful words that caused Mom to scold him. After she interrupted his stories a few times, an argument would break out. He'd call her a holier-than-thou goddamn, shanty Irish Catholic. Mom would retaliate by calling him an English sot and Thames River scum. She didn't have the adjectives Pa had but she didn't need them; his ego was more delicate. It didn't take much to send him stomping off mad. Then we wouldn't hear from him for another year, finally, not at all. He may have died or been killed for all we know."

"Surprising isn't it how the hatred and armed conflict between the Irish and the English goes on," I said. "There must have been a lull between battles, though, during which they managed to marry and reproduce."

"Yes, but what surprised me most about their squabbles was that they both were born in this country; neither had ever seen Ireland or England. After one of Pa's angry departures, I asked Mom how they ever stayed together long enough to get married. She said, 'I didn't realize what he was like when I met him. He was already working for the carnival. I guess you know your father was a good-looking man; he was charming and led an exciting life compared to mine in Bellevue, Ohio, so when he asked me to go off with him on the carnival circuit, I went. I ain't sayin' I didn't love him back then; but not long after I got pregnant he sent me back home. He came up with enough money to settle me into this dump and it's been a struggle ever since to make the rent.'"

"Yes, I can see why she wouldn't rank marrying young—or even marrying at all very high on the scale."

"Yes, but Mom never took marriage off her list of careers for me. She was desperate to get me out of the nest or at least to have me add more money to the pot. I was doing some baby-sitting and giving her half; it was only after a bitter argument that she let me keep half so I could buy new clothes once in a while. Even before I was old enough to quit school, Mom started studying the help wanted ads. She expected me to quit school and work fulltime as soon as I was 16. Anything she found that I might be able to do, she read aloud: house-cleaning, babysitting, serving hamburgers—all promising opportunities for me. She assured me that if a tenth grade education was good enough for her it was good enough for me. But, I knew quitting school without a high school diploma would mark me for the same desperate life my mother led. There were times when even Mom would admit that her succession of low-paying jobs didn't have much to recommend them; but that didn't keep her from pushing me to pay my own way."

"So based on that you went to live in a convent?"

"That was one reason; there were at least two additional reasons, though." She smiled and continued, "You see, Paul, a long time ago—before I entered the convent—I had an interest in boys. I wasn't anxious to give that up, even though Mom wouldn't allow me to date. She was really negative about sex and to her that's what boys represented. She let us all know that any expression of sex, even in its mildest form, was sinful and filthy. She never told us what sex was, though; and since our school wasn't very expansive on that subject, I had only a vague notion of what she was talking about."

"I would think television would have cleared that up for you?"

"There wasn't much sex on television back then, besides our set was an old black and white that a neighbor gave us. The sound was OK; but the screen had so much snow on it that if sex was happening, we wouldn't have known. For quite a while mom didn't pay attention to what we were listening to; but one evening, she walked by and overheard some profanity. We were immediately ordered to take the T.V. out to the curb for the trash pickup."

"Didn't the kids at school talk about sex?"

"A little, but not like now. You'd see boys huddled together smirking and laughing but, the nuns would break them up as soon as they saw what was going on—no coeducational opportunities there," she laughed. "It wasn't long after I left high school that foul words and filth became the common language of teenagers, but based on the rise in venereal disease and pregnancies, I suspect teenage sex talk doesn't have much educational content."

Annette paused. A smile coaxed the corners of her mouth until it released the next secret. "I did have one experience in sex education, though, before I entered the convent. A high school senior named Eric, who used to sit next to me on the bus, told me he had a jalopy. He kept pestering me to go to the drive-in theater with him. I knew from some of the other girls at school that going to the drive-in with a boy meant hugging, kissing and other things; but no one ever said what the *other things* were; they'd just roll their eyes when I asked. Anyway, I told Eric I couldn't go out with him because I had to stay home with the younger kids while my mother worked. It was true, too, because at that time she had a job in a store restocking shelves from 7:00 p.m. to midnight."

"I'm sure it was easier for you to tell Eric that than to say, 'My mother doesn't let me go out with boys.'"

"Yeah, but the next thing he wanted to do is come over and watch T.V. with me. When I told him we didn't have T.V., he didn't believe me and kept trying to get me to give in. I can't say I wasn't flattered by his attention. At night in bed, I allowed my mind to imagine what it would be like to go to the drive-in with Eric, to have him kissing me and running his hands over me."

As Annette described her horny teenage longings, I struggled to adjust my erection to a more comfortable position; at the same time, I understood Eric's desire for Annette, as well as his frustration over her denial.

"Eric didn't give up easily," Annette said. "One night, after I had the kids settled in bed, I went back down to the front room to do some school work. After about ten minutes, I looked up from my book and there was Eric. He was on the front porch looking in the window. When I opened the front door, he said he was just driving by and thought I might like to go for a spin. He said this as though we hadn't already had that conversation, so I explained to him again that I had to stay with my brother and sisters until my mother came home around midnight; by then it would be too late. Next he wanted to come in. I told him my mother wouldn't like for him to be here when she's not home. 'Just for a few minutes,' he pleaded."

"Oh, God, Annette, you let him in."

"Worse than that, Paul, wait 'till you hear what happened. First I made him promise to leave as soon as I asked him to. Then, as you probably guessed, he wanted to turn the lights off. I made him leave the kitchen light on so I could see the clock. Once we were seated on the couch, Eric didn't take long to progress from the kissing stage to the stage where I was struggling to hold him off. After so long, though, just as my resistance was beginning to weaken, I heard footsteps on the porch. We didn't have time to straighten up or anything. I heard the door open, then Mom call to me like I was in the kitchen where the light was, 'Annette, how come you didn't have the porch light on? I tripped and almost broke my leg coming up the steps.' When she found the light switch and turned the light on, there I was struggling with my bra which was caught in my blouse; Eric was still buttoning his shirt. I said, 'Mom, you're home early; this is Eric. Eric this is my Mom.' Without saying a word, she walked past us into the kitchen and made herself a cup of tea."

"Hard to know what to do next, huh?"

"I'll say. When we finished putting ourselves together, Eric called, 'Goodnight, Mrs. Devon' and I let him out the door."

"Did your mother respond to his good night?"

"No, she was too busy stirring her tea—making sure we could hear the angry clacking of her spoon against the inside of the cup."

"Did you join her in the kitchen?"

"No, I wasn't very brave about facing up to my mistakes when I was a teenager. I just went upstairs to bed. I knew she wouldn't come up and holler at me for fear of waking my brother and sisters. In the morning I left for school before she or any of the others were out of bed. Later, the incident was never mentioned."

"What was Eric's reaction?"

"At first he was apologetic about getting me into trouble; but it wasn't long before he was telling me how much he loved me and that he had to have me or he would die. I guess I was pretty naïve; I didn't understand what he meant. I thought he was proposing to me. I sort of made a fool of myself. I asked him: Do you plan for us to quit school and get jobs to support ourselves or do you expect us to live with your parents or what?"

"Without knowing what Eric had in mind, your answer was really quite good."

"I suppose so, now that you mention it, but what I said didn't stop him. He told me he wanted to marry me as soon as he finished college and got a job, but meanwhile, he did not think we should wait that long before we made love. I was even uncertain what he meant by making *love*."

"Maybe he just wanted to play house in the back seat of his jalopy."

"I guess that's what he was saying. Anyway, once I convinced Eric I couldn't go out with him, he fell in love with another girl."

"Were you upset?"

"Only for a short time. Not long after that, I told Mom she could quit worrying about Eric, that we broke up. She didn't say anything, just sort of nodded her head; but I felt relieved."

"Maybe she decided it wouldn't be so bad after all if you became pregnant and left the nest to get married?"

"I don't believe Mom ever had such optimism. What she probably thought was she'd end up with one more mouth to feed. She wasn't without a plan, though. My first clue came when one of the nuns, who had befriended me, began encouraging me to consider a life serving God, I was flattered. But, when several other nuns, who barely knew me, also began to encourage me, I suspected that Mom was stirring the pot."

"I would have resented that and become obstinate."

"I might have, too, except that with this scheme, I could finish high school, and with it also, came a vague promise that I might some day go to college; the idea didn't seem that bad. I began thinking about majoring in elementary education or maybe in sociology. I always enjoyed working with children, but I also saw in our neighborhood what a struggle old people have and how little it would take to make their lives better. The sisters assured me that as a nun I could work with either children or the elderly. They said that young and old alike, who need help, find their way to us and education for me beyond high school would be encouraged."

"It looks to me, Annette, like your interest in helping people didn't disappear when you left the religious life."

"There will never be a shortage of people who need help. But, I don't want to give you the impression that I went into the convent solely to help people. The experience I had with Eric made me realize how vulnerable I was. I didn't even love him; yet when I was with him I lost control of myself. If my mother hadn't come home when she did, I know I would have given in to him. I could have become pregnant. In the fall after Eric went away to college, I would be left with a baby and the Devon household would have another mouth to feed. It really scared me. I felt I would be safer with the sisters."

"Your joining up doesn't sound like it was a result of God calling you."

"It wasn't, but I was pretty young then; I wasn't as inclined to examine my motives as I am now. I remember that in addition to feeling safer, I was sort of taken in by the aura of mystery associated with life in a convent—you know, the ritual, the way nuns dress and live in a community dedicated to doing good."

Annette went on to tell me about her experiences in becoming a nun and her life during that time. She said, "While I was a postulant, which was for the first six months, I was with other teenage girls. At first, we behaved like normal teenagers. We stole the communion wine for secret parties, played tricks on the Mother Superior and fell in love with young priests from afar. Soon, though, we weren't allowed to talk with each other about such things. Our celibacy and obedience training were supposed to repress all sexual thoughts. Discipline, oppression and mind control were to cure us of self-pride. It was hard for me to understand how they could claim that pride was a bad thing when it looked to me like most of the nuns and priests who achieved higher levels in the Catholic hierarchy were well endowed with pride. While I was a novice, these attempts to suppress and remold my personality often brought me to the edge of rebellion or flight."

"Your experience with discipline, oppression and mind control sound surprisingly like basic training in the Army, except in basic, when we were allowed to talk, we got to swear and talk about sex. But, what about Vatican II, didn't that reform movement have a mellowing influence on life in religious orders by the time you joined?"

"I entered the convent in 1974; even though the Second Vatican Council opened in 1962, it was a long time before its impact was widely felt. There were mixed opinions on what this revolution was about. Different priests had different interpretations; sometimes I thought it had more to do with their desires or weaknesses than anything else. You know, when Pope John XXIII said he wanted to 'throw open the windows and let a little light in,' I didn't know what that meant and neither did a lot of other nuns and priests. That light was slow to reach us, and what little did was awfully dim. Later I discovered that reform in most Roman Catholic orders was well ahead of ours, in fact, the others looked down on us for adhering to the old traditions."

Annette seemed to be having difficulty getting to her buried pain. Dinner came, and while we ate she talked about working with underprivileged children and their families, older people and inner city kids. As a social worker she seemed to have enough knowledge and common sense to do a good job even though she did not have a degree in the area.

Melba came and took Annette's order for dessert and asked if she wanted a doggy bag for her unfinished chicken. I passed on the dessert. "You sure you don't want dessert, Hon?" Melba urged. I declined again and she said, "OK, Hon, if you don't want to grow up to be big and fat like me that's up to you," and she went off with our plates.

I asked Annette, if when she was a sister, she wore a nun's habit."

She smiled and said, "Yes, my order continues to wear the habit; I guess you know most nuns no longer do."

When Melba returned, she put Annette's chocolate sundae in front of her, then offered me the doggy bag in one hand and an extra spoon in the other. "Take your pick," she said. I took the spoon and she handed the doggy bag to Annette saying, 'We had a baked potato left over so I put that in the bag, too, then with a knowing smile added, 'tell your dog I said you're welcome.'"

Annette insisted that I sample the sundae while she picked up our conversation where she left off. "One of the things we used to do is take city kids on nature hikes or to the beach for a swim and a picnic. The parish had a minibus that was driven by a retired a man, a volunteer. Usually Sister Carol and I organized these trips. We were often accompanied by one of the young priests, Father

Thomas. He would drive out in his own car and meet us at the site we planned to visit. Carol and I provided him with an itinerary, so if he was detained by church duties, he would know where we would be so he could join us."

"Where did you take the kids?"

"Sometimes we took them to the Natchaug State Forest. We had two localities we liked: one was a beaver pond where the kids could hike around the pond and see marsh birds, muskrats and beaver dams. Aunt Lettie had brought me there some years ago and I had found it interesting. I could even tell the kids about how beavers build dams. The other place was the ruins of an old farm that had been reclaimed by forest. We took the kids to the farm first. It was built on a hill probably in the early 1700s. Not much was left now, only the stone foundations of the house, barn and a couple of outbuildings. The boundaries of the original fields were still marked by the remains of stone walls meandering through the woods. It was interesting for the kids to try to imagine what life was like up there without the trees and to be working the fields with horses or oxen."

"Do you spend the whole day at this site and a whole day at the other site?"

"No. We finish exploring the abandoned farm a little before noon then drive the few miles to the second site where there is a nice picnic area near the river. Sandwiches and soft drinks are supplied by parish volunteers interested in our project. On this occasion Father Thomas arrived as we were spreading the lunches out on the picnic tables. In trying to get to the old farm, he had become confused by the tangle of country roads, so when time ran out he headed to the picnic site. The kids were still talking about farm life in colonial days and a couple of them were even brave enough to tell Father Thomas about things they saw. When

Father Thomas expressed disappointment about missing that part of the trip, Sister Carol suggested that I take him back to see it while the rest of them eat lunch. If she and the kids finish before we get back, we can catch up to them along the trail. Father Thomas and I agreed, so we took our sandwiches and drinks with us and started back to the farm. Along the way we talked about things—some of them more personal than what we usually discussed—I mean not real personal; I don't even remember now what we specifically talked about only that I felt a little awkward about the conversation. I had recognized earlier that we were dangerously attracted to each other but I hadn't worried about it because we were never alone before. He was a nice looking man, reminded me of Montgomery Cliff—you remember him?"

"Yeah, I saw him in *From Here to Eternity* and *Rain Tree County*."

"Well, like Montgomery Cliff," Annette continued, "Father Thomas was slight of build. He had a sad, serious look; but when he smiled, it was like he was favoring me with a special reward. He came from a family of seven children, but his father was vice-president of a big company. You could tell he didn't come from poor folk by the way he talked and his mannerisms. Even though he was younger than I, I have to admit that I recklessly enjoyed his stealthy glances. Here alone with me in the car he was less guarded about the way he looked at me."

"Did he ask if you found celibacy difficult?"

"Paul!" she said as though I had committed a venal sin; but after a moment of silence, she said, "As a matter of fact he did."

I acted surprised, as though it was a lucky guess. I thought it was more gentlemanly than explaining to her that if this guy was planning to seduce her that would be a way to introduce the subject."

"Yes, he did ask me that but less directly than you did. He seemed awkward about how much we were enjoying each other. I guess you would say that, in a clumsy, inexperienced way, we were flirting with each other."

Annette paused, but I did not interrupt her; clearly she was struggling. Finally she said, "Paul, I did something very stupid. When we arrived at the farm, I pointed out a foot path to Father Thomas and suggested that we take our lunch down to the clearing where we can look out across the river valley. He agreed, and added, 'We can take my beach blanket from the back seat to sit on while we eat.'"

"By now had you guessed what was about to happen?"

"I'm not sure. I had such a mixture of emotions ranging from excitement to fear that I don't think I knew. I have reviewed the events of that day many times and usually end up taking full blame for what happened. I don't think either of us was aware of the risk we were about to take. Like me, he probably just wanted to continue our pleasant interaction. I carried the lunch and he carried the blanket as I led the way down the heavily shaded trail through an orderly stand of huge spruce trees planted years ago. When we emerged from the forest into the sunlight we found a small grassy clearing with a good view of the valley. We spread the blanket; and while we ate lunch, we talked about superficial things. I had become too conscious of our situation and the forbidden fruit to focus on anything else. When we finished eating, I started to stand up but he took my hand and gently drew me toward him. I was off balance and fell into his waiting arms. As soon as we came together, we lost control, but then in the midst of the frenzy, I froze up and stopped. It was close but we didn't actually have intercourse."

"How close can you come and not really do it?" I asked trying hard not to show the anger welling up in me. I don't know why I was angry. I'm not a Catholic, so I didn't feel betrayed by my church. Neither did I seize on the event to justify disliking the church. That was not an issue with me, but I still wanted all the details. Why? I asked myself. You stupid ass, Paul, it's because you are jealous.

"How close, Paul? I won't embarrass either of us with the details; but toward the close of summer and the end of our program, I went to a doctor. I wasn't knowledgeable about female physiology, but even I knew that missing two periods wasn't normal for me. I couldn't believe, though, that I was actually pregnant. The doctor had difficulty convincing me it could happen. I guess he could tell I was embarrassed about talking with him. He spoke very professionally like he was reciting something from a text book. He said, 'Impregnation can occur without penetration if ejaculation occurs in the vicinity of the vaginal opening.' Those words weren't part of my regular vocabulary, but based on what seemed to have happened, I knew what he was saying."

"How did Father Thomas react to this news?"

"After our picnic in the woods, I never saw him again. Carol and I received a message from the secretary telling us that we will have to continue the inner-city program for the rest of the summer without Father Thomas's assistance. He must have been transferred but I didn't want to inquire about it."

"Did you rejoin Sister Carol and the kids?"

"Oh, yes, I guess I didn't tell you what happened next. Anyway, we didn't spend any time looking at the ruins of the farm. I think we were both too concerned about our own ruins."

"You mean you were concerned about breaking your vows?"

"Yes. Or being found out. While we returned to the car and for most of the drive back to the tour group, Father Thomas didn't have anything to say; I couldn't tell if he was mad at me, overwhelmed by guilt or also afraid of being found out."

"Maybe he was waiting for you to speak."

"Yes, I guess that's what it was. When we turned off the highway on to the road into the picnic area, he slowed the car to almost a creeping pace and asked, 'Should we talk about it?'"

"I said, 'Yes, if you want to'; but Father T. was silent. Finally he said, 'I don't know what to say. What do you think?' I said, 'I don't know either.' He resumed normal speed and pulled into the picnic area. The group was still there. Lunch was over but several boys were down by the river bank throwing flat stones, skipping them along the surface of the water. Sister Carol was calling them to rejoin the group. Father Thomas said he was going back to town. I said, 'I'll see you later,' but I didn't—like I said, I never saw him again."

Annette became quiet. Tears appeared to glisten in her eyes but the light was too low at Little Eddy's to be sure. I asked her, "How did you really feel about what happened?"

"That's a hard question, Paul. On the long run, how I felt about it kept changing as events unfolded. At first, it was exciting—the most exciting thing that ever happened to me. I had never been with a man before. I forgot about everything—but then I got scared and I pushed him away, probably denying myself an even greater experience. Later, that same day my mind began to play the *what if* game. Like, what if Father Thomas wants to set our vows aside and have a secret love affair, how will I respond? I vacillated between renewed excitement and the nausea of panic."

"Would you have quit the church and married him?"

"I didn't seriously consider that; we barely knew each other; we didn't have time to fall in love. We just sort of collided—clumsy, inexperienced and unrestrained. It would have been hard to identify an ounce of romance in what we did. As for marriage, in looking back, I didn't think either of us would have been equipped to make a living. Both of us had spent our adulthoods serving the church. Living in a convent, I rarely made any decision regarding my own life; I still have difficulty with it."

Annette was very intense as she examined this disturbing episode in her life. I found myself completely absorbed in her struggle, but at the same time, I was aware of how beautiful she was even when she was upset. I wanted to hold her; I wanted her to love me and to have our relationship move beyond that good night kiss that ends with her tensing up and pushing me away. But now what? Not only is it likely that her years of celibacy were impacting our relationship, but her experience with that priest probably adds to it. Or maybe it is time for me to consider that I am just not her type. After all, the circumstances of Father Thomas's situation were far less opportune than mine yet . . .

Annette had paused briefly; but now she continued to the next stage of her thinking, which began when she was sure Father Thomas had disappeared. "Up to that point," she said, "I was still feeling warm about him and thought a lot about what it would have been like to have gone all the way. I even imagined that by chance it might happen again—and how it would be. But, that fantasy gradually gave way to wondering what happened to Father Thomas. I decided that he must have told the bishop what we did and was immediately transferred to another parish; or maybe he just quit the church and quietly left in shame. Since he never tried to see me again, I felt deserted. I even began to think I loved him and disappointed him. On top of that, if he had been punished or transferred, I felt it would be my fault—that I was totally responsible."

"Weren't you at all concerned about what might happen to you? If Father Thomas confessed, he may have identified his playmate."

"Yes, I was a whole lot concerned. If he had told any part of the story, whoever listened to his confession would not have had much trouble guessing who his lover was; everyone in the parish knew we were working together. Sister Carol would have been ruled out because she was considerably older than Father Thomas; I was only somewhat older than he."

"And what about going to confession, how did you handle that?"

"I put a pretty soft light on my behavior, as much as I could and still be within the bounds of truth. I confessed that as a single woman I had been passionate with a man. I didn't acknowledge to myself that, in making this confession in a church some distance from my parish I was being deceptive. I was wearing my hiking clothes and didn't tell the priest I was a nun. My guilt over holding back the details wasn't large compared to my feelings of responsibility over the event itself. By then, I was already thinking that maybe I wasn't cut out for a life of celibacy."

"So, what you're saying is that from the time of the picnic to the time you discovered you were pregnant—what two months later—no one said anything to you about it?"

"Nothing. Not a word. Meanwhile, I received a letter from my mother telling me that Aunt Lettie wasn't doing well. Mom and I had not been close from the time I left home—for that matter, we never were very close, so receiving a letter from her was a rare occasion. She didn't say what Aunt Lettie's problem was, but I already knew her health and mental state had declined."

"How long had it been since you had seen her?"

"A little over a year. Already at that time her health and memory were failing. What struck me especially was her tendency to withdraw. She had always been outgoing, now she no longer visited old friends. She had lost interest in weaving and most other things she used to enjoy. She fed and watered the sheep but apparently nothing else was done for them. Anyway when the summer program ended, I thought that with my pregnancy and the deterioration of Aunt Lettie's health this would be a good time for me to take a leave of absence. Mother Superior wasn't receptive to my request; she had other plans for me and wanted me to postpone my leave for six months. Each time I tried to address the subject she became more insistent. My frustration mounted until there seemed to be no other choice than to tell her why I had to take a leave of absence."

As Annette spoke, that frustration and her pain were clearly registered on her face; she was near tears. But then, she said in all seriousness "—or I suppose I could have just allowed the muffin to rise in their ecclesiastical midst."

I could not hold back my laughter. At first Annette was startled by my reaction, but then she realized what she had said and joined me. We laughed until tears came to our eyes. Everyone in the restaurant was looking at us including Melba who announced to the other customer, "No use waiting, folks. I don't think they're going to share their joke."

When we regained control, Annette picked up where she had left off. Now that we had become the center of attention, she spoke in almost a whisper, "I suppose I should have just flat out quit the sister business at that time, but it would have caused an even greater hubbub than trying to get an extended leave of absence. My plan really was to resign but I was too cowardly about it and thought it would be easier to do it by mail. After more delays and haggling, Mother Superior found alternatives and agreed to my leave. A few days after I settled in at Aunt Lettie's, my periods resumed."

"So, were you really pregnant?" I asked.

"I don't know. The doctor, who had pronounced me pregnant hadn't run any tests, so who knows whether I lost the baby or never had one?"

Most of Little Eddy's guests were leaving so we decided to go back to Annette's house for a nightcap.

7

When we pulled into the driveway, the sheep were calling. Annette went to feed them; and I went into the house to build up the fire in the fireplace—already we had a routine for what to do when we arrived at her house. I put some small sticks on the remaining embers and was puffing at them with the bellows when I gradually became aware that I was not alone. Had I heard something? If I had, I was not conscious of what it was. The only lights that were on in the house were in the kitchen. I looked around and did not see anyone, so I decided it was my imagination and returned my attention to the fire. When the twigs caught fire, I added larger pieces of wood then stood up to stretch my back. I still felt I was not alone. I looked more carefully into the corners of the kitchen, then through the open door into the unlit dining room. That is when I saw her, a slender figure standing back in the murky light, barely visible. I felt she wanted me to see her but not too well. I stared at her without comment. Neither of us moved. Finally, I waved, ever so slightly; but she did not respond, so I remained silent and continued to stare. I was afraid if I moved toward her, it would frighten her. Was this a spirit or what? I had never seen a spirit before; until now, I had not believed in them. The longer I looked at her, the better I was able to make her out. She was wearing a dress that came a few inches below her knees. It was the dress, obviously, that had unconsciously set me to thinking of this spirit as a woman. Now, I also saw that she was wearing a short coat; for some reason I thought it was fur; but I was not certain. Before I could establish if it was fur, I heard Annette open and close the outside door into the entrance way. I glanced toward the sound briefly; and when I looked back to the dining room, she was gone. Had I seen a ghost, or had I imagined the whole thing?

When Annette entered the kitchen, she said, "That woolly pair gets so irritated with me when I'm late with their dinner—it's a good thing their vocabulary is limited to one word. Even with that, they're able to make me feel like a bad mother." Then she noticed the fire and said, "Hey, nice fire; maybe it wasn't so bad for me to take that long to get them settled."

I looked back at the fire and was surprised, too, to see how well it was going; I was also surprised that Annette thought she had been gone a long time. Perhaps I had been in contact with the ghost longer than I thought. I decided not to tell Annette about the apparition—struggling now with whether I had seen anything or just imagined it. So I just said, "Yes. The fire is cozy but if you'll excuse me I think I'll use your bathroom. Those two beers have caught up to me."

"Sure," she said. "You remember where it is?" Before I could answer, she said, I think I'll go, too; I'll use the one upstairs."

While I was in the bathroom, I remembered that I had left Annette's doggy bag on the counter in the kitchen. I had meant to remind her to refrigerate it before the kitchen warmed up. When I returned, Annette had not come down yet, but apparently she had spotted the bag and put it away before she went upstairs. I wandered around the kitchen while I waited for her and ended up being especially attracted to a weaving on her loom. It was colorful and had dancing figures bordering the outer edge. They made me think it was for a little girl. When Annette returned, I told her how beautiful it was.

"Thanks," she said. "It's a poncho for my plumber's 12-year-old daughter. During the worst cold snap this winter, a water pipe froze and split. The plumber was willing to fix it if I would make a poncho for Kathy. Her birthday is next week; I'm almost finished."

"Kathy is a very lucky girl. I'm just so amazed you're able to do that."

"Thanks, but it really isn't that hard. I'll let you watch me sometime and demystify the process for you. Right now, though, it's time to relax. I'll get our bottle." I presumed she was fatigued after the stressful telling of her life's story.

I put the goblets on the table and when she returned poured the brandy. Once we were seated, I asked Annette if she felt any relief from talking about her experience with Father Thomas.

"Yes, but after putting it into words, I wonder if my feelings of guilt and pain weren't exaggerated. My limited experience with men and the moral setting where this took place probably magnified it for me."

I nodded and said, "It could be, I suppose." I was glad to hear her put the experience in a more reasonable perspective. I didn't want to say so though; it was certainly real and upsetting for her.

She took my hands in hers and drew them toward her; she put her head down and rested her forehead on our folded hands. Then she kissed my hands and said, "Thanks, Paul, for bearing with me. You are a good friend."

I wished she had said something more endearing. I would have known how to respond to that—but, a conventional response like *you're welcome* seemed trite. Finally, I said, "I'm more than just a friend."

She said, "Yes, you are. I care about you more than any man I have ever known."

I stood and drew her to me. When I kissed her, I felt her body respond, but when I let my hand slide down to her buttocks, she drew away from me. "I'm sorry Paul. I'm very attracted to you but I'm just not ready yet. I need more time."

I said, "OK." But, it was not OK; her repeated rejections were really bothering me. Our relationship seemed to be going nowhere. All of a sudden I blurted out, "The reason you don't think it's time for us to make love—is because you're afraid the ghost might see us?"

"What ghost?"

"The one you gave your doggy bag to."

"I gave my doggy bag to a ghost? Paul, ghosts don't eat—you know that."

"They do if you warm their food in a microwave oven."

Looking down at the table, she said, "I thought I was being very sneaky about that."

"Oh, you were sneaky, all right. But, when you turned on the oven, the house lights dimmed briefly; and a few minutes later, I could smell chicken and baked potato as the odors drifted by my nose on their way up the fireplace flue. Besides, I saw your ghost."

"You saw her! When? Where?"

"In the dining room, while you were feeding the sheep. She materialized there in the dark room. I could barely see her but she stood there for quite awhile. She didn't move or say anything and neither did I. For a moment my attention was briefly distracted by your coming into the house; when I looked back, she was gone."

Annette swirled her brandy, took a sip, put the glass down and looked at it, then picked it up, took another sip and put it down. "That's the first time she's been downstairs for a long time." After a pause, she said, "Guess you caught me in another lie. . . . What can you expect from a fallen nun?" She was crestfallen.

"I don't think of you as a fallen nun; nor am I bothered that you told me Aunt Lettie is dead, when she isn't—I assume that was Aunt Lettie."

"Yes. It was Aunt Lettie. She isn't dead. . . . It was her lie, though, not mine."

I waited for Annette to explain but she apparently was still troubled over being caught in a lie. Meanwhile, I was sorry I had not stuck to my original thought of not mentioning the ghost; but with its image foremost in my mind, it slipped out. I said, "I'm sure you had a good reason for telling me Aunt Lettie is dead. It wasn't a casual thing for you to weave a story like that into our relationship."

"No. It sure wasn't. The issue first came up about a year ago when Aunt Lettie asked me to tell people she had died. I ignored it then but now she has become insistent. We argued about it for days starting with when I told her I had invited you out here to ski. At first she was delighted that I had a date with a man and asked all kinds of questions about you; but then, she became worried that I might invite you in. I told her it would be nice to have you in for beans and hot dogs after we finish skiing. She agreed but continued to hold her mouth in a tight line. I asked her what was bothering her. At first she wouldn't tell me but I continued to coax until she admitted that she was worried I would call her down to meet you or bring you upstairs."

"If she didn't want to meet me, wouldn't it have been less complicated to tell me she was asleep or something?"

"I tried that but she had already decided our relationship was going to be long-term and that she needed a permanent solution to deal with you or any other guests I might want to bring to the house. I told her a dozen times it wouldn't work to selectively tell people she's dead. That took her back to her original request of a year ago when she wanted me to tell everyone she had died, been cremated and sent back to Ohio."

"Wasn't she concerned about the legal implications like a public announcement, execution of her will and dispersal of her property?"

"No, she wasn't concerned about those things, but I was. I used those arguments and every other I could think of. I told her I didn't want to lie for her, especially such a dumb lie; but it became an obsession with her. It wasn't enough for her to withdraw and become a recluse. She said people will drive by and know she's in there and talk about her, even call her strange names. She insisted that I either tell people she has passed away or help her to die, knowing full well I wouldn't do that. Until now, you and Todd are the only ones I have told Aunt Lettie's lie to. I'm hoping the issue will pass before I get in too deep or she insists that I make a public announcement of her death."

"Believing that Aunt Lettie and Uncle Matt are dead didn't make any difference in my case, but it does to Todd if he thinks he's the sole heir to the property. Did you tell your aunt about Uncle Matt's bastard son and his claim to the estate?"

"No, and I don't plan to tell her either unless it becomes necessary. I don't think she would take it well to find out that Uncle Matt had a son. I did ask her, though, if Uncle

Matt left a will. She said he did and that she inherited all but a small amount of cash; that went to people she didn't know, not relatives but people she had never heard of who apparently had done favors for him in the past. So that's why I'm not worried about Todd's claim; ownership of the property was legally transferred to Aunt Lettie."

"Todd must believe his right to it has something to do with bloodline but I think that's only if there isn't a will. Did Aunt Lettie show you Uncle Matt's will? It would be interesting to know if Margo Bowen was one of the people mentioned in the will, maybe one of the names Aunt Lettie didn't recognize who received a small amount of money."

"Margo Bowen? Oh, you're talking about Todd's mother's name before she married Trish? Yes, that would be interesting but I haven't read Uncle Matt's will."

"Are your going to tell Todd that Aunt Lettie is still alive and legally owns the farm?"

"I won't unless his nuisance level forces the issue. I'm afraid if he finds out she's alive he'll try to get to her and pester her to see the will. In a way it's good that she doesn't come downstairs anymore. I used to be able to coax her down with a special dinner, but now she insists I bring all her meals up. She's afraid someone will visit unannounced and she won't be able to hide fast enough. I bought a microwave oven and a small refrigerator for her some time ago because we aren't always on the same schedule. For awhile she made her own tea and warmed food from the refrigerator but then she started having trouble with the microwave. She'd get mad and yell at me because the goddamn microwave doesn't work. I'd review again each step you have to take to turn it on but she was too angry and impatient to listen—or remember."

"I can't say I blame Aunt Lettie for getting irritated. If her microwave is like mine, it takes seven or eight clicks to set the timer and temperature level."

"Yeah, but I wish she wouldn't yell at me."

"I would have trouble with that, too. In terms of her being dead, though, haven't the neighbors or her friends asked about her?"

"A few have, I tell them she's failing and too sick to see anyone. I don't tell Aunt Lettie they asked about her."

"I would think she would become lonely with only you to talk to. I had the impression from things you said earlier that she used to be pretty outgoing."

"Yes, she used to have friends and a lot of attention. Now she complains about being bored. She's sick of T.V., and the books and magazines I bring her aren't any good. The problem is she can't remember earlier parts of the story long enough to understand later parts. At first she was interested in knitting and crocheting doilies; but when she would make a mistake she would become angry. If I tried to help, she wouldn't listen or would get mad at me. I was glad when those activities came to an end."

"Even then, it sounds like she's pretty demanding."

"I'll say, I spend as much time with her as I can; but it's never enough. You remember, Paul, I told you earlier how she likes to talk about old boyfriends, well she still does. She repeats herself a lot; but if I'm patient, she often rewards me with more explicit details of her love affairs. Her life was very rich and colorful—colorful, at least, compared to my ascetic life. I suppose it's the vicarious experience that holds my attention. I get to feel what living is like without risking too much of myself in it."

Once Annette stopped worrying about her lie, her conversation flowed along without me prompting her. She told me, "Auntie had a flare for the dramatic in both her dress and her conversation—and I suspect in her flirtatious behavior with men, too. The dining room is pretty dark without the lights on; how well were you able to see her?"

"Not well enough to decide if I was looking at a ghost or a person. I also think I was mesmerized by what I was seeing. You said it took you a long time to get the sheep settled. It all seemed like a very short time to me; without realizing it, I must have stared at her for quite awhile."

"Mesmerized, huh? Well, I'm sure Aunt Lettie loved every minute of having you see her—of having a man's eyes on her. She would especially enjoy it if I told her you were mesmerized by her. She had put a lot of preparation into her appearance. When I delivered her doggy bag dinner, she hadn't had time to change. She must have barely made it back to her room before I went up. At the time, I wondered why she was so breathy. I couldn't figure out what she was up to. There she was all decked out in a party dress and wearing her mink stole. When I asked her about it, she said, she just felt like putting them on. I told her she looked great and asked her if she was thinking of coming back to life; but she said, no, that she wanted to be remembered as she was, and gestured toward a large portrait on the wall that captured her beauty at an earlier time. She didn't say a word about her little escapade into the living world and she didn't seem concerned either about having blown her cover."

I asked Annette what she thought Aunt Lettie expected me to do, if I'm supposed to pretend, too, that she's dead.

"I don't know. She probably considers us family now—a man, a woman and a ghost. She would expect you to protect the family lies. Except she doesn't know yet that you thought she was a ghost. That might be her solution; if she ever decides to join us, she will simply materialize; but only so you and I can see her."

Having recovered from being caught in a lie, Annette could now see the humor in Aunt Lettie's appearance. I asked her what she had told her aunt about me that made her curious enough to blow her cover.

Annette said, "Everything."

Startled, I repeated, "Everything?"

"Yes, everything. I hope you don't mind. You know, after listening to Aunt Lettie tell the same old love stories over and over again, I wanted to have something to tell her. She doesn't want to hear about my life in the convent, so my short fling with Father Thomas and now our relationship are the only experiences with men I have to talk about—except of course, that little bit of petting I did with Eric while I was a teenager. As for the Father T affair, I had to tell Aunt Lettie about that, since when I came to live with her, I still thought I was pregnant and was going to have the baby here at her place."

Suddenly, Annette stopped talking and looked at me carefully. "You look irritated. Shouldn't I have told her about us?"

I was momentarily angry about Annette discussing our private relationship with Aunt Lettie; but then I realized how naive Annette was about this sort of thing, and what did it matter anyway, so I said, "No, I'm not mad. I'm just surprised you would tell her everything about us—but then I guess there isn't much to tell, is there?"

"I thought there was; and based on what I told Aunt Lettie, she must have thought you were interesting enough to get all gussied up before revealing herself to you."

"C'mon, Annette, what did you tell her?"

"You really want to know the details? OK, I told Aunt Lettie I thought maybe you love me, that every time you kiss me you seem to get aroused and anxious to go to bed with me."

"Oh, God. You really told her I become aroused when I kiss you and right away want to take you to bed?"

"Well, not exactly in those words. What I said was, 'I could feel you becoming hard and pressing against me.' Aunt Lettie laughed and said, 'If he gets a hard-on over you, that's a good sign but it doesn't necessarily mean he loves you.' When I used that word now, I was experimenting; I wanted to see if I could say it."

"Oh you did fine. I'm getting a hard-on now just thinking about it."

"Really?" she said. "It happens that easily?"

"It does when I'm around you." I stood up, went around the table and raised her to her feet. When I embraced her, she pressed herself against me and allowed me to rub against her. We did not kiss. We just held on to each other like the wrong move might break the spell. This went on for awhile. I could feel Annette begin to breathe heavily— suddenly she tensed up and pulled herself away.

"That's enough, Paul, maybe too much." She went back to her chair, put her elbows on the table and buried her face in her hands while she calmed down. I went over and gently placed my hands on her shoulders. She reached back, patted one of my hands and said, "I'm sorry, Paul, this just isn't the time or place." When her breathing slowed, I returned to my chair across from her. She looked up with a smile and asked, "Paul, was that love?"

I said, "Yes, but that's just a beginning. Love is more than that."

"Really?" she said with a sly smile, "I'll ask Aunt Lettie what she thinks."

8

A couple days after my encounter with the *spirit*, I went to visit Annette with a six-pack of beer and a large enough pizza to share with the apparition.

Annette met me at the outer door and held the pizza while I took off my coat and hung it in the entranceway. She said, "I asked Aunt Lettie if she would like to join us for pizza, but she declined. After you left the other night, I told her how you thought she was a ghost when she suddenly appeared in the dining room, and that you were mesmerized by her presence. She smiled slightly and appeared pleased; but then her smile faded and she flatly denied having been in the dining room or downstairs at all. She thanked me for inviting her to join us, but said, 'You and Paul should be alone. I may have a piece of pizza and a beer later if there is any left.'"

"Along with her pizza, she'll also want an update on the progress of our love affair."

As Annette put the beer mugs on the table, she asked, "Do you mind? I mean, after all, it isn't like she's going to spread a rumor all over town and ruin your reputation."

"No, that doesn't worry me."

"Something's bothering you; I mean if you don't want me to tell Aunt Lettie about us, I won't. By the way, she assured me that she did die last year and hasn't changed her mind on that nor does she have any interest in coming back to life."

"I'm not bothered about what you tell Aunt Lettie. It just takes me a little time to get used to sharing our privacy—even with a ghost."

"I thought guys didn't concern themselves about privacy. I thought they liked to brag about their conquests. Is it that girls aren't supposed to be proud of theirs? Is that what bothers you? Girls aren't supposed to tell?"

I stood shaking my head in wonder not knowing what to say, while Annette grinned. I countered with, "You can't really call it a conquest until you get me into bed with you."

"I suppose that's so, but that wouldn't be a problem, would it? I mean getting you to go to bed with me?"

"Not at all if you could ever settle on an appropriate time and place."

Instead of answering me, she said, "I think we better put the pizza in the oven for a few minutes." When she returned to the table, she took a sip of beer, looked at me with an innocent smile and said, "I suppose you would like to have me give you some clues as to what *appropriate time and place mean*s. The fact of the matter is, Paul, I'm a 39-year-old woman completely ignorant about having a relationship with a man. Until recently, my thoughts and emotional feelings about sex were pretty much suppressed by my mother and the Catholic Church. Now that I'm trying to overcome the effect they have on my emotions, I'm left without a social or moral system I can depend on. The feelings you bring out in me are a little scary; but I think if I could overcome the fear, I would really enjoy just turning myself over to you. So against that background, how am I supposed to know when, where or if I should share my intimacy with you? I would like to, Paul, because even right now the thought of being with you is exciting to me; but something keeps telling me this isn't the time or place so I freeze up. I hope you'll be patient and help me find my way in what is really a new world for me."

The things Annette said would not have occurred to me; but I could see now they would be true. I should not have been in such a rush to get her into bed even though that is what men do. But, this is different; I really love Annette—it's not just mating time. Annette must have been able to tell that I was giving serious thought to what she said. I may have nodded in agreement—I do not remember. Anyway, Annette came over and kissed me, her mouth slightly open. But we embraced for only a moment before she broke off and went to check the pizza. Patience, Paul, I told myself as my barometer rose another notch; but at the same time, I wondered how she could do something like that after claiming naivety.

As I watched Annette work on the salad, I said, "You told me you've been living with Aunt Lettie for three years. Has she given you a lot of advice on how to live outside the convent? You don't seem completely ignorant about the facts of life."

"Yes, Aunt Lettie helped me quite a lot. She got me my first job, you know, the one at Old Sturbridge Village. With her interest in crafts, she got to know a lot of people who work there. Before I started, she helped me brush up on the gardening, pottery and weaving skills she had taught me as a child. At the same time she encouraged me to look things up in books and pushed me to read more than I normally would have. Confidence building was also part of her program. She repeatedly told me that I have a natural talent for working in the crafts."

"Is it any easier for you to read and write now than it was when you were in school?"

"I've learned a few more tricks that help me unscramble words. I took some basic college courses and some psychology and sociology courses while I was a nun. These pushed me beyond my high school reading ability. Writing my garden article, too, has done more for me than just keep me from sliding back. But, of course, what you were really asking me, Paul, was if Aunt Lettie helped me with my courtship skills. It wasn't my craft skills you were inquiring about."

"Yes, I guess that was the original question."

"Aunt Lettie pushed me to overcome my reservation about dating and advised me on how to attract a man's interest; but she didn't give me much hands-on information. Anyway, Todd Bowen was the first man I ever dated, if having a beer with a man is considered a date. I might have given up right then if Aunt Lettie hadn't insisted I try again—and look, Paul! You're the winner." With a flourish she set the full salad bowl in front of me and went back for the pizza.

I said, "Yes, I'm the lucky winner. You know, you were so cool about it out there in the *Chronicle* parking lot last winter. I had no idea what you were up to. You put more planning into that than I ever suspected at the time."

She laughed as she wiped pizza sauce from her face, "Aunt Lettie kept asking me about eligible men, as she called them. I kept telling her there aren't any; they're all married. But during that time, I was already doing research on you. Beth Turbot was my main source of information. She told me you were single; and if she weren't so G. D. old, she'd go after you herself."

"She said that! How did you manage to talk to Beth about me when my desk is right next to hers?"

"I happened in on days when you were off on assignment. She loved talking about you. She agreed with me that you are a good-looking man and probably more sensitive and intelligent than your run-of-the-mill guy. I had already decided to try to get to know you; but I didn't know how, beyond saying 'Hi, Paul,' when I walked by your desk; but that didn't get me anywhere. Our encounter in the parking lot, when I invited you to go skiing, was pure chance. It did go well, though, didn't it? I went right home and told Aunt Lettie. She was so delighted you'd never guess she was dead."

"That is funny. She must still be interested in your courtship or she wouldn't have sneaked down to peak at me."

"Oh, yes, she's more than just interested. Like you said, after you leave tonight, she'll want me to sit with her while she has her pizza and beer. She won't let go until she knows every detail of what we did and what we said to each other."

"If she's so interested in life, it's surprising she wants to remain withdrawn from the world."

"I often think that, too; but as I told you earlier, she was quite a beautiful woman. After all the attention she received when she was younger, it was hard for her to accept being old. If you could see her room, you'd know she enjoyed her good looks to the fullest. Dozens of framed photographs occupy every available space and she's in every picture, some with famous movie stars. She and Uncle Matt went to expensive restaurants in Boston all year around; and during the summer, they often went to Newport, Rhode Island. He knew a lot of people. When they were out to dinner and encountered his acquaintances, they would often ask Uncle Matt if he and his lovely friend would join them. The way Aunt Lettie tells these stories; it was because these people were anxious to meet her. She thinks Uncle Matt used her for bait to get to know influential people."

"With all that attention, I would think the memories would give her enough momentum to carry her gracefully to the end."

"Yes, you would think so; but back when I was still in the nun business, she was already showing signs of depression and disappointment with her life. She complained about not being able to go to Boston shopping and how shabby her wardrobe had become, and how the men who used to drop by were now dropping dead or had become old and ugly. She didn't like old people and couldn't accept the fact that she had become one of them. The final disappointment came when she had to admit to herself she was having trouble remembering day-to-day things. She was embarrassed about it and was afraid people would find out. Her recollection of the past at that stage, though, was phenomenal."

"Would she remember Joe Esposito?"

"Based on what Aunt Lettie told me not long ago, I'm sure she would. She said Joe had an eye for her. She thought he was a creep, though; but, yes, she would remember him."

"Do you think that after I'm around for awhile Aunt Lettie will get used to me enough to tell me about him?"

"I don't know. Why? We've established that Todd's interest in me has to do with his heritage, not with Esposito's hidden money, so let's talk about something else?"

"Sure. I'd like to go back to discussing the sexual rehabilitation of a former nun."

"You can't rehabilitate something that never was."

"Yes. You're right. So, tell me about the pot of gold. You know something about it, don't you?"

"Paul, do you remember how shocked you were when I called you a 'turd'? Well, right now you're being a pushy turd. You don't have any reason to pursue that issue unless you're hoping for an interesting story to publish—and I don't want that to happen—but, I'm going to tell you anyway about Esposito, so we can get on with our lives. I want you to promise, though, that you won't publish any of it; and when I ask you to tell me something about your secret life, which is most of it, you'll remember you owe me."

Not until I said, "OK," did she begin.

"Uncle Matt made a lot of money. Whatever his business was, he had a lot of cash stashed in the house—money he hadn't paid taxes on. There's no point in asking Aunt Lettie where the money came from. I already tried that. She told me she stopped asking Uncle Matt that kind of question early in their marriage when she found his answers were always a bunch of babble about working for the government—secret stuff she shouldn't know about. Anyway, during the construction project on the house, while Aunt Lettie was staying with my mother, Uncle Matt had a hidden wall safe installed in the dining room. After a while, it turned out the safe wouldn't hold all the money, which was mostly in low denomination bills, so he loosened panels of the wainscoting and tucked some of the money in the walls. A couple of years before Uncle Matt died he and Aunt Lettie came home from a trip to Newport to discover that their house had been broken into. The safe had been chopped out of the wall with an ax and the wainscoting pulled loose. The money was gone."

"Did they take anything else?"

"No, just the safe and the money. Aunt Lettie had left expensive jewelry lying loose on her dressing table and in an open jewelry box."

"Maybe the burglars didn't have time to go through the whole house."

"There was probably only one burglar and he wasn't in a hurry; he knew when they would be back. There were signs he looked in all the rooms. Aunt Lettie said he especially made a mess of Uncle Matt's room. He emptied all the dresser drawers onto the floor and tossed everything out of his closet. But, Aunt Lettie's room was left in an orderly condition. She could tell things had been removed from her chest of drawers and put on the bed; but when the burglar returned them to the chest, it wasn't always to the right drawer. So, what do you make of that, Paul?"

"I think somebody liked Aunt Lettie better than Uncle Matt. In fact, that somebody must have liked her quite a lot to pass up the jewelry and put her things back in the drawers. I presume they were either looking for the safe combination or for money hidden in drawers with false bottoms."

"Yes, that's what Aunt Lettie thought, but she went one step further. She thought it was Joe Esposito. Uncle Matt pooh-poohed it; he said Joe was too loyal to do anything like that. Of course, Uncle Matt couldn't bring the police in on the theft because he hadn't paid taxes on the money."

"Yes, and that sort of spoils the lie he told your aunt about working for the government, since the money would have had the taxes already deducted if it was a regular job."

"Aunt Lettie didn't believe Uncle Matt worked for the government and he knew she didn't believe him; but he also knew she wouldn't dare call him a liar. Anyway, not long after the robbery, Joe was arrested—not for robbing Uncle Matt—but for racketeering and a lot of other stuff associated with it."

I said, "Well, if that's the end of Aunt Lettie's story, it leaves a lot of loose ends, doesn't it? For example, was Uncle Matt working for the government as an FBI informant and being paid under the table? If Uncle Matt had ties to the mob and knew a lot about Joe Esposito's criminal activities, he may have given Joe to the cops to punish him for burglarizing his home or for having too much interest in Aunt Lettie.

In treating Aunt Lettie's belongings with such respect Joe was either stupid or he was intentionally leaving insulting clues so Uncle Matt would know who violated him. Joe and Uncle Matt may have had a falling out earlier and the robbery itself was an act of revenge."

"If Uncle Matt revealed Joe's racketeering activities to the FBI, wouldn't he have placed himself at some risk? He and Joe did seem to be in business together."

"Except Uncle Matt as a paid informant may have been protected by the FBI."

"Of course, so he really was working for the government."

"That was a very interesting story, Annette, why were you so reluctant to tell me about it?"

"Because I knew that Uncle Matt's robbery and occupation would make such a juicy news story it would torment you not to be able to publish it. And if you were to throw in a ghost and a runaway nun, the state would redirect Route 171 past this house so tourists could gawk at it. I couldn't tell you when you first wanted to know about this because I didn't know you very well back then. For that matter, I still don't know you. The only thing that's different now is that you know all about me. I must have taken it as a hopeful sign that you've accepted me in spite of my peculiar background and current way of life. I guess I am also still impressed with the way you tried to help the Lynns; it shows that you do have the capacity to care about others."

As I listened to Annette evaluate the growth of our relationship, I didn't admit that what I did for the Lynns was a favor to her; it was what she would have wanted me to do. Instead, I asked her if she had heard from the Lynns recently.

Annette said, "I stopped by yesterday on my way home from work. They're doing OK."

"That's less than good, isn't it?"

"I wasn't going to tell you. I knew you would be irritated, but obviously, I've already demonstrated that I'm not able to keep anything from you—so why hold this back? As soon as I arrived at their house, Mr. Lynn started grumbling about what a poor job you did in hooking up the pump. He said you had the water line going out the doorway above ground. When he closed the door he had to leave a two inch gap for the hose and couldn't lock the door. After you left, he disconnected it—so Mrs. Lynn's back hauling water from the lake."

I just shrugged and remembered previous experiences when I had tried to help people and how often it turned sour.

"Aren't you angry?" Annette asked.

"Yeah, sort of. The ground was still frozen hard; we couldn't bury the water line. The door into the kitchen from the shed had a lock, so I didn't think they were in any danger. I suppose he was worried someone might steal the junk in his shed. That must have bothered him more than having Mrs. Lynn haul water from the lake."

"Well, anyway, Mrs. Lynn appreciated what you did. She filled every container she had with water from the faucet before he disconnected the pump."

"Warm as the last few days have been I expect he can get someone to bury the line for him now or maybe he'll just scratch it down an inch or two underground, the way it was when it froze." I tried not to show how irritated I was. Instead I asked Annette how she felt about what he did.

"I didn't like the way he blamed you and how willing he was to leave Mrs. Lynn without running water; but during those years as a nun, when I worked with old people, I found that my attempts to help them often didn't go the way I planned. Anyway, here I am back spending nearly half my time trying to help old people. At least Mrs. Lynn appreciates my efforts."

"How about Aunt Lettie, doesn't she give you credit for what you're doing for her? She wouldn't survive if you weren't living with her."

"She doesn't admit she needs help. Big egos aren't exclusive to men—let's go to your place."

I was startled by her non sequitur—and was left scrambling for words. I did not want to appear inhospitable, but neither did I want her to see my place—not now anyway, so I said jokingly, "By the time we go over there and then get you back home it will be too late for you to tell Aunt Lettie what we did. Why don't we do that another time, Annette—when we can get an earlier start?"

"Aunt Lettie can take a nap if she needs to. Besides, don't get the notion we're going to do anything fun, at least not anything that would take long to tell her about it. I'll run these two pieces of pizza up to Aunt Lettie; and then we'll go—don't worry that you left your dirty underwear on the bathroom floor and dishes in the sink."

9

As we drove toward my house, Annette said, "Paul, you told me earlier that you and your family lived in Danbury, Connecticut. Do your parents still live there?"

"My mother does—as far as I know. My father died before I went in the army. He was a lot older than my mother."

"I guess you're like me about not staying in touch with your mother and not having a father."

"Yeah, sort of. Actually, neither of them are my real parents. They adopted me shortly after I was born. I spent most of my growing up years trying to figure out why."

"Why they adopted you?

"Yes?"

"What did you decide?"

"The closest I could come was that my father wanted an heir to his plumbing business and my mother wanted to have someone with poor English to harp at."

"Neither of them loved you?"

"I don't think so; at least they never said they did and never showed it; but then, I didn't know what love was until I met you."

"That's a different kind of love," Annette said as she patted me on the leg. "Did she have a job or anything?"

"Sort of, but more like self-employed. She wrote romance novels."

"Really," Annette exclaimed as though that was special. "Were they good?"

"She wouldn't let me read them. She used a pen name and wouldn't tell me what it was."

"But you found out, didn't you?"

"Yes. On a couple of occasions letters came in the mail addressed to Martha Lovejoy. The first time I saw one, I asked Mom, 'Who the hell is Martha Lovejoy?' She swept the letter from my hand and said, 'I'll see that she gets it.' She didn't even scold me for saying hell. The next time a letter came for Martha, I noticed the return address was the same as Mom's publisher. It was probably a secretary who had trouble remembering the author's pen name versus her real name."

"If your father owned his own plumbing business and your mother was a successful author, your family must have been fairly well-off—or maybe the books weren't that good."

"They were OK, I guess. I read several of them. But as a teenager, I couldn't judge romance novels. I did find her use of foul language interesting, though; I thought she must have learned it from me. The major love scenes in her books always took place behind closed doors, so I couldn't tell if she knew about sex, only that my imagination at that age wasn't sufficient to fill in what she left out."

"They must have been a nice supplement to the family income, though."

"Not really. Although my mother published at least ten books and received royalty checks, the checks were small and they dribbled down to almost nothing in a short time."

"How about your father's business?"

"Not much better. He kept busy but most of his customers were from a poor neighborhood. He couldn't charge them much and even at that they were slow to pay their bills—if ever. My dad was always in debt to his suppliers. He insisted I help him with his work when I wasn't in school so I could learn this valuable trade with the promise that one day I would own the business. Becoming a plumber never became a goal for me."

"So you took up writing, more in your mother's footsteps."

"I suppose you could look at it that way but I always saw journalism as enough different from writing romance novels that I didn't have to give her any credit for my life."

I recognized that my part of the conversation had turned negative. I wished we could change the subject, but I knew if I did, Annette would accuse me of trying to hide my life from her. I was saved by the sign announcing the town of Chaplin. At that point, Annette began to overflow with expectations and good cheer. I tried to explain to her, "My place isn't that grand, Annette, just a three-room bachelor's pad."

"Whatever it is, it will add to the things you just told me. I may even get to know you before the night is over. . . . Paul, if I seem pushy about going to your place tonight, it's because I didn't want to schedule a visit and give you time to hide things you don't want me to see. I was also hoping that since I revealed an embarrassing and troubling part of my life to you, that you might be willing now to open yours to me. I think it's working."

"Come on, Annette, I'm not that secretive." She smiled and nodded indicating that I am secretive. As we drew closer to my place, I became conscious that my mind was racing through a list of things Annette would see—things she would ask about—not dark secrets, just things I did not like to talk about.

We pulled into the drive; and as the car lights flashed across the house, Annette exclaimed, "That's not an apartment; it's a cute little house." I thought to myself, I suppose you could call it cute. It is a small Cape Cod with a steep, dark-gray roof and white clapboard siding. The front door is red and two windows with red shutters are equally spaced on either side of it. Three huge pine trees shade most of the yard and carpet the ground with needles. "So this is where you live," she said.

"Yes. Gordon and Barbara Filmore built it. They live around the corner on the street we came in on. This was their starter home; they built it to live in while they worked on their dream house next door—the one they planned to raise their family in. They were going to tear the dollhouse down once they finished their dream house; but luckily for me, they weren't able to discard the memories of their earlier life. The rent is about the same as I would pay for three rooms in an apartment building. I like this better since most apartment buildings around here are full of college students who like to party. I've outgrown the party days."

"I don't see any house next door. What happened to the Filmore's dream?"

"Before they started to build it, one of the 1820s colonial homes around the corner went up for sale. They bought it and ended up spending more money and effort renovating it than they would have building a new house, but I think what they have now is nicer than most new homes."

When I opened the front door and Annette stepped inside, she exclaimed, "Wow, its all in one room!"

"Well, at least the kitchen, dining room, living room and my study are all in the front room; but there are two small bedrooms and a bath in the back." What Annette was looking at is a house built on a concrete slab; most of the floor is covered with beige carpeting except where the oil-fed space heater rests on its fireproof pad in one corner and a tiled area sets the kitchen apart from the rest of the room. Annette inspected the kitchen area first, which was pretty ordinary: refrigerator, stove with oven and a small oak table with four chairs. After asking for permission, she opened cupboard doors, drawers and the refrigerator. All of this inspection was carried out with a look of amusement. When she was finished, I said, "So what do you think, Annette? Kind of boring, huh?"

"Not at all," she responded.

"So, what do you know now that you didn't know before?"

"You don't eat out as much as I thought; and in fact, you must do quite a lot of cooking. I'm hurt that you haven't invited me to one of your dinner parties."

"I haven't had anyone to dinner since I moved here. I'm not that confident about my cooking although I must admit sometimes my dishes are pretty entertaining. One thing about living here, though, I'm only ten minutes from the Chinese take-out place, so if dinner is a complete flop, they can bail me out. So how about it, would you be willing to take a chance on one of my dinners next Saturday night?"

"Paul, I'd love to have dinner at your place."

"OK, so it's dinner at my place Saturday. How about Aunt Lettie? Would she be willing to come?"

"You can count on me, but Aunt Lettie—not likely. I wouldn't even know how to convey the invitation to her; you're supposed to think she has quit eating."

While all this banter and house investigation was going on, Annette did not seem to notice how tense I was about her visit; she still wore the look of cheerful expectation that she brought in through the door. Next she turned down the short hallway that separates the bedrooms and ends in the bath-room. Annette turned left into the guest room, looked at it briefly. Then without comment she walked past me into the other bedroom where I sleep. "Yes," she said, when she entered, "that room across the way doesn't have anything to do with you; this one does."

"You mean you like the way I make my bed?" I had just pulled the blankets up to the pillows and unceremoniously dropped them without bothering with the wrinkles.

"It's more formal than my process. Now that I have my own room, I just get out of bed and leave the damage behind like I'm rebelling against my ascetic life. How come you have double beds in both rooms? I would think single beds would give these small rooms a better balance."

"I didn't furnish this place with much thought. When I decided to rent the house, the people at work donated furniture from their garages and attics; Gordon and Barbara also loaned me things. In total I bought very little furniture. All this will tell you about my character is that it's too weak to generate a taste of my own. I guess you're right, though, single beds would look better."

"Oh, God, Paul, don't look to me for advice. Living in convents and Aunt Lettie's museum doesn't qualify me to pass out advice on interior decorating."

"Maybe you developed some common sense guidelines from Old Sturbridge Village." Annette did not answer. By then she had spotted the picture on the nightstand next to my bed. She picked it up and was studying it carefully. I could feel the back of my neck getting hot and the hair prickling up.

"When was this taken?" she asked, not taking her eyes off the picture.

"Fall of 1971," I answered. My voice sounded funny to me, a little tight and high pitched. The picture she held was in a five-by-seven frame so the 12 men in the photograph were pretty small. Annette was probably having trouble finding me among them.

"You were a sergeant?" she said.

"Yes."

"How old were you?"

"Twenty-one."

"Are you still in contact with any of these guys? She was looking straight at me; her eyes serious and penetrating. I looked away for a moment; but when I looked back, she was still looking at me, waiting for my answer.

"They're all dead," I said . . . "except maybe for the guy standing next to me. Last I knew he was in a hospital in Arkansas. I went to see him the year after I got back. He was just a vegetable; he's probably dead now." Annette looked back at the picture for a while, put it back on the table and led the way back to the front room. She stood next to the stove looking serious and thoughtful; the excitement of discovery had turned grim. I went over to my desk, opened the center drawer and swept some loose things from the surface of the desk into it. Although I closed the drawer quietly, she either heard or saw me do it and came over to where I was standing. She said, "Paul, you just hid something you didn't want me to see."

I asked her if she did not think she had sampled enough of my hidden life for one night; but she said, "No, Paul, I want to share it all with you. If it's painful we can cry; if it's funny we'll laugh, if it's shameful we'll accept it and rationalize it. Please open the drawer, I want to see what you thought you had to conceal from me."

I went over, sat on the couch and patted the cushion next to me hoping Annette would join me. She remained standing at the desk shaking her head no without smiling. I remained seated for a moment; gradually her words soaked in and I realized that what she was trying to tell me was that she cared enough about me to want to share my pain as she had shared hers with me. I went back and opened the drawer, then returned to the couch. She looked down for a few seconds at the scrambled pieces of metal where they had landed in one corner of the drawer, then asked if she could pick one up and look at it. I told her she could. I got up from the couch and joined her at the desk where I knew the inquisition was about to begin. Annette turned on the desk lamp and picked a piece of brass from the drawer to hold under the light. Reading the tiny words below the cross she said. "Paul, it says, 'For Valor.' This is so beautiful; what's it called?"

"The Distinguished Service Cross."

She laid the medal carefully on the desktop as though it might break, then asked if she could pick up another one. Successively she ran through the Silver Star, Bronze Star, two Purple Hearts and some lesser medals all of which she arranged on the surface of the desk. When she was through, she stood back and looked at the assemblage. Then she went over and sat on the couch. I picked the cigar box off the side shelf of the desk and swept the medals back in the box where I usually kept them.

Annette asked if I look at those medals very often. I told her, "This is the first time I had them out since I moved here two years ago."

"I guess you didn't have them out to show me, did you?"

"No."

"Who do you show them to?"

"I have never shown them to anyone."

"Why not? I would think you would be very proud to be so honored by your country."

"I was thinking about throwing them away."

"Why on earth would you throw them away?"

"I don't know," I shrugged, hoping she would stop talking about them. "Do you have to work tomorrow?" I asked hoping to derail the direction she was headed.

"Not until afternoon. Why, is it getting late?"

"I guess not. You want a beer or coffee?"

"How about tea? I'd like to talk some more if you feel up to it. You didn't answer my last two questions, you know, why you never showed your medals to anyone and why you were thinking of throwing them away."

While I put the water on, I tried to be casual about explaining to her that when I got home, opposition to the war was pretty strong; I didn't think anyone would be interested in my medals.

"What year was that?"

"Nineteen seventy-two."

"You didn't show your medals to your fiancée?"

"No, Emily made me feel like I was the enemy. She wouldn't have been impressed."

"That must have been tough to take."

"She wasn't the only one who made me feel that way. At first, while we were over there in Nam, we thought we were doing something worthwhile, even patriotic. But, later it became almost as difficult to face coming home as it would have been to stay there."

I tried again to change the direction of our conversation by pouring the tea; but as Annette joined me at the table, she said, "It must have been especially difficult for you,

Paul, while you were there putting your life on the line. I remember how strong opposition to the war was at that time. My community was instructed not to become involved in the protests but I know quite a few sisters in other orders did."

"Yes, some of the news clippings Emily sent me included nuns among the demonstrators. Remembering those pictures fortified my reluctance to talk with you about the war."

"The pictures I have seen of Vietnam suggest that it's a beautiful country. As I think back on what you told me earlier about your job of trying to upgrade facilities in the villages and helping the families of soldiers in your unit, you made it sound like you were a social worker who on your days off took walks in the countryside with your buddies. What about the two Purple Hearts, Paul?" she asked, gesturing toward the desk.

"Yeah, well. . . . By the time my first wound healed, my tour of duty was nearly over. I could have gone home. But I began to think, well, once you're wounded that takes care of that, it couldn't happen again; besides, I'm smarter and more careful now. I also thought about the platoon. You know, when you put 20 guys together, some are assholes and some are OK; but then it eventually turns out that even the assholes have become important to you. Once you've been down a few rocky paths together, they become like family. You know what to expect of them and they know what to expect of you. Interdependency, I guess is what it's called. Anyway, those are the things I thought about in the hospital as my tour of duty was about to run out, so I reenlisted and went back to my platoon—I thought they needed me—or maybe I needed them. I don't know."

10

I was anxious to stop talking about Vietnam; but before I could change the subject, Annette said she had watched a television documentary recently that showed combat scenes from the war. "I found them so upsetting I couldn't watch the program to the end."

I said, "Yes, some of those documentaries were able to incorporate the worst of it. Let's talk about something else."

Annette was persistent about the subject of the war. "What happened when your platoon was wiped out, Paul? Had the enemy taken you by surprise?"

"No. We knew they were out there; we were ready. That's what we thought, anyway. There were just too many of them." I did not think Annette would want me to describe how the bodies piled up in front of our position—and on both sides and behind us, too, so I just said, "We were overwhelmed. We couldn't hold them off. At one point I realized Corporal Nhu and I were the only two from our sector returning fire. He was about seven feet from me. I glanced at him just in time to see a grenade land next to him. Nhu didn't see it. When it went off, his body blocked a lot of stuff that would have hit me, at which point I lost track of what was happening. I was probably unconscious for a while; when I became aware of what I was doing, I had Nhu's gun. Mine must have run out of ammo and I had picked his up. I could still see a little out of one eye. I guess I was still firing. I felt the recoil but I couldn't hear anything. It seemed like Charlie was all over the place. The last thing I remember was lying on the ground thinking about a small culvert that ran under the road near where we had set up a machine gun the night before. When I regained my senses again, I could hear a little out of one ear. People were talking, running and yelling orders in Vietnamese. I knew enough of the language by then so I could tell they were Viet Cong and North Vietnamese. It was pitch-black. While I was feeling around trying to find my weapon, my hand came in contact with corrugated steel. I realized I was in the culvert but I couldn't remember how I got there. I moved my head around so I could see the opening. It was dark out, and there weren't any stars; but I could see the glow of lit cigarettes moving around. The culvert was less than 20-feet long and barely wide enough to accommodate my shoulders. As best I could tell, my head had not reached the halfway point through the tunnel which meant my feet weren't far from the opening at the end where I had entered. I was afraid that when daylight came they would look in and see my boots. I tried to wriggle forward but my legs weren't much help and one shoulder wouldn't support any weight. I discovered, though, that I still had Nhu's gun; it was slung over my shoulder and lying on my back. I struggled to move it forward so it would be ready if I needed it but I must have kept passing out."

"What were you planning to use it for?"

"I don't know; but if you're wondering whether I was planning to shoot myself, no; that never occurred to me. I think my foggy mind was still at war. If I was attacked from the front, I wanted to be able to defend myself. If I was attacked from the rear, though, I couldn't have done anything about it because the rifle was longer than the diameter of the tunnel. I couldn't turn it around—good thing—about all I would have been able to do in that direction is shoot my feet off."

"Were you ever able to get the gun off your back and point it at the opening of the tunnel?"

"Yes, by the time daylight came, I was ready to resume combat; but none of the enemy approached my hiding place. I think I waited most of the day; I really don't know. The next thing I remember is waking up in a field hospital. All I could learn was that the American forces retook the position. Somebody from our side must have looked in the tunnel and saw a pair of GI boots. The following day I was on a plane to Hawaii. They sort of patched me up there; but I needed a lot of long term reconstruction work, so I was put on a plane to Walter Reed Army Medical Center in Washington, D. C."

Annette was thoughtful. Then she stood up and said, "Paul, in a way I'm sorry I put you through all this tonight. I know that my pushing you to relive that experience had to be terribly painful for you, but your sharing it with me makes me feel close to you—like what you said about going down that rocky road with your platoon caused you guys to feel close to each other."

I stood up and was about to comment on what Annette said; but decided not to—I did not know what my voice would sound like. I felt that my eyes might be a little moist. Fortunately, she did not seem to be looking for a response. She took me in her arms and hugged me for a long time. Then she said, "I better be getting home; it's late."

"Why don't you stay here? I'll make you a nice breakfast in the morning."

"Could I sleep in the guest room?"

"If you insist, but my room is nicer."

"In what way?" she teased.

"It's cozier—and friendlier, too," I assured her.

"Hum," she said, "regarding our time and place issue, maybe your dollhouse is the right place. I think it may be. The whole house feels cozy and friendly. But is this the right time? I mean what we went through tonight was pretty hard. I don't know about you, but it's going to take me awhile to sort this out and find the right corner in my brain to store it. I'll have to rearrange a lot of stuff that's already there. I know you spared me a lot of details but my mind insists on trying to visualize all you went through. Some of the images I'm concocting probably include parts of that television documentary I mentioned; that, too, is rummaging around in my mind looking for a place to fit. No—this isn't the time for us to sleep in the same bed. We wouldn't be able to resist trying to make love. We would probably bungle it."

"I guess you're hoping it will be perfect the first time?"

"Yes—why, is that a fantasy?"

"I don't know. I thought we might have to practice quite a lot to make it perfect."

"Paul, you're really bad, you know."

I laughed and asked if she was concerned that Aunt Lettie would worry about her not coming home tonight.

"When I delivered her pizza, I told her I was going over to your house for awhile."

"What did she say?"

She smiled knowingly and said, "How nice."

I asked Annette if she would like to borrow a tooth brush and a pair of pajamas and she said, "Maybe the pajamas, I put a tooth brush in my purse—just in case. You go first, though."

While I brushed my teeth, my mind was not on the disturbing things we talked about earlier; it was totally on Annette's spending the night in my pajamas. For some reason that aroused me—and the thought that she would be right across the hall further stimulated me. I wondered if she would leave the guest room door open when she went to bed. If she did, what would that mean? Would it be an invitation for me to visit her in the night or morning or would it just be a friendly connection. When I finished using the bathroom and announced to Annette it was available, she emerged from the guest room carrying her tooth brush and my pajamas. As we met in the narrow hall, I stepped back so she could get by and tried not to let the bulge in my jeans show; but as she passed, she innocently let the back of her hand brush over it. For one so inexperienced about sex, Annette always seemed to know what to do or say to keep my libido well tuned.

While I was putting on my pajamas, I left my bedroom door open so I could hear her brushing her teeth and running water in the bathtub. I looked down at the bulge in my pajamas, which was even more prominent than in jeans. I sat on the bed and tried not to think about Annette so the bulge would go away; but now I was focused on why she thought we should not sleep together tonight. In consideration of her opinion, I felt it would not be gentlemanly for me to have this hard-on standing between us when we said good night. Based on our previous good night kisses, my guess was that as soon as she felt me press against her, she would freeze up and retire behind her closed bedroom door.

I picked up a book from the nightstand and tried to read but I had trouble finding where I left off. When I listened to the water running in the bathtub, I envisioned Annette taking her clothes off and stepping naked into the water.

Next she would lie down and soap herself all over, turning this way and that, drawing one leg up and soaping it, then the other, and carefully lathering her private parts. After a bit, I heard water draining from the tub followed by Annette rinsing the soap from her body with fresh water. When it became quiet, I pictured her drying herself with the towel. I tried to think where I should be when she comes out; but by the time I swung my legs to the floor to sit on the edge of the bed, she was standing in the doorway wearing only the top to my pajamas; it hung halfway to her knees. Through a mischievous smile she explained, "I couldn't keep the bottoms up. I was afraid, if you decided to chase me around the dollhouse, I would trip over them—then what?"

"If you were hurt, I would have to kiss you everywhere you hurt."

"What if I hurt all over?"

"I would try hard not to miss any places." When I stood up, my pajamas protruded so much Annette could not have helped noticing. Without comment, she turned and went into the guest room. I thought to myself, "oh shit"; but within a second, she was back. She had just turned off the light. Now she stood inside the door to my bedroom apparently waiting for me to make the next move. I took her in my arms and held her close. She pressed against me as though she wanted as much body contact as possible. Then, as if that was not enough, she drew back slightly and unsnapped my pajama bottom. When it fell to the floor, she resumed our embrace.

When I awoke in the morning, the room was full of bright light even though the shades were down. Annette was lying on her side facing me, still asleep. She seemed so natural lying naked beneath the thin sheet. Last night she took me totally by surprise. I had assumed that, if we ever made love, it would begin with the lengthy process of Annette letting go of her past, one step at a time with periods of atonement in between. As I looked at Annette, I thought about how much I loved her, even before last night. I would have been willing to wait for her. I leaned over and kissed her gently on the cheek and nuzzled my face against hers.

"Do you love me, Paul?" she asked still half asleep.

"So much I don't know what to say or do."

"Is that because I let you do it?"

"Oh, God, Annette, don't ask me to evaluate why. It's too big for that. Let's just be glad for what it is and make it last forever."

"You know I didn't reach a climax, don't you?" She sounded worried.

"Yes, but I don't think that's unusual the first time, that will come?"

"I don't know," she said. "Did it spoil it for you?"

"Annette, I was so carried away nothing could have dampened the experience." It was then I realized how selfish my lovemaking had been and that this may not have been such a great experience for her.

Hesitantly she said, "I just imagined that "perfect" would include us reaching a climax at the same time—and here it didn't happen at all for me."

"That was probably my fault. I was too fast. Let's try again." I kissed her soft and tenderly and she responded affectionately; but then she said, looking at the clock, "Not now, Paul, it's too late. I have to get home and feed the sheep."

"You have time for breakfast don't you?"

"Just a quick bowl of cereal and a piece of fruit. Then I have to run."

"It's too far to run. I'll drive you," Annette was too deep in thought to pretend my lame joke was funny. She was slipping back into my pajama top for the trip back to the bathroom where she had left her clothes. She was so lovely, I must have been gawking. I know I was still aroused.

Annette smiled, and spoke to my bulge under the sheet like it was a separate entity, "Another time, perhaps, I have other animals to feed this morning, but thanks for the good time."

I responded for my animal, "You did enjoy it then, at least somewhat?"

"Oh, yes, Paul, I thought it was marvelous—don't think because of what I said about perfect that I didn't enjoy it."

I hoped she meant it and was not simply tending to my bruised ego.

As we drove back to Annette's place, we were both quiet until Annette said, "Paul, don't worry about perfect— if that's what you're doing. Let me tell you what had me concerned all along; it will explain why you shouldn't assume too much responsibility for the direction of our lovemaking. You remember when I told you about Sister Carol, who participated in the inner-city children's project with me?" I nodded and she said, "Well, she, too, had left the convent; but after several years, came back."

"I didn't know you could do that."

"Yes, but don't start worrying about my going back. The point I was going to make is that during my life in the convent, I didn't learn much more about sex than I knew when I went in. As I already told you, what seems like a long time ago, talking about such things was strongly discouraged. Carol, on the other hand, did talk about it, mostly in short bursts. Desire for a normal sex life was the reason she left the convent. Failing to find gratification for her sexual needs was one of the reasons she came back. Even though she was 60 when I knew her, she still had not resolved that issue. One time she told me that for several years before she resigned, she and a priest had been attracted to each other. This was long before I knew her. Anyway, she claimed they resisted having sex until their desire and feelings became overwhelming, at which point, they both resigned."

"Do you think they did actually abstain for several years?"

"I think they did. They probably would have been better off, though, if they had tried it before they quit the church, at least as far as Carol was concerned. She said they never did marry; they just moved in together. Carol told me they tried everything, nothing worked for her; she simply could not have an orgasm and was left frustrated by it, so they split. He eventually married someone else."

"Did she define what everything meant?"

"No, Carol wouldn't tell me. She said I was too naïve to be able to imagine it. She did say, though, that after they split, she dated a lot of different men; and then, wondering if maybe her problem was that she was a homosexual, she had an affair with a woman, but that didn't satisfy her either. What started me to worrying about myself was Carol telling me that during the period after her resignation she was in contact with six other nuns who had resigned. She said that eventually each of them had opened up to her and admitted to having problems with sex."

"And so, your time and place issue was born out of a concern that you might become number seven on Carol's list?"

"Yes. And the perfect issue, too; I guess it was sort of the same thing. I wanted to make sure the situation was perfect, as well as, that our mental states didn't distract us—You're amused! You think all this planning is silly."

"Yeah, sort of; but I guess I can see why you're anxious about it in view of the guilt trip your mother and the church laid on you, topped off with Carol's doomsday message."

"You aren't bothered by any sexual hang-ups?"

"No. I guess you can always tell when I'm aroused. As soon as that happens, my animal takes over and does all the thinking for me."

"I guess men have it easier."

"If they have problems, their macho won't let them discuss it. No, I take that back. When I was a junior in college, Dave, a friend of mine confessed to me that he was worried he might be a homosexual. I was surprised; he seemed like such a normal guy. So, I asked him why he thought that."

"Did he tell you?"

"Yes. He said, 'One night, me and a couple of guys were driving around drinking beer; Fred suggested we give Irma a call. Tim said, Yeah, good idea. Fred explained to me, that sometimes if Irma has a couple of beers, she'll put out. Well, that night she needed only one beer. We started to take turns with her in the back seat; but when it was my turn I couldn't get it up.'"

Annette said, "Does that mean he didn't get an erection?—On the basis of that he thought he was queer? That's such an ugly story. I don't know how a man with an ounce of sensitivity could have sex under those circumstances. What did you tell him?"

"I don't remember exactly but I think it was along the same lines as what you just said."

Annette was silent for awhile; she seemed to be deep in thought. Then she said, "Paul, when I asked you if you had any hang-ups, I was also thinking about religion, but I guess that's not a problem for you. I know you're not a Catholic, but do you have any religion?"

"How do you know I'm not a Catholic, Annette? I didn't know you were a Catholic until you told me."

"Yes, but I've been working hard for the past three years to take a neutral stand on religion while I sort out what's good about it—and what's bad. My problem is that I don't know what I believe intellectually versus what is based on indoctrination. I've been attempting to determine if any of it is for me."

"Have you attended Mass since you resigned?"

"A few times. It's not that easy to kick a habit, you know." I didn't catch her pun at first until she smiled and I realized she was playing off the nun's attire. "But, don't be evasive, Paul, unless of course you really don't want to talk about it. I sort of think you don't have any religion; but I have heard so many stories about foxhole conversions, I'm wondering if you experienced anything like that."

"Annette, I rarely talk about religion because as you suspected I don't have any—or at least nothing conventional. When I was in college, if I said I was an atheist or an agnostic, it usually led to a long argument. I didn't mind then; but by the time I graduated, the arguments had all worn thin and boring. Eventually, I decided, that if a person gets something out of religion, I shouldn't risk spoiling it for him with my views. And, yes, I have seen foxhole conversions; if they make it easier to die, that's fine. But when people offer such emotional declarations as proof of God or even take satisfaction that eventually they will win the debate with me when I'm on my death bed, I don't find any intellectual food in that."

"When you were lying wounded in the culvert, Paul, did you think you were going to die?"

"I don't know. I guess so."

"What did you think about at that time?"

"During my periods of consciousness, I thought about getting Nhu's M-16 off my back and up where I could use it; and I thought about trying to move forward in the culvert where I might get a shot at Charlie."

"You didn't think at all about God and the hereafter?"

"Like I say, some of that may have passed through my mind, but I was kind of busy trying to make use of what time I had left."

"So what do you call yourself now, atheist, agnostic or what?"

"I've never liked either of those terms. Like I said to admit to one or the other is like waving a red flag. Immediately people want to attack you or save you. Agnostic is the better of the two because fewer people know what it means and are less inclined to take issue. I think I might be an existentialist but I'm never sure because I keep forgetting the name or what it is."

Annette looked amused then said, "OK, I'll bite. What is it?"

"Well, I see the word from time to time and occasionally look it up in a dictionary. Each dictionary defines it differently, though, and the definitions are so filled with intellectual gobble de gook that I have trouble understanding what they mean, anyway the part of the definition that I think pertains to me is: A philosophy that doesn't believe in supernatural authority but emphasizes the freedom and responsibility of the individual." Since some of the rest of it I don't believe or I don't understand, I changed the subject and asked Annette, "What will you tell Aunt Lettie about what we did last tonight?"

"I don't know. I've been wondering about that. I suppose it will depend on the amount of detail she insists on. How much do you think I should tell her? Or, maybe you don't want me to tell her anything?"

"Would she let you get away with that?"

"No," Annette said.

"For my part, tell her whatever you like. I don't think Aunt Lettie's going to scold us for anything we did last night."

"Me either, unless it would be for passing up your offer to do it again this morning."

11

Annette called and told me that over the past four days Todd left three more notes, two at the back door and one in the barn by the sheep. Since her trouble with Todd, Annette had become more careful about locking the house; otherwise he probably would have left a note on the kitchen table. Who knows what would have happened if he ever encountered Aunt Lettie?

I visited Annette two nights after her call about the notes. She told me that yesterday Todd was waiting for her when she returned from work. He slipped into the passenger side of her car; and before she could order him out, he flooded her with how glad he was to see her and how great she looked in her early American costume.

Annette said he smelled like beer and that once he got his conversation warmed up with layers of flattery—he asked to borrow $2,000 to tide him over "until this estate thing gets settled." Annette thought he was having trouble finding a lawyer to take his case without a retainer. After she told him she did not have that kind of money and that she would not lend it to him if she did, he wanted to borrow $20 dollars until payday. She told him she did not lend money to casual acquaintances. He laughed and reminded her, "Hey! We aren't casual acquaintances; we're cousins," whereupon he picked Annette's wallet from her open purse on the seat and removed all the bills. Then he returned five dollars to her wallet and pointed to the gas gauge saying, "You need gas." The rest of the money he shoved in his pocket and said, "I owe you $18. I'll pay you Saturday."

Annette told him not to bother and that if he ever sets foot on the property again, she would call the police. Todd laughed and said he did not think the police would drive all the way out to put a relative off her property, especially one who had come to repay a loan. He said, "If I were to molest you that might be a different matter. I only bring that up because I find that flash of anger in your eyes kind of exciting. It makes me think how much fun it would be to take you down and see what's under that fetching costume you're wearing. How about that, Annette! We could have a good old-fashioned toss in the hay some time over there in the barn."

Annette was still upset but less so than I would have expected, maybe because it was a day later. She related the incident more like it was an interesting story than a threatening experience. She was annoyed by Todd's behavior and seemed somewhat frightened; but she was also sympathetic—and that is what I did not understand. I also worried that she underestimated who she was dealing with, or maybe I was too concerned over what Todd might do. Anyway, I had to be careful that my thinking was not driven solely by jealousy.

I offered to stay with Annette until Todd is no longer a threat but she declined. She said Uncle Matt had fortified the house adequately after the robbery so she was not afraid Todd would break in. "If he attempts to, I'll call the police," she said.

I told her I could get there faster. She said, "I know, but it frightens me what you might do if you got to Todd first."

I tried not to reveal my disappointment over Annette's rejection of my offer to help; but she continued to assure me she would be OK. I was certain she was aware of my feelings about Todd and how I might react. Eventually, I realized she was right; it would serve no purpose for me to pound Todd into the ground. Once I calmed down to a point where I was rational, I asked Annette why she felt sorry for Todd. She said Todd was raised without a father. He only recently discovered that he grew up less than 15 miles from his father—a man who had rejected him—a man whose mother had told him was dead.

"Did Todd tell you these things bothered him?"

"He didn't dwell on it anymore than I do over the absence of my father during my younger years; but when I reflect on my childhood, I am saddened to think how much better my life might have been with a real father. My life's direction may have been less muddled than what it turned out to be."

I did not discuss Todd further. Annette was now calm about the incident; all I could have done is cause her to worry. But, Todd's main goal, after discovering the identity of his father, was to turn his misbegotten birth into profit. And, his only interest in Annette was to get into her pants—and that is what inflamed me.

When I started to make movements and sounds about going home, Annette said, "You mad at me?"

I said, "Heavens no, Annette. You know how much I love you. I couldn't get mad at you. Why would you think that?"

"Because it's so early and you seem angry, even though you're trying to hide it. Do you think I should have given Todd more static about his taking my money?"

"No that was the least of my concerns; you handled that just fine."

"Something is bothering you. I bet it's because I have a small measure of sympathy for Todd or are you jealous because he said he'd like to pull me down in the hay? Paul, you don't have to worry about this guy, he's all puffery and flattery."

Hearing Annette's naïve evaluation of Todd pinpointed for me why I was so concerned over her safety, but she was right about the basis of my jealousy.

It was about 7 p.m. when I left Annette and went out into a windy and rainy night. I had not gone far on Route 171 when I saw flashing lights ahead. I eased past a police car and parked at the end of a small line of spectator's cars. I grabbed my hat from the back seat and walked back to the accident wishing I had my raincoat. A sports utility vehicle had missed the curve, plunged down a 12-foot embankment and landed upside down. One State police officer was holding back the spectators while another with a flashlight was going back and forth between a figure lying on the ground and the wrecked vehicle.

I introduced myself as a reporter to the officer who was holding back the crowd and asked him what happened. When he turned his flashlight in my direction, he said "Hi, Paul, I didn't recognize you in the dark." It was Officer Bill Burger whom I had met on several other occasions. He told me they had been at the accident scene for only a short time. He did not know much about it except that the driver, who was the only occupant, was traveling north at a pretty fast speed, missed the curve and went off the road on the opposite side. Apparently he had been tossed from the car when it turned over.

Another police car pulled up with two more officers followed by an ambulance. The scene had more light now, so I could see the wrecked car. It was an older Bronco, a light beige color like Todd's. I waited at the scene until the accident victim was brought up to the road. It was Todd. He had been fitted with a collar to keep his head still in the event of a neck injury. After they slid him into the ambulance, one of the spectators said, "I'm Todd Bowen's cousin; How serious is he?"

A paramedic responded, "Bad enough." Then he rushed to the passenger side of the vehicle. The cousin called after him, "Where you taking him?"

"Windham Hospital," he called back as they drove off.

Most of the crowd left; a few new people filled the vacated places but there was not much to see now. Most of the lights were turned off. Officer Burger and his partner had put up a yellow crime scene tape. I went over to chat with the police hoping Burger's partner, who had spent more time with the accident victim, might give me some information about Todd's condition. After Burger introduced me to Officer Garceau, I told him that when they put the driver in the ambulance I thought I recognized him. "It is Todd Bowen, isn't it?"

Garceau said, "That's what his driver's license claims; he a friend of yours?"

"No, it's more like he's a friend of a friend of mine. How badly is he hurt?"

"Hard to tell, he's been deep dipping in the sauce; I don't think he feels much pain even with a broken leg."

By this time, I was so wet the water was dripping off my underwear and running down the inside of my legs into my shoes. I went back to the car to call Annette; but I was shivering so hard I decided to put off calling her. I drove home, took a shower and put on dry clothes. I had stopped shivering but instead of calling Annette, I sat with the phone in my hand and the dial tone humming while I wondered why I was reluctant to call her. Was I concerned the news would upset Annette? Was I afraid I might feel called upon to assure her Todd would be OK? Actually I thought it possible that Todd may not make it. He did not look good to me. I could not help thinking that if Todd died it would solve the problem of his claim on Uncle Matt's estate, as well as his sexual interest in Annette. But, since Annette did not seem alarmed by either issue, she and I would view her cousin's accident differently from each other. "Yeah, OK, and that makes you the asshole, so go ahead and dial, and try to be nice."

Annette was glad I called even though it was late. She had just heard on the news there was an accident on Route 171 and that it occurred about the time I left her place. She said she tried to call me to make sure I was all right but my phone was busy. I did not admit the phone was off the hook while I was adjusting my attitude. When I told her the accident occurred a few minutes before I got there, she was relieved. "I was worried that the rain along with the bad mood you were in when you left my place may have distracted your attention from the road. The report I heard had just come in and not much was known about the accident except that it involved one car and a single male driver, so you can see why I was panicky. When your phone was busy, I settled down some—but let me tell you, Paul, I am glad to hear your voice—you are OK, aren't you?"

"Yes, I'm fine but the news isn't all good; it was Todd. He smashed up his Bronco."

"Did you stop? Is Todd OK?"

NEITHER THE TIME NOR THE PLACE

I told her that I did stop, that Todd was alive and the ambulance took him to the hospital.

She wanted to know if she should go there and see if he is OK. I told her she probably would not be allowed to see him or to find out much until the doctors have had time to examine him. I said I would go to the hospital now and call her in the morning before she goes to work.

When I arrived at the hospital, a police car was parked in the emergency area. Inside, in the waiting room, a half dozen people were seated in two groups. The man from the accident scene, who said he was Todd's cousin, was there with his wife. Their names turned out to be Scott and Terry Webber. They had been joined by an attractive older woman that Scott introduced to his wife as Aunt Margo. This, of course, was Todd's mother. I recalled that the Lynn's had spoken of her as Margo Trish. The remaining three people were huddled in another part of the room speaking Spanish. From where I sat, I could hear most of the conversation of Todd's relatives. Scott and Terry had already seen Todd briefly and were telling Margo about it. Scott said that Todd told him he had been out to Grandpa's farm practicing archery with Melissa. At dusk he had dropped her off at Grandpa's but on the way home he had run off the road. Scott said the nurse let him talk to Todd for a few minutes. "He was pretty drunk," Scott added.

A nurse came into the waiting room and told Mrs. Trish she could see her son, but for only a moment. When she returned, she told Scott he was right about Todd being intoxicated. She said she had trouble understanding what he was saying, but she thought it was pretty much the same thing Todd had told him. The nurse had assured Margo that except for a broken leg and a lot of bruises Todd did not seem to have any life threatening injuries; she also said that when the effects of the alcohol wore off, he was going to have a lot of pain. The nurse suggested they all go home and come back tomorrow after Todd had a thorough checkup.

Scott and Terry talked with Margo for a few minutes, about the accident scene. Then, as they prepared to leave, Lt. Ted Dylan of the State Police came into the waiting room from the emergency area. I had known him for a couple of years from previous crime investigations we had covered. His interest in Todd's accident caused me to suspect that it involved more than a drunk running his car off the road. Dylan scanned the waiting room said, "Hi", to me then went over to talk with Todd's relatives. He said, "I've been talking to Todd and there are things he wasn't clear about. Perhaps you could straighten me out on a few family relationships?"

When they agreed, he asked if Melissa was Todd's cousin. Scott said she was actually Todd's second cousin; Melissa's mother, Cheryl Carpenter, is Todd's first cousin.

"And the farm where they were shooting bows and arrows?" Dylan asked.

"That belongs to our grandfather, Arnold Witter. Carpenter's house is on the same piece of land."

Dylan said, "Oh, yes, now I remember that's the Witter Farm in Eastford. Carpenter's house is down by the road and the Witter's house sets back a couple hundred yards up the hill."

"Could you tell me a little about Melissa, like how old she is and whether she and Todd had a close relationship?"

Scott said, "She's 12; I don't think Todd knew her well. Why are you asking about Melissa? You don't think she was in Todd's car and wandered off after the accident? Todd told me he dropped her off at Grandpa's."

"That's what Todd told me, too," Margo added.

Dylan said "The reason I'm asking about Melissa is that she hasn't been seen since she left to go bow shooting with Todd. Neighbors and relatives have been combing the woods and fields looking for her since 8:30 p.m."

Dylan thanked his stunned audience, then came over and dropped into the chair next to me. "What a miserable night to be searching the woods for a lost girl," he said. I agreed and told him that I had stopped at the accident scene on the way home and how soaked I had become in a short time. As soon as Todd's relatives left, Dylan said, "Just between you and me, Paul, I don't have a good feeling about this Todd Bowen guy. Do you know him?"

"Only from a distance and comments from a friend; the message I get concurs with you that there is real cause for alarm."

"Is this anything you can tell me about?" Dylan asked.

"Not much beyond what you probably already know. You were at the hearing over the disturbance at Four Corners where Todd's stepfather had a squabble with Todd and three of his drunken buddies. I assume you've seen his rap sheet where it says that Todd has a manslaughter conviction for shooting a house guest when he was a college student in Massachusetts."

Dylan nodded and waited a few seconds, then said, "Don't quit, Paul, whatever you've got, even if it's only gossip, let's hear it."

"Yeah, well, I guess I can do better than gossip. Todd has been stalking a friend of mine. The reason I hesitate to tell you about it is because she thinks she has it under control and would be angry with me for mentioning it to you. She wouldn't want me to get this guy in trouble. The bastard aggravates and frightens her; but at the same time, she feels sorry for him."

Dylan said, "We've exchanged confidential information before, Paul, with neither of us getting hurt. I'm trying to develop some kind of profile on this guy to help me assess how strong the link is between Bowen and Melissa's disappearance. I would appreciate whatever you can give me about his behavior."

"OK, I can't give you the name of my woman friend; but I'll tell you as much as I can. Later, if circumstances justify it, maybe I'll be able to get her to come forward." Todd had been leaving notes at the back door of my unnamed friend's house and in her barn. He had waited for her in her driveway, then got into her car, took money from her purse and told her he'd like to have sex with her in the hay."

Dylan said, "This guy has advanced beyond stalking. Your description of Bowen's attitude toward women fits well with other things we know about him. As a matter of fact, let me return the favor with an interesting tidbit. It turns out that Officer Garceau found a .38 Taurus revolver in Bowen's wrecked vehicle and a knife lying a short distance from him on the ground. Garceau thought Bowen must have taken the knife out of the sheath on his belt and tossed it as far as he could to get rid of it. You shouldn't publish these two items until they're brought up at Bowen's court hearing. But it will give you something to pass on to your ladyfriend so she'll know this guy isn't a safe playmate. Maybe it will encourage her to talk with us."

As we walked toward our cars, we heard a call come in on Dylan's radio, so I waved goodbye to him and continued toward my car. Dylan called, "Hold on, Paul." When I returned, he said, "If you're planning to go out to Witters tonight, the search has been called off until daylight."

I had planned to go out to the farm but was relieved that I could wait until morning. When I arrived the following day, a gloomy dawn was breaking; but at least, it was not raining. Two search parties of neighbors, friends and relatives were being told what specific areas to cover. A truck with two bloodhounds followed by a State Police car pulled into the yard. Mrs. Carpenter provided the police with some of Melissa's clothes so the dogs could sample her scent. After last night's rain, I wondered if her scent would be strong enough for the dogs to detect.

The dog handler and one police car with two officers proceeded down a muddy farm road for about a quarter of a mile. They parked next to an abandoned building, visible from the farmhouse. Arnold Witter, an elderly but powerful looking white haired man, who was helping to coordinate the search parties said, "That's where Todd left his Bronco when he and Melissa went into the woods with their bows." After the search parties set out, I went back to my car and called Annette. She was shaken when I told her where I was and what was happening. Annette said she knew Melissa, that she had given her a couple of weaving lessons last year. "She's just a little girl, Paul. I can't believe Todd was involved in her disappearance." Annette resisted what I was telling her. She insisted there had to be another explanation. She suggested that when Todd dropped her off at home, Melissa may have gone, to spend the night at a friend's house. I let it go. However, when she wanted me to call her back if the searchers found anything, I knew she was not totally persuaded by her own argument. I asked her where I should call her—if she was going to work today. She said, "I'll ask Agnes to fill in for me. I'm going to stay home and watch the news and wait for you to call. I would ask you to come out, but I guess you're pretty busy—this kind of thing is at the height of what you do, isn't it?"

"It could be a very busy time for me. The yard is rapidly filling up with T.V. trucks and reporters of all kinds. Local stations are already talking into their microphones and cameras are scanning the people and grounds. I expect you can hear it live as it happens, but I'll keep in touch with you and come out as soon as I can".

"You think it's bad, though, don't you, Paul? You think Todd did something to Melissa."

"I think there's reason for alarm." The quaver in her voice stopped me from telling her about Todd's gun and knife being found at the accident scene.

When I stepped out of the car, I could hear the deep voiced "ahloop" of the hounds in the distance. The police were not letting anyone go down the road, but a cluster of people stood at an imaginary line designated by an officer. They were looking across the field toward the abandoned building, waiting for the hounds to tell them something. Mostly the spectators did not speak, but when they did it was in hushed tones.

Twice the dogs went silent; but within less than a minute, one hound would start up again, quickly joined by the other. At one point they both let out a couple of yelps and were not heard from again. While the spectators waited, the television announcers whispered softly into their microphones that something was happening. But, it was not long before they abandoned their hushed tones and began pumping hype into the microphone, excitedly asking people what they thought was happening. The two main opinions were that the dogs lost the trail or they found Melissa. In spite of the redundancy of the questions and answers, the process continued.

While this was going on, I chatted with an elderly couple in the same age group as Melissa's grandfather. They introduced themselves as Zetta and Ben, and said they were Melissa's great aunt and uncle. Zetta said she was Adele Witter's sister and that she and Ben had driven in from Providence last night as soon as Adele called that Melissa was missing. Ben said they were at the Witter Farm before the police arrived and were up all night with Melissa's parents and grandparents.

In the distance, the dog handler returned to his truck with the hounds. One of the two police officers returned, as well, and went to the police car where I assumed he would call in a report on the results of the search. I went back to the farmhouse where the cars were parked and spotted Lt. Dylan and his partner Officer Diaz listening to their car radio. It was what I was looking for. I assumed the message concerning the canine search would be relayed to Dylan. I couldn't hear what was being said, though; and as soon as the call was over, Dylan and Diaz went up to the house. Dylan knocked on the door and was let in but Diaz stayed on the porch. The news people and neighbors quickly regrouped around Diaz and began pounding him with questions. Repeatedly he told them Lt. Dylan will be out shortly to make an announcement and answer their questions. They kept asking the same two questions in different ways, wanting to know if Melissa has been found and if she is alive. While this was going on, the truck with the dogs drove by and went down to the highway. Officer Diaz asked the group to maintain a "respectful distance" from the porch. His choice of words, along with the dogs being withdrawn, struck me as ominous.

Ben and Zetta apparently thought the same thing. They went up on the porch and conversed softly with Officer Diaz. When they returned to stand with the rest of us, they looked upset. Several reporters tried to find out what Diaz had told them; Uncle Ben said, "He just told us we should wait until Lt. Dylan comes out." Zetta was shivering and appeared fatigued so, after the reporters settled down, I pointed to my nearby car and invited them to wait with me there. They were hesitant at first but then decided to join me. Ben explained they had left their car on the other side of the house.

I invited Zetta to sit in front with me close to the heater. Both she and Ben were anxious to talk about Melissa, who was foremost on their minds. They spoke of her mostly in the present tense, but every once in a while they would catch themselves referring to her in the past tense. Finally Zetta broke down and cried. When she regained her composure enough to speak she said, "This is ridiculous Ben; I'm going to tell him." He nodded, and Zetta, still half sobbing, said, "Paul, that policeman on the porch told us Melissa was found; but she was dead. He said we shouldn't tell anyone until Lt. Dylan makes the announcement. The officer on the porch said Dylan has to tell the parents first and will probably give them all the information he can so they won't hear it first on T.V. He said it may take awhile."

Once that was out of the way, they went back to telling me about their niece; clearly they loved her and knew her well. Ben said, "Melissa was a real tomboy. She was close to her stepdad, Rutledge Carpenter; everyone calls him 'Rut'. He supported her interests in all kinds of things like archery and go-cart racing. She'd drive that go-cart hell a flying all over the farm. Rut entered her in the go-cart race at the Woodstock Fair where she won a second-place ribbon. She gave it to her younger cousin. People always commented on what a generous girl she was. Grease and dirt were more a part of Melissa's life than getting dressed up. The 'No Fear' T-shirt she wore yesterday along with her jeans and boots—they were Melissa."

Zetta quickly pointed out the other side of their niece, she said, "Melissa loved music. She played several instruments: guitar, violin and cello. The cello was her favorite. Six months after she learned to play it she soloed in the school concert. Her upstairs bedroom had four or five musical instruments lying about, as well as, concert posters stuck to the walls announcing events come and gone. She had a small loom up there, too, and last year took weaving lessons from a woman up the road."

"Don't forget the baseball," Ben said.

"Yes, Melissa has a baseball autographed by a Red Sox player, Cal something or other; she keeps it in a glass case in her room." Zetta's voice wavered as she added, "Melissa had a framed picture of herself shooting her bow at a target on that building where they started searching for her with the dogs."

Just then Dylan came out on the porch. After Diaz spoke to him, he looked over at us getting out of the car and waited until we walked the short distance to the porch. Then he said to the group, "I'm sorry to have kept you waiting so long out here in the damp cold. I'm even more sorry at the news I have to deliver. Melissa has been found. I guess you all know when that was—when the dogs stopped barking, about ten minutes before they were brought back to the truck. Before a lot of rumors start to circulate, I'm going to tell you what happened as far as we know; but I warn you, it's upsetting.

"Melissa's body was a hundred yards north of that shed out there where the cars are parked." Dylan waved his hand in that direction. Then he paused before he said, "The 12-year-old's body was naked and handcuffed to a sapling. . . . I know you wonder if she was molested. We don't know yet. How was she killed? We don't know that either. Do we have any suspects? Yes. And that's it—that's all we know at this time."

A dozen hands went up as the T.V. cameras ground away. Oh, God! I thought, Annette is watching this and remembering the little girl she gave weaving lessons to—the little girl Zetta and Ben so lovingly described to me. This is going to be hard on Annette, not only because she knew Melissa but because she also knows that Todd is the suspect. Although Dylan did not say so to this audience, it was clear from what he said last night that it was Todd.

Most of the questions from the group came from reporters. Dylan had already answered them with his few brief statements, but they were not satisfied he had told them everything. They were hoping Dylan would let something else slip that he was holding back. I suppose I could have hung around pestering friends and relatives for more information about Melissa and her family but I was beginning to feel sick to my stomach. I had been lucky enough with Zetta and Ben who had provided enough material for today's column. Before I left, I told Melissa's uncle and aunt that Melissa's former weaving teacher is a dear friend of mine and that she will be taking it hard, too, so I was going to go up there now to be with her. I hugged Zetta, who was in tears, shook Ben's hand and left.

As I approached the place where Todd had run off the road, I had to slow down. An unmarked State vehicle was parked on the road and two plainclothes investigators were watching the Bronco being drawn up the embankment by a tow truck.

A few minutes later I knocked on Annette's door and went in. She was so focused to her television set in the kitchen that she had not heard my knock. When she saw me, she said, "Oh, there you are. You disappeared. I saw you hugging Aunt Zetta and shaking hands with Uncle Ben. Then you disappeared. I didn't know where you went."

"How did you know who they were?"

Annette's eyes were red around the edges. She hugged me and said, "The lady with the microphone said that's who they were when you took them to your car. Paul, this is so awful, I can't believe this is happening." Just then an ad came blasting out of the T.V. and Annette said, "I'll shut it off; I don't need it to keep track of you anymore."

Annette poured me a cup of coffee and said, "You look so tired, Paul. Did you get any sleep last night?"

"About two hours. How about you?"

"I don't know, I didn't think I slept at all; but then, I remembered a stupid dream I had that didn't have to do with Todd or Melissa, so I must have dozed off. . . . Paul, Melissa was such a sweet girl, so full of enthusiasm you could not help loving her. How could anyone do this to her?"

"I thought she must have been a very fine girl the way Zetta and Ben spoke so glowingly of her."

"I guess that's what you three talked about in the car?"

"Yes. You must have seen everything I did out there."

"Probably. There were long periods with nothing happening and nothing for the camera to focus on. I was always glad when it found you."

"One of the things Melissa's aunt mentioned in the car was that Melissa took weaving lessons a year ago from a woman up the road. It pleased me to know who her teacher was from what you said last night. When did you see Melissa last?"

"Her mother drove her out about a month ago. She wanted to show me some things she had made on her loom. Why?"

"I'm still trying to answer the question you asked about how anyone could have done this to a 12-year-old girl."

"I guess you're still pretty sure Todd did it, huh? Is Todd the only suspect the police are considering?"

"I think so. Todd apparently was the last one to see Melissa alive. When Officer Dylan addressed the group from the porch he didn't tell them that the family saw Melissa go off in Todd's car yesterday afternoon for archery practice and later saw the car parked by that abandoned building where the tracking dogs started out. Could you see the building on television?"

"Sort of, I guess, but not very well."

"Anyway, toward dusk Melissa's mother and sister saw Todd get in his car but they didn't see Melissa. They were initially concerned, but then thought maybe they just didn't see her because she got in on the other side. When he didn't let her off at her grandparents' house nor at Melissa's parents' house where her stepfather was—that's when they really became alarmed. Shortly after Todd left the Witter Farm, he ran off the road. I overheard his mother and cousin at the hospital discussing how Todd smelled of alcohol and how incoherent he still was two hours after the accident. Todd told Officer Dylan last night that he dropped Melissa off at her grandparents' house on his way out but Melissa's mother and sister were standing in the yard and saw him go by and knew that he hadn't stopped to let her out."

"If he is the one who left Melissa handcuffed to a tree like they found her, he must have been terribly drunk, so drunk he didn't know what he was doing. You asked me when I saw her last. Was that because you wanted to know if she looked sexually mature?"

"Yes, 12-years-old is kind of borderline, isn't it?"

"I guess so. I was startled when I saw her last at how much she had developed from when I had seen her less than a year earlier. At that time she was a pleasant-looking, slightly overweight girl with only the suggestion of breast development; but the last time I saw her, she was quite well developed. Otherwise, though, Melissa was still a loveable little girl with a little girl's enthusiasm for life. Would boobs be enough to drive a drunk predatory male to do what he did?"

Not knowing how to respond, I shrugged and went on to tell Annette more about what Zetta and Ben had said in support of her "little girl enthusiasm." Most of the while I was talking, Annette had her back to me frying eggs and making toast, but I could hear her softly crying.

When she set the plate in front of me, I asked, "How did you know I was starving?"

She sniffed a little and said, "On T.V. you looked like you hadn't had breakfast this morning, and I know you're still pushing yourself. Any minute now you're going to rush off to write your column, so eat now while you have a chance. And when you get ready to leave, don't worry about me; I'll be OK now that I've had a chance to feed you and talk with you. I know you have to do your job even though sometimes I act like I resent it."

She was right regarding the urgency of what I had to do, but I still did not know how upset Annette was about Todd's role in Melissa's death. When I asked her, she said,

"Paul, I understand how bad I feel about what happened to Melissa but what I feel about Todd isn't that simple. I don't want to talk about it now."

12

Six weeks later Annette still was not ready to talk about Todd, but the State of Connecticut was. A court hearing was scheduled for tomorrow to determine if sufficient evidence is available to try him for capital murder and rape. I thought by now Annette might be able to talk about it or even attend the hearing where she could listen to the evidence against Todd and decide for herself. Her initial response was surprise that she would be allowed to attend the hearing, that it was open to the public. After I assured her she could sit right there in the courtroom and listen to the lawyers and judge and watch Todd's reaction to what they say about him, Annette thought about it for a moment then said, "No, you can tell me about it. I know he's guilty; I knew as soon as they found Melissa's body, especially when that came on top of what you told me the night before about her not returning from their outing together."

At the Danielson Court House, Todd was brought in wearing an orange jump suit. He was manacled and wore leg irons chained close together, which forced him to walk with mincing steps. Three marshals came in with Todd, one at either elbow to prevent him from falling and the third close behind him. Two more guards covered the back of the room as well as the closed door. Outside the door another marshal watched the hallway. I asked one of the guards whether the accused was thought to be a serious flight risk. He said,

"Probably, but there's more concern about some of his buddies." From that I still did not know if they thought Todd's friends might try to help him escape or whether the guards were just prepared to expel disruptive members of the audience. When I asked him, all the guard would say is, "Whatever".

As Todd was ushered to the defense table, I searched his face for a sign of depravity; but Annette was right when she told me that he is simply a pleasant, nice looking man. Even bound in chains he did not appear harassed or anxious, if anything, he seemed mild mannered and at ease.

Donna, a reporter for the *Hartford Courant*, who was sitting next to me, drew my attention to three young ladies in the audience. They were smiling at Todd as he took his seat at the defense table; one waved at him ever so slightly and he smiled back. I asked Donna if she knew who they were and she whispered, "Members of his fan club."

I replied, "He really is a charming son-of-a-bitch." She smiled and nodded, and I thought to myself that it is easy to see why Annette was willing to go out for a beer with him.

Once Todd was seated at the defense table, he chatted amiably with his two public defenders like they were old friends. If this case goes to trial, I felt that the jurors are bound to have a good impression of him; all they need to do is ignore the likelihood that he murdered, raped and sodomized a 12-year-old girl.

The state's attorney Patrick Cobb came across in court as concise and business-like; outside of court I know him as a calm, pleasant man. I have seen him jogging occasionally along local country roads, which accounts for the youthful build he has carried into his late 50s. Even his hair has co-operated with this image, most of it still brown and well distributed over his head.

Cobb began with a brief synopsis of what took place at the time Melissa was killed: that she and Bowen had gone four-wheeling over the hilly terrain of her grandfather's farm in Eastford, and that her naked body was found the next day with her wrists handcuffed above her head around a tree. Cobb said she had a stab wound in her abdomen, a six-inch knife wound under one breast, and she had been shot in the mouth. The painful effect of the prosecutor's dialog registered heavily on Cheryl Carpenter and her other daughter Pamela, 17, as well as her husband Rutledge, who looked like he was in his late 40s. They were seated near the front of the room.

When Cobb finished, he asked Melissa's mother to describe for the court their family situation: where they live, immediate family relationships and circumstances leading up to Melissa's disappearance.

Cheryl Carpenter was a youngish, slightly stout woman with long black hair. She was dressed simply in a green, short-sleeved blouse and brown skirt. She indicated that the family had recently moved into a house on the 120-acre farm where Melissa was killed. She said, "There are two houses on the property; we live in the one near the road, on Route 171. A gravel drive next to our house runs up a hill about 150 yards to where my parents live."

Cobb asked, "What are your parents' names?"

"Arnold and Adele Witter." She explained, "The house we live in used to belong to Todd Bowen's grandmother; Todd and I are cousins. When we were children, our families were close. We kids used to play together on the farm until Todd went away to school. When he stopped by the house, I hadn't seen him for over 20 years."

"Do you recall the time and date of Mr. Bowen's visit, Mrs. Carpenter?"

"Yes, it was September 25, 1997, about 1 p.m. The girls had come home from school early that day. Anyway we talked about old times for a while. Then Todd said he was going up the road to ask my dad for permission to bow hunt on the farm when the season opens.

"Todd came back a half-hour later and told me Dad had given him permission to hunt and also to practice archery that afternoon. Todd asked if any of us wanted to go with him. Neither Pamela nor I wanted to go, but Melissa said she would like to. She had a bow of her own and loved archery. Melissa was still in her school clothes, so she went upstairs and changed into her boots and jeans. When she came down she was wearing her favorite T-shirt that said 'No Fear' across the front. I told her that wasn't warm enough. But, they were in a hurry, so Todd loaned her the plaid shirt he was carrying in his hand; and they drove off in his Ford Bronco."

Were you home for the rest of day, Mrs. Carpenter?"

"Later, about 3:30 Pamela and I went up to my parent's house to help Mom prepare a birthday dinner for one of her younger grandchildren. I could see Todd's Bronco in the distance parked near an old shed where Melissa usually went for target practice. When it started to get dark, Pamela went out and honked the car horn three times, a signal for Melissa to come home. She didn't come, so Pamela went back out and honked the horn on her grandfather's truck, which is louder. A few minutes after that, I joined Pamela to see if the honking brought any results. We saw Todd climb into the Bronco and assumed Melissa had gotten in on the other side, so we went back in the house. When Todd didn't let Melissa off at Grandpa's, we assumed he would drop her off down at our house.

"Around seven o'clock, we finished helping Mom and went home. Melissa wasn't there. When Rut told me he had not seen her, I freaked out. I called the police, the neighbors and family members. Those who lived nearby came immediately and started searching the area around where the Bronco had been parked. By then it had turned dark and started to rain."

Cobb reviewed Todd's accident based on the report filed by Officer Burger. The report indicated that at 6:55 pm on September 25, 1997, Burger and his partner, Officer Garceau, saw that a car had run off the road on a sharp curve a few miles north of the Witter farm on Route 171. The driver, Todd Bowen, had driven his Bronco over a 12-foot embankment and landed upside down. Bowen had been tossed out and was lying injured about 15 feet in front of the vehicle. Apparently he had crawled some of that distance. Bowen was taken by ambulance to Windham Hospital in Willimantic. He was charged with driving under the influence of alcohol.

Cobb said the report indicated that while Burger and his partner waited for the ambulance, they looked in the car and searched the surrounding area to see if anyone had been riding with Bowen. They did not find anyone but they did find a .38 caliber Taurus revolver in the car and a six-inch knife on the ground another eight feet beyond where Bowen had crawled.

Public defender Ben Forgash interrupted Cobb to ask if Officer Burger had a warrant to search that vehicle. Cobb looked at Burger, who was sitting in the front row. Burger said, "No Sir. But, we had to make sure there wasn't anyone still in the car. That's when we found the gun."

"And that's when you found the gun," Forgash mimicked, "just lying there on the passenger seat?"

Burger said, "The car was upside down."

"So it fell off the seat and was lying on the inside of the car roof?"

Burger became red in the face and seemed reluctant to answer. Judge Albert Thornton looked annoyed with Burger and asked him if the gun was in plain view. Burger admitted he found the gun by running his hand between the two front seats.

Thornton said, "The gun is out. It may not be used as evidence in this case." Then the judge said, "And while we're at it, Officer Burger, is there anything else you found in Mr. Bowen's vehicle you might like to have the court rule on at this time?"

"Like the handcuff key I found in the glove compartment, Your Honor?"

"Yes, Officer Burger." Then, Thornton looked at the prosecution table, and said, "The key, of course, is also poisoned fruit and is inadmissible."

Cobb frowned, apparently over the loss of two choice pieces, then asked Burger if he found anything in plain view that might be construed as evidence. Burger said, "The six-inch sheath knife, I guess that's OK; it was lying on the ground eight feet beyond the driver. Officer Garceau and I thought the driver may have tried to get rid of it but he was too injured or too drunk to throw it far."

Forgash went after Burger again, "What made you think it was Mr. Bowen's knife? Couldn't it have been dropped by a hiker or hunter?"

Burger started to become rattled again. Forgash's blustery manner affected witnesses that way; but Burger got a hold of himself enough to respond, "We tried the knife in the empty sheath on Bowen's belt. It fit well and was tight enough so it wouldn't have popped out and flown eight feet through the air. Besides, the knife didn't have any sticks or pine needles lying on it."

Forgash nodded acceptance; but he jotted down a note, probably to remind himself to discredit Burger for tampering with the crime scene if the knife came up in a trial.

Cobb resumed by questioning Lt. Theodore Dylan about his visit with Bowen in the emergency room shortly after the accident. Dylan indicated he had heard on the car radio that Melissa Carpenter was missing. The proximity of Bowen's accident to where the girl had disappeared suggested that he should talk with the driver. Dylan said, "Bowen freely admitted that he and Melissa had been shooting their bows out at the Witter farm but said that before he left the farm he dropped Melissa off at home."

Dylan said he read Bowen his Miranda rights and asked him for permission to collect forensic samples. When Bowen agreed, hair and blood samples were taken, as well as fibers from his clothing, the empty knife sheath from his belt, and the red plaid shirt Bowen was wearing during the accident. Dylan told the court that Bowen appeared calm but he had a strong odor of alcohol on his breath and his speech was slurred and sometimes disconnected.

Attorney Cobb then talked about the autopsy report filled by Dr. Theodore Osborn. It indicated that the 12-year-old victim weighed 150 lbs and was 5 feet, 4 inches tall, that she died of a gunshot wound to the head and that she had been stabbed. The .38 caliber bullet had entered her mouth and was found imbedded in the back of her skull.

Cobb showed several large photographs to the judge, then handed them to the defense. I could see them when Forgash and Cobb were looking at them. One showed a naked girl lying on her back with her arms raised above her head and her wrists handcuffed behind a small tree. The stab wound in her abdomen was evident, as well a cut across the bottom of her left breast. The other pictures were taken during the autopsy. Todd looked at them like a curious stranger viewing the body of someone he did not know. For a 12-year-old, Melissa was well developed. Her aunt and uncle had spoken of her as being a little plump but attractive in her own way. They felt it was her vivacious, sweet personality that made her so popular both at school and in the neighborhood.

Forgash attempted to get the judge to suppress the pictures, claming they were too inflammatory for jurors to see but the judge said the pictures would be entered as evidence.

Melissa's blood alcohol level was .07; the legal limit to operate a motor vehicle in Connecticut is .05. Cobb suggested that Bowen attempted to get Melissa drunk so he could have his way with her. The autopsy report, though, did not confirm that Melissa had been raped. Although her anus and genitalia were dilated, there was no evidence of sperm in the genital tract, anus or mouth. Cobb argued that discharge of the gun in the victim's mouth might account for the absence of semen there and that the dirt and scruff marks on her knees seen in the pictures suggest she had engaged in oral sex.

To charge Todd with capital murder, the prosecution would have to prove that Todd had killed Melissa during the commission of another crime; in this case, sexual assault or attempted assault would serve that purpose. A capital murder charge could result in the death penalty for Bowen.

The crime scene investigators had found a stick at the crime scene that had been whittled with a knife into the shape and diameter of a penis. Cobb indicated it may account for the dilation and scratch marks involving the victim's vagina and anus.

Forgash tried to convince the judge to disallow the stick as evidence; but Thornton allowed it.

So far Cobb's case for capital murder was substantial but it was not iron clad. I had mixed feelings about seeing Todd get the death penalty; but with only a murder charge and the potential for early release he could still be a future threat to Annette. Prison would not cause Todd to abandon his dream of fortune any more than it did Joe Esposito.

Next the court talked about a report from the State crime lab. It turns out that a swab taken from the victim's pubic area contained a mixture of DNA that could have been contributed by two people, one of them consistent with Melissa's DNA and the other consistent with the defendant's DNA. The analysis would exclude 86 to 90 percent of the population as possible contributors to this mixture.

Forgash ridiculed this with a confident smile asking, "How many thousands of people in the vicinity would not be excluded by this analysis?"

Cobb said if you narrowed that down to the number of people on the Witter Farm the afternoon Melissa was . . . The judge interrupted Cobb before he could finish, "I think you have both made your points. Let me remind you this is a hearing; maybe if there's a trial you'll be allowed to examine this issue until the jury falls asleep, but for now let's take a lunch break."

In the afternoon Cobb began by describing the execution of a search warrant of Bowen's apartment. State Police investigators had found a belt with an empty handcuff case, two packs of Best Choice Cigarettes, and an empty box for a .38-caliber Taurus revolver as well as some .38-caliber cartridges. Cobb was doing his best to make up for the loss of the revolver and handcuff key the judge had disallowed as evidence.

The state's attorney went on to describe additional evidence collected by crime scene investigators which included articles of Melissa's clothing: boots, underwear, the 'No Fear' T-shirt, and her jeans, as well as butts from Best Choice Cigarettes and a bottle of Old Overholt rye whisky.

Forgash wanted to know if Melissa's clothing was torn or badly soiled. Cobb said, "No, the crime scene investigators made note of the fact that her clothes were casually folded and stacked in a pile next to her boots."

Forgash said, "So there was no evidence of a struggle?" Forgash's tone and hand language implied that the girl may not have been assaulted, that she may have willingly taken her clothes off and submitted to a sex game in the woods.

Cobb said, "If someone was holding a gun on me and told me to take my clothes off, I'd take them off. Besides we're talking about a 12-year-old girl, whether she was willing or forced into this, it's still rape."

Next Cobb called a witness wearing a tweed sport jacket and a tie. He spoke with a Cambridge, Massachusetts, accent and was introduced to the court as Derek Hutchens, owner of Hutchens' Guns and Sporting Goods located southeast of Boston, near Dedham—just inside the beltway. Cobb asked him if he sold a .38-caliber handgun to Ester Hurk on January 29, 1994. When he agreed that he had, Cobb asked Hutchens how he remembered that.

"For one thing," Hutchens answered, "I still have the paperwork on the sale; but I also remember that she was an employee of the Massachusetts Department of Corrections at the prison in Walpole."

"Was she alone when she bought the gun?"

"There was this guy helping her decide what to buy. I remember being irritated by him. He expressed a lot of confidence about what would be the right gun for her. I had a feeling he was more interested in what would be the right gun for him. Hurk finally bought a .38-caliber Taurus revolver."

"Mr. Webber, do you see the person today who was with Mrs. Hurk when she bought the gun?"

Webber said, "Yes," and pointing at Todd Bowen added, "that's him, the defendant."

Next to testify was Gary Hurk, Ester's former husband. Cobb asked him under what circumstances his former wife knew Todd Bowen. Hurk said, "Ester met Bowen while he was an inmate at Walpole. Ester and I were divorced before Bowen was released from prison. She rented an apartment in Norwood, Massachusetts, north of Walpole. When Bowen was released, he moved in with her, that was sometime in May of 1994. They lived together almost a year. She called me to say she had taken a position in Arlington, Virginia, with a security company and was moving down there. She said Bowen had already moved to Connecticut."

I did not appreciate the full significance of Hurk's testimony at the time. I was too anxious about whether or not the prosecution would be able to place Todd at the crime scene with more substantial evidence than inference. My remaining hope was that the empty rye bottle collected by the crime scene investigators would have Todd's fingerprints on it, but it did not.

The prosecution had done its homework, though; Cobb said that a paper bag was recovered from Bowen's wrecked Bronco with a sales slip in it from Fred's Liquor Store. The date on the sales slip indicated that Fred had sold a bottle of Old Overholt rye whisky on September 25, 1995, the same day Melissa disappeared. Cobb said Fred did not remember selling the bottle to Bowen but said Bowen was an occasional customer in his store. He also said Old Overholt is not a popular brand in the area and he had this one bottle in the store for over a year and was glad to see it go.

At this point Judge Thornton called for a break. As I headed for the men's room, I thought that if Fred is called to testify he would not firmly cement Todd to the crime scene either; but if his testimony is added to the other inferences, it could go a long way toward convicting him. By the time I flushed and was washing my hands, I had convinced myself that Bowen was headed for trial and conviction. That is when Forgash came in. After we exchanged greetings, I said, "It looks like you have your work cut out for you."

He laughed and said, "I suppose you think Cobb has this case all packaged for a jury?"

I shrugged and said, "I don't know about that but he scored some pretty good points today."

Forgash said, "Yeah, I thought he did about as well as he could; but I hope you know this'll never go to jury."

"Well, so far I've heard only one side. I'll be anxious to hear your side of it." At which point, I began to worry that Forgash was holding something that would get Todd off without a trial, maybe even before day's end.

Out in the hall Uncle Ben was stretching his stiff limbs. He asked how I thought the hearing was going. I told him, "I thought enough evidence had been presented to send Bowen to trial and convict him, but I just talked with Forgash who told me with irritating confidence that the case will never go to trial." Ben's expression became dejected, so I said, "I suppose a lot depends on how the judge interprets the DNA evidence. Most of the other evidence tells us Todd and Melissa were out there together but we already knew that. I would think about all Forgash can do is try to convince the court that someone else killed Melissa."

"Oh yes," Ben agreed sarcastically, "some stranger grabbed her after Bowen dropped her off and dragged her back out in the woods where she and Bowen spent the afternoon."

13

When the hearing resumed, the state's attorney asked to have Gary Hurk recalled. Cobb asked him if to his knowledge his former wife, Ester Hurk, had a set of handcuffs. When Hurk said, "Yes," Cobb asked if he would be able to identify them if he ever saw them again. Hurk replied, "Yes, Ester had her name engraved on them, 'Ester Hurk.'"

For the first time, since the hearing began, Todd looked worried. He raised himself from his slouched position and looked directly at the judge then at his attorney.

Forgash asked Hurk if he knew where the handcuffs are now. Hurk said he assumed Ester took them to Virginia with her.

After Hurk left the stand, Forgash said, "Your Honor, I would like to point out that the prosecution has submitted no evidence that Mr. Bowen was ever in possession of the handcuffs with Ester Hurk's name on them or that he was the one who restrained Melissa Carpenter with them. They could have been stolen from Mrs. Hurk before she moved to Virginia or she could have given them to most anyone; and that's who the police should be searching for."

I thought Forgash's statement was desperate and absurd. Even though the handcuff key was disallowed, the handcuff case found in Todd's apartment was still in evidence. I was amazed Forgash would bother to make such a flimsy remark; possibly his mind was focused on what he planned to ask next: "By the way, Attorney Cobb, were Mr. Bowen's fingerprints on those cuffs?"

Cobb said, "No, the only print found was a partial thumb print left by the officer who removed them."

Forgash's face lit up and with a burst of excitement he said "So, the crime scene was contaminated! I move to suppress the handcuffs as evidence."

Judge Thornton said, "Mr. Forgash, I believe I mentioned earlier that this is a hearing and not a trial." Waving a hand toward the jury box he said, "Look, no jury."

The defense attorney was not in the least put down. His delight over the absence of Todd's fingerprints on the handcuffs was followed by a lengthy debate between the prosecution and defense over previous legal rulings on crime scene contamination. While it was going on—and it must have been for nearly an hour—Todd listened attentively, looking back and forth from judge to attorneys as they spoke. In the end, Judge Thornton indicated that since the handcuffs were removed inadvertently and not willfully, in an attempt to conceal evidence, he would allow them. With that the prosecution concluded its presentation.

The court waited while a flurry of anxious whispering went on at the defense table. Then Forgash arose and asked the judge to drop the capital murder charge claiming that the prosecution did not have any evidence that Melissa Carpenter was raped or that Mr. Bowen was her killer.

After listening to a rehash of the issues from both sides, Judge Thornton ruled that the original charge accusing Bowen of capital murder would stand but with modification. He said, "Although the accused may have forced the victim to have oral sex with him, subsequent discharge of the weapon in her mouth would have destroyed the evidence. Also, the autopsy results revealed no evidence of vaginal or anal penetration. Dilation was observed; but, semen was not found inside the body. The DNA evidence showing a mix of the victim's DNA with that of another person was inconclusive. Therefore, the original charge of capital murder in the commission of rape, sodomy or attempted rape or sodomy is amended to 'capital murder in the commission of attempted rape or sodomy.' The revised charge does not alter a jury's option of recommending the death sentence."

Thornton asked Forgash if he plans to present evidence to contest the state's case. Forgash said, "Not at this time, Your Honor."

Judge Thornton looked at the defense and prosecution and said, "If your calendars are open Wednesday afternoon, at two o'clock I'll rule on whether this case will go to trial." Both attorneys agreed to Wednesday and the guards came to take charge of the accused. When Bowen arose from his chair he appeared expressionless, perhaps stoical. Before he moved to follow the guards, he turned to look at the audience. Briefly our eyes made contact; he recognized me, but from where I wondered, and was there any other message? When his eyes moved on, he spotted his mother; he raised one of his restrained hands slightly to wave, but neither of them smiled or spoke before the guards led him away.

Late in the afternoon I gave Annette the details of what happened at the probable cause hearing. She did not ask any questions until I finished. Then she said, "He's going to trial, isn't he?"

"Yes. Thornton could have told us that this afternoon— I guess he did sort of; but I suppose he wanted to organize his comments in a formal way before officially presenting them."

"How did Todd take it?"

"Not well, the prosecution had saved the engraved handcuff evidence until last. From that point Todd's attitude changed. The casual air he wore during most of the hearing was gone. He seemed suddenly surprised at how much evidence the State had against him and how little his attorney was able to defend him against it. If Todd really was so drunk that he blacked out, he may not have been completely aware of what he did or the clues he left behind."

"Unaware of most, but not all, huh?"

"No, not all. Getting dead drunk doesn't happen suddenly any more than what he did to Melissa happened suddenly. Todd played with her before he killed her. He had her smoking and drinking whisky. Her clothes were neatly folded and stacked. The prosecution claimed her dirty knees indicated he had forced her to have oral sex with him and then he cut her under the breast. Even after it was all over and he drove off and cracked up his Bronco, he had the presence of mind to try to get rid of his knife."

"Will Todd have any chance at all at the trial?"

"If Forgash continues as his attorney, he might have a slim chance. Forgash is good, dramatic enough to confuse jurors and careful enough to find technical reasons to suppress evidence as he did with the gun and handcuff keys."

"But deep down you really think Todd has become concerned over the engraved handcuffs—enough to worry about the death penalty?"

"Yes, it was when the prosecution made the connection between the cuffs and Todd's former girlfriend that he began to look worried."

"Paul, when it first looked like Todd might be connected with Melissa's disappearance, you asked me how I felt about his involvement. I wasn't able to answer you. Even after she was found horribly murdered and Todd became the only suspect, I still didn't understand my feelings enough to put them into words. For a long time, I had trouble accepting the fact that Todd killed Melissa, especially in such a hideous way. But now that I have accepted it, I still struggle with my feelings. Visualizing Todd being strapped to a gurney and delivered a lethal dose of something—just isn't easy for me. You know I did care about him in spite of his uncontrolled behavior?"

I nodded and kept myself from saying, "Yeah, I know and it used to piss me off."

"Perhaps, if I knew how aware Todd was of what he was doing to Melissa and how much control he did or didn't have over himself, or even how much remorse he has now, I would know how to feel. . . . I don't suppose you allow your mind to wander down such a muddled path. You always seem to know what you think."

"Not really. During the hearing, I sat behind Todd but off to the side where I could see a little of his face. Even still, my thoughts kept drifting away from Todd and visualizing the little girl that so many people loved. I wondered if there was anything the court could do to Todd that would make Melissa's loved ones feel at all better. I felt that killing Todd or not killing Todd wouldn't help these people. So next, I asked myself if there is anything the court might do that would cause Melissa's loved ones to feel worse. I knew there was. The court could find Todd not guilty or guilty of a lesser charge that would let him off with a light sentence."

"Neither of those things could happen, could they?"

"You know that they do happen."

"Yeah, I know it happens with wealthy celebrities who have teams of high-priced lawyers but Todd will probably have a public defender."

When I assured Annette that guilty defendants, even those with public defenders, sometimes get off, she said, "Paul, if Todd were to get off, it would be terrible for Melissa's parents and everyone who knew Melissa—I mean with all that evidence against him. But killing him? That's plain and simple revenge."

"I've always seen *justice* verses *revenge* as a murky line. If the court gives Todd the death penalty, it will be called *justice*; but if Todd is released on a technicality or by a flaky jury and Melissa's stepfather kills him, the law would call it revenge and charge him with murder."

"But you would still call it justice—don't answer that. Just tell me how you would have dealt with Todd if he did to me what he did to Melissa."

I was glad she asked that question. I had wondered if Annette ever considered how vulnerable she was during her association with Todd. His "toss in the hay" comment still bugged me. I didn't say anything about that, though; instead I said, "You would never imagine, Annette, how much I worried about you and what Todd might be capable of, even before September 25th. Anyway, I'm sure my visceral response would be to shoot him. But, I really don't know what I would have done. In Melissa's case, Todd was already in custody before the relatives knew she was dead. That cooling-off period could make a difference."

"You actually worried that he was capable of doing something like that to me? I knew you were bothered by him but I thought you were just jealous over the attention he was giving me."

I told Annette how Todd had looked at me in court and that I wondered how he recognized me. At first Annette said she was not aware he had ever seen me. Then I asked if she had ever told him she was dating someone, and she did admit that she had mentioned it. I asked how he reacted and she said, "He seemed annoyed and asked me a lot of questions about you. I told him it was none of his business. That didn't stop him from asking, though, it just meant his questions became more taunting than curious."

"How come you didn't tell me about it?"

"I almost did but you were already angry enough over him."

I did not know whether she was afraid I would do something stupid to Todd or become angry with her. The following day, while Annette was at work, I drove slowly along the road in front of her house. Fifty feet beyond the driveway I saw that someone had pulled off the road into the brush and parked—more than once. A rough trail led through the woods toward Annette's backyard. I found three Best Choice cigarette butts—his brand—two near where he parked his car and one along the trail halfway to Annette's yard. Yes, he had seen me before, if not in her driveway then through the kitchen windows.

I saw Annette a half-dozen times over the next couple of weeks, but I did not mention that Todd had been spying on us. Her spirits were already low enough. Several times I asked what was bothering her, and she either said nothing or that she was worried about Aunt Lettie, who apparently had declined another notch.

Meanwhile, Todd had been bound over for trial, held with a bail set at a million dollars. A few weeks later, Annette seemed to recover from her low mood. She told me she had been to visit Todd at the Montville prison, which is about 50 miles south of where she lives. I was amazed she had been bold enough to take on such an experience all by herself; but, she explained she had visited prison inmates previously, as a nun and was familiar with the place and its procedures. She admitted, though, she had been pensive about talking with Todd but insisted she was not depressed like I seemed to think. When I asked her why she didn't tell me what she was up to, she said, "Your way of looking at Todd and his situation is different from mine. I didn't want to be persuaded by you."

I nodded but I must have smiled a little because she asked, "Is that smile to cover your annoyance with me for not telling you about what I was planning to do?"

"No, I was just amazed you took on this scary adventure by yourself but mostly I'm pleased to see you in a better mood. Your visit must have gone well."

"I suppose as well as it could but mostly I'm relieved it's over. Actually I made two visits to Montville. Initially, I tried to appear casual, hoping to cheer Todd up; but that didn't work; he was too hostile, defensive and depressed. Right off he said, 'I suppose your boyfriend told you all about the trial and what a bad boy I am.'"

"I said, 'Paul told me about the evidence the prosecution presented; he said he felt you were in serious trouble.'"

"Todd said, 'You know that evidence is all bullshit, don't you? If you'd of been at the hearing you would know it's was bullshit. I didn't do anything to that girl. Why weren't you there?'

"I told him I didn't go to his hearing because I was afraid of what I might hear; and what's more he can turn off his sour, defensive attitude that I didn't come to judge him."

"'So, what the hell did you come for?' he wanted to know. 'If it was to collect the 20 bucks I owe you, forget it—they're going to have a trial, then put me on death row until everybody forgets who I am, then kill me.'

"Todd, you don't know that's what's going to happen."

"'Yeah, they found those goddamn handcuffs with *Ester Hurk* written on them.'

"I asked, 'Who's Ester Hurk' and Todd said, 'You know goddamn well who she is. Your boyfriend told you; if he didn't, it was in all the newspapers and was broadcast over every T.V. station in Connecticut.' Then he went silent, just looking down; when he finally looked up he said, 'Ester was an old girlfriend. I met her when she was a guard up at Walpole. The cops found her ex-husband, Gary Hurk, and got him to tell the court that the handcuffs belonged to his former wife. He also told the court that I had lived with Ester for a while. Forgash, my attorney, doesn't think he can get rid of that piece of crap.' I think Todd meant both the engraved handcuffs and his relationship with Ester.

"He said, 'There's other bullshit, too, that's pretty damaging; but Forgash says the worst thing of all is that there aren't any other suspects. So, sure, I was out there with Melissa. We were shooting our bows. I gave her a cigarette and a couple snorts of Old Overholt; but, goddamn it, I didn't do what the prosecution says I did. I don't know who did it, but it wasn't me. The cops and that goddamn prosecutor aren't bothering to look for anyone else; they'd be happy enough to see me get the needle—looks like that's what's going to happen.'"

I asked Annette if Todd wasn't aware that even if he is convicted of capital murder, the jury can recommend life without parole instead of the death penalty.

"Todd said his lawyer told him, but Forgash thinks that with his life on the line the stakes are too high to leave the decision to a jury. Todd also said Forgash told him that once the jurors 'get a look at the pictures of that nice plump little girl staked out in the woods naked, they're going to be hot to see me get the juice.' I'm sure these were Todd's words, not Forgash's. Anyway, based on what you told me earlier, Paul, about the pictures of Melissa, I can see they would be a serious threat to Todd's life; but at the same time what you also told me about juries letting guilty defendants go, I too had doubts about leaving this issue to chance."

"I wondered why you went to visit Todd."

"Yes, I wanted to find out if Todd was worried enough about his situation to consider a plea. I wanted to prevent Todd from getting the death penalty, but at the same time make sure he is never released from prison."

"Were you successful?"

"I think so. In talking with Todd, I became reassured that he is guilty and that the only remorse he has is from being caught. At one point during our conversation he became kind of weepy over being executed, so I took that opportunity to suggest he talk with his lawyer about a plea bargain. Based on things Todd told me, I felt Forgash was already trying to steer him in that direction."

"Yes, I'll bet that's what Forgash was hinting at in the courthouse men's room when he told me Bowen's case would never go to trial. At the time I thought it was just Forgash bravado about winning with a hidden card he had yet to play—I fell for it. But, Forgash knew all along Todd's case was hopeless and was trying to maneuver him toward a plea."

"Yes, when I brought it up, Todd's response suggested he had already thought it out; he sort of repeated what he had said earlier, 'I know if I go to trial, the jury will find me guilty and recommend a death sentence'; but then he added, 'regardless of what they might recommend after a trial, it may be two years before they get around to a trial. I'd be loony by then; and if that didn't drive me over the edge, sitting on death row for years with endless appeals would complete the job. Goddamn it, Annette, I don't want to die and I don't want to go nuts.'

"After putting that into words, he seemed less angry; he even appeared glad that I came to see him. When it was time for me to go, he asked me to call Forgash and tell him what we talked about and arrange a time when his attorney and I could both come back."

"Why did he want you there?"

"That's what I asked him, he said, 'I want someone to be here that I can trust and I don't mean my mother. You're smart; you'll pay attention to what Forgash has to say. I'm never sure about his motives. I know you'll look out for my interests.'"

"Did he know what your real motives were?"

Annette said, "He should have; I told him pretty much the same thing I told you. Basically, I said, 'Whether you blacked out when you were in the woods with Melissa or whether you knew exactly what you were doing, the evidence against you sounds compelling and the crime so horrible you should never risk being in a position to do it again.'"

"How did he take it?"

"He stared at his hands for a moment, then said, 'In addition to what I told you earlier about being smart, Annette, you're also painfully straightforward, so I know you wouldn't let Forgash do me in just for his own convenience. I know he tried to get out of taking my case, and I sense that he isn't anxious to defend me in front of a jury.'"

"Funny thing about Todd, isn't it? When he's sober he seems to be pretty sharp—even has some sense about right and wrong."

"I'm glad you noticed that, Paul. I was afraid you might think I had become demented that I even bother with him."

"No, reckless, and maybe a bit of a tease the way you used him to make me jealous." She laughed and denied that she intentionally tried to make me jealous, so I moved on to ask her how the second meeting went.

"Forgash was pleased to hear that Todd was finally ready to talk about a plea that he hadn't been willing to discuss earlier. I felt Todd was right about his attorney being anxious to get rid of his case. Forgash even changed a couple of appointments so we could go out the next day. When we arrived Todd was still receptive and readily agreed to plead guilty in exchange for life without parole. It was strange, though; at no time during these two conversations did Todd acknowledge what he did to Melissa. It was as though, if he hadn't heard about it in court, he wouldn't have known."

"Maybe he really was blacked out from the alcohol when he committed it or maybe he blocked the event from his mind immediately afterward. I felt that during most of the trial he behaved like a curious bystander unaware they were talking about him until the very end."

"Forgash told me the same thing on the way home, that Todd found it difficult to enter a plea because he had trouble visualizing his guilt."

"After Todd talked with Forgash, did he ask you if it was still all right for him to plead guilty?"

"As a matter of fact, he did. After Forgash explained the process and how it would involve the prosecution and the judge, Todd asked me, 'What do you think Annette?' I told him I couldn't advise him on any of the legal issues but that I think he should feel proud about having the strength to do the right thing. Then he wanted to know if after he is settled somewhere I would visit him once in awhile. When I said I would, he turned to Forgash and agreed to a plea. Forgash said he would talk with the officers of the court as soon as he could, then get back to him."

We were both lost in our thoughts for a moment. Finally I said, "Annette, the way you dealt with this horrible tragedy has been a lesson for me in compassion. My mind doesn't usually work the way yours did in dealing with Todd; I have to confess you have turned some of my anger into something I'm more comfortable with." I hugged her and we both held on for a long time.

As I listened to the court proceedings, it was clear that Forgash's negotiations prior to the hearing had gone well. Todd was allowed to enter a plea of no contest to first degree murder, which was based on his admission that there was sufficient evidence to convict him without his having to plead guilty to the crime. He would spend the rest of his life in prison with no possibility of parole. In return he would be spared the risk of a death sentence at the hands of a jury. And, I thought to myself, he can continue to deny any recollection of Melissa's sexual assault and murder.

Todd stood patiently and listened to Judge Thornton explain the conditions under which the court would accept his no contest plea and acknowledged that he understood each of the stipulations the judge presented. Afterward, he requested permission to speak to Melissa's family. When it was granted, Todd faced the Carpenter family and, stammering for words, did his best to express his sorrow for the pain he had caused them. He did not specifically mention Melissa, which I am sure would have been as difficult for him to do as it would have been for the family to hear him speak of her. When Todd finished, he looked at Annette, who with flooded eyes, was standing next to me. Todd seemed to be making a visual appeal for Annette's approval for the way he dealt with his crime. Annette nodded slightly and Todd turned to his mother, who was working her way out of a row of seats toward the aisle where she could reach over the railing to her son. The guards looked to Thornton for agreement then they led Todd over to where he could extend his cuffed hands to his mother. They exchanged a few words and the guards lead Todd away. Annette went to talk with Melissa's mother and I went over to where two other reporters were throwing questions at Todd's mother. She would not respond to them, so they joined the cluster of reporters gathered around Melissa's family. I introduced myself to Mrs. Trish as a friend of Annette's.

She said, "I know who you are," and tried to walk away from me; but the aisle was clogged with people talking and barely moving toward the door. So, I stayed with her and explained that Annette and Todd were friends, and that through Annette I felt I knew Todd but I never really met him. I told her I was sorry for what she and Mr. Trish are having to go through.

"You're sorry for me and Mr. Trish, huh? You don't see him here, do you? Hell, no you don't. Herb hit the road the day after the police found that dead girl and arrested Todd. You can put that in your goddamn newspaper, Mr. Reporter; that's where Herb read all about Todd—right there in your newspaper. You didn't miss a damn thing, Mr. Hurst; it was all there."

Annette and I had come to the courthouse in separate cars but we had parked in the same lot. As we left the building, neither of us had much to say except to agree on how sad and hopeless this was for everyone. But, before we reached our cars, Annette said, "I'm glad Forgash was able to arrange it so Todd didn't have to plead guilty to a crime he apparently has no recollection of."

I agreed, even though I still was more skeptical than Annette about what Todd was aware of while he assaulted Melissa or how much he remembered afterward. I did congratulate Annette, though, for her success in getting Todd to recognize the threat he might represent to society if he was not confined.

"Do you really think I did right, Paul, or was I just being self-righteous?"

"Your role in this could not have been played by anyone else, and without you we could not guess what would have happened. I admire what you did and add that to the long list of reasons why I love you."

"Thanks, Paul, this has been nagging me." I took her in my arms for a good-bye hug cut short by Annette, who reminded me that people will see us. Then she left for home and I went to the newspaper office to write a brief column on the court's action. When I returned home, a message from Annette was waiting on my answering machine. It sounded urgent; she wanted me to call her back as soon as possible. I dialed and she picked up immediately, "Paul, Aunt Lettie is acting strange—I don't know what to do."

Within 20 minutes I was in her driveway; Annette was outside waiting for me. She said, "When I got home from Danielson, Aunt Lettie was acting like she was having a heart attack. You remember, Paul, I told you how she plays these games for attention. Well, this seems different."

"Have you called an ambulance?"

"She never lets me call anyone for her."

"What's she doing that's different this time?"

"I'm not sure. The other little games she plays—like being certain that her intestinal gas is an ulcer, or a severe headache is a stroke; and chest pains are a heart attack—all of these things I can cure by sitting with her for ten minutes or so. This time, though, along with the chest pain, she added a pain in her shoulder that runs down her left arm. I just don't know; there's so much medical stuff in magazines nowadays she may have found something new to add to her repertoire. But what really frightens me this time is the flicker of a smile between surges of pain. Aunt Lettie may seriously think she's dying and is just perverse enough to enjoy the effect it's having on me. On the other hand, she may be pleased with how well the new additions to her little act have caught my attention."

"Is she perspiring? I've seen that listed as one of the symptoms of a heart attack?"

"No, but then she never does perspire. Another thing that bothers me, though, is the sheep. You hear them? They won't shut up. They aren't just greeting your arrival. They've been carrying on like this since I came home over an hour ago. I fed them but they didn't eat and they won't stop bleating."

When I told Annette she should call an ambulance, she said, "Aunt Lettie would just have a fit on top of whatever else is bothering her. I did raise that old issue again, but she wouldn't hear of it."

"Annette, I don't think you should place yourself in a position of being responsible for her death through your negligence. You shouldn't leave this decision up to her."

"I know you're right, Paul; when I was a nun working with old people, I frequently made this kind of decision; but going against Aunt Lettie isn't the same. She makes me feel like a child without the authority to act unless I have her permission."

"If Aunt Lettie gets mad and dies because you call an ambulance, that's not your fault; but if she dies from a heart attack because you didn't call an ambulance that *is* your fault."

"I know you're right. I guess I just needed to have you tell me. Paul would you mind calling?"

"No, I don't mind; I'll call."

By the time I finished giving instructions to the dispatcher on how to get to Annette's, she returned from another visit upstairs. She was trembling as she said, "She seems worse. Aunt Lettie is really dying, isn't she, Paul?"

"I don't know. If she gets to the hospital soon enough, they may be able to do something. Was she watching the news when her attack came on?"

"No. When I came home, the TV was off. Aunt Lettie was lying on her bed fully clothed. I asked her if she had listened to the news. She said in a flat voice, 'Bowen pleaded guilty.' She was breathing funny; she seemed short of breath. That's when she told me about her chest pain and shoulder pain."

"Had this just started or what?"

"I don't know. She wouldn't talk about it. When I told her I was going to call an ambulance, she said, 'You are like hell!' That was the only time she had any inflection in her voice, the rest of the time it was weak, almost monotone—her sick voice I call it because that's what she uses to get my attention.

"I sat with her in the chair near her bed for a little while; when I started to get up to leave, she said, 'Where're you going?'"

"Was she afraid you were leaving to call an ambulance?"

"I think so, but I told her I was going to call you. She wanted to know if I was going to ask you to come out and I told her, 'I will if it's all right with you.' She nodded slightly then said, 'Yes, he should be here.' So, that's when I called you."

"Maybe you better check on her again."

Within a couple of minutes, Annette was back. "Aunt Lettie wants to see you," she said.

This must be serious, I thought. Annette entered the room first and reaching back for my hand said, "Auntie, this is my friend Paul." Aunt Lettie did not look well. She was so frail and colorless.

"Pull up the chair, Paul," she said in a weak, flat voice. When I sat down next to the bed, she reached out. I took her hand with both of mine. She studied my face for awhile, then said, "You're a good man, Paul. I hope you will continue to love Annette and take good care of her. Move in if you wish, this house is too much for one little girl to manage all alone."

I nodded and she seemed satisfied; at least she closed her eyes and relaxed her hand. I did not know what my nod meant to her, whether she thought I was thanking her for saying I was a good man, or if she thought I was agreeing to continue loving Annette and would move in. If it were not for an almost imperceptible rise and fall of her chest, I would have thought she had died. After a minute or so, I released her hand and started to get up. Without opening her eyes, she said in a barely audible voice, "Thanks, Paul."

I signaled to Annette that I would go downstairs and watch for the ambulance. Before it arrived, Annette came downstairs. She had tears in her eyes. I held her for awhile; neither of us spoke. When she was able to talk, she said, "After you left, I took Aunt Lettie's hand and held it but she didn't respond. I wasn't sure if she was alive or not. She jerked once like a fly had landed on her then she was still. I checked her pulse but couldn't find any."

"Here comes the ambulance," I said, "They'll know what to do."

14

After Aunt Lettie died, I thought Annette would need my support. Instead, she seemed to be avoiding me. When I called, I usually got her answering machine; or on those few occasions when I did reach her, she said she was awfully busy with arrangements and all. I finally had to accept the fact that I needed her more than she needed me. I thought she would have had at least a little time when we could get together. I had things I wanted to say to her; I wanted to hold her and help her. Even if she did not think she needed my help, I wanted to be part of what was going on during this difficult time in her life.

When at last Annette did agree to meet with me, it was late afternoon. She was waiting for me in the driveway, still wearing her Sturbridge Village costume. As soon as the car stopped, she surprised me by opening the passenger side door and getting in. I tried to kiss her but she offered me her cheek, then asked me to drive out past the Lynn's place.

"We don't have to stop," she said, "just drive by." It was not that she was cool toward me; I felt we were still good friends—but not lovers. Was she feeling guilty about having slept with me, or was she preoccupied? I told myself, that it is the stress of Aunt Lettie's death and the arrangements that keep her so busy; once that is attended to we will return to the previous warmth we shared.

But what are all these arrangements? That's what kept gnawing at me; I assumed Annette would tell me when she was ready. They could not all be about Aunt Lettie; she had made it clear there would be no funeral and no memorial service. "Do whatever you want to with my ashes," Aunt Lettie had said, "just don't let the wind blow any of them toward the cemetery where I planted Uncle Matt. And don't let anybody know that I have died again, or they'll think I was loony or something."

As though Annette could read my thoughts, she said, "I didn't get the ashes back from the crematorium, yet. They told me it will probably be another week. When I have them, will you help me decide what to do with them?"

I said, "Yes." But as we were having this conversation, we drove right by the Lynn's property. Usually I spotted the house through the trees and slowed down well before we reached their house but this time we went right on by. It was out of the corner of my eye that I realized there was no house, just a pile of ashes. When my mind caught up to my vision, I was stunned. Annette had not cautioned me to slow down. I glanced at her; and by the way she was enjoying the expression on my face, it was apparent her omission was intentional.

"The same thing happened to me," she laughed.

"Annette, I can tell from your amusement that the Lynns weren't in the house when it burned. What happened to them?"

"That's exactly what I wondered—probably even more than you—since the ashes were still smoking when I zipped by. I had to stop the car and go back to make sure Mr. Lynn and Mrs. Lynn weren't in it."

"How could you tell?"

"Because the car wasn't where the garage used to be—and there wasn't any sign of Mrs. Lynn's precious stove or Mr. Lynn's guns and tools. But, I had to consider that they sold those things, so I still wasn't sure until one of the neighbors stopped and told me the Lynns moved to South Carolina. I didn't know the woman, but she said she recognized my car as one frequently parked here and assumed I was a friend of the Lynn's. She said that Dr. Malak, up the road bought the property; and not long after the Lynn's left, had the fire department burn it down."

"How come the Lynns didn't let you know they were leaving?"

"I received a letter from Mrs. Lynn yesterday telling me they arrived in South Carolina safely. She explained that they sold their property and as soon as they closed, she and Mr. Lynn filled the car with as much stuff as it would hold and headed south. Mrs. Lynn wrote that she wanted to stop at a phone booth to call me before they left Connecticut, but Mr. Lynn had a full tank of gas and was not about to stop the car 20 miles after they started."

I found a place to turn the car around a couple hundred yards up the road. On the return trip, I drove by the place slowly. I felt sad but I was not sure why. Maybe I didn't dislike the old goat as much as I thought I did. He really was part of history; both of them were. I said to Annette, "Well, I guess we should have known they were serious about leaving. The last time we were out Mr. Lynn was expressing satisfaction over having sold a number of things like his tractor and farm implements at the price he paid for them 20-50 years ago. I wonder what happened to Mrs. Lynn's stove."

Annette said, "Yeah, I'd like to know, too. Mrs. Lynn never said anything about selling it, but I can't imagine they shipped it to South Carolina to use in their house trailer."

"Did you ever think about having it for your kitchen?"

"Don't laugh, Paul, I loved that stove and did think about it. I wanted to be prepared in case she offered it to me; but I couldn't think of how to vent it except into the fireplace chimney or out the side of the house; either way would have been ugly."

I agreed.

Annette said, "I didn't have any contact with the Lynns between the time Aunt Lettie died and they left for South Carolina. Guess you know I've been pretty involved. I thought their preparation was just part of their lifestyle and that the move would never happen."

"Yes, that's what I thought, too. I guess the key to the whole thing was the selling of the property. You remember, Annette, not long after I met Mr. Lynn, he offered to sell the place to me? His main selling point was so I could live closer to you."

"Yes, I remember he offered to sell it to you and that you said the price was more than you could afford. I heard Mrs. Lynn tell you later, when you were out of Mr. Lynn's hearing range, that prices have a way of going down for the right person, especially if the seller's time is running out. But, this is the first I heard that Mr. Lynn was offering me as bait."

"Maybe I was a little shy about reporting it to you. We hadn't known each other very long; but already Mr. Lynn must have seen I was quite attracted to you. Interesting, though, that in the end they sold the home to Dr. Malak. I bet they didn't know he would burn it down. I hope the Lynns never find out but I suppose it won't take long before one of the neighbors lets Mrs. Lynn know. Her friend Gladys from Four Corners would want to be first to tell her."

On the return trip to Annette's house, she did not talk anymore about what was going on in her own life. She talked mostly about things Mrs. Lynn had written regarding their lives in South Carolina. When we pulled into the yard, a couple of baas came from the barn. Annette said, "Don't worry about the sheep. I fed them before you picked me up. They're just welcoming us home. Paul, I have a casserole in the oven if you're interested."

"That sounds good. I was hoping you would invite me to stay so I brought a bottle of wine."

After we were in the house, I said, "You know Annette, the only rooms I have seen in this house are the kitchen, dining room, and downstairs bathroom, and recently, of course, Aunt Lettie's room."

"I know; but I couldn't very well show you around while we had a ghost in the house. Unfortunately, the house is currently in a mess; but if you don't mind that, let me check the casserole; and we will take a tour. It looks OK; I'll shut the oven off and leave the pot in to stay warm."

Annette started for the main staircase to go upstairs, but I cried, "Whoa."

"What's wrong?"

"Isn't your bedroom downstairs?"

"Yes, but you don't want to see that."

"Why not? I showed you my bedroom."

"That's not all you showed me."

"It's your tour, Annette. If you want to show me some of your other things while we're visiting your room that would be good."

She paused for a moment while she watched the bulge form in my jeans. Then smiling slightly, went past the stairwell to a small room located in back of the kitchen. It had a single bed with no box spring. It would be a cot, I suppose, except it had a wrought iron headboard. Contrary to what Annette had told me at my house about never making her bed, it was carefully made. It did not have a bedspread, only a blanket, which looked like an army blanket. The top sheet was folded back over the blanket about four inches. A second blanket of the same drab color was folded neatly across the foot of the bed. The rest of the furniture consisted of a simple wooden desk and chair, a chest of drawers and a floor lamp. The walls were bone white and totally bare except for a crucifix in the center of the longest wall—no pictures and no mirror. The room had a very serious effect on me. I could not think of anything appropriate to say. Annette broke the silence. "Paul, you've lost your hard-on. We may as well continue the tour." As she went past me to lead the way out of her room, she let the back of her hand bump against my crotch and said, "So now you know what it was like for me to hope for an orgasm with eight dead guys watching us from a picture on your bureau."

"Oh, God. I did do that, didn't I?"

She nodded without looking back and started up the stairwell. The first room we entered was Aunt Lettie's. The closet door was open and the floor was covered with boxes of clothes. "I'm getting Aunt Lettie's clothes ready to go off to Charities and Family Services." Her photographs, jewelry and other personal things were gone. I admired her window seat, which I had not had a chance to look at when I visited her the night she died.

We entered the guest bedroom next, which Annette told me was never used. "Aunt Lettie and Uncle Matt never had overnight guests, except for me. Even as a little girl, I always preferred the room downstairs. I liked to get up earlier than they did and didn't want to awaken them."

The guest room was small like those I had seen in the Victorian homes I had visited in Willimantic during the last annual house tour. When I mentioned that to Annette she reminded me that at the time Uncle Matt had the downstairs rebuilt, he didn't change the upstairs except to have the window seat built in the turret where it opened up into Aunt Lettie's room.

The guest room looked like it had been pleasant at one time, but now it seemed to be a catchall room for things that might be needed later. I thought some of the pictures and furniture, including a single, disassembled four-poster bed and a beautiful dressing table were probably from Annette's room downstairs before she relapsed to her earlier ascetic life but I didn't ask. In fact, I was not saying much of anything; mostly I was waiting for the tour to be over. After seeing Annette's room, I had slumped into a low mood.

"I haven't done anything with Uncle Matt's room, yet," Annette was saying, still chipper. "Aunt Lettie got rid of most of his personal stuff long ago except for his books. She always had trouble throwing away books. If you want any of them, take your pick."

I glanced at them and thought there were a few I might like to have, but I was not in the mood to go through them now. "I don't think so now, maybe another time if you haven't thrown them out yet."

"Here," she said, "at least take this one." She handed me a large, heavy world atlas. I opened it, and there was her Uncle Matt's gun. "I don't know what to do with this. You can keep it or maybe find a home for it if you don't want it."

I said, "OK, thanks." My thoughts about whether this could be traced back to any unsolved crimes were interrupted when my eyes fell on the little computer on Uncle Matt's beautiful cherry desk. It was a Mac SE. The screen was so small I had forgotten how tiny they were. I told Annette, "I used to have one like it. Is that what you use?"

"Yes. Uncle Matt bought it but I don't think he ever used it. I just use it for word processing. You can tell I was the user by the way the chair is cranked up all the way to the top.

"Paul, I was going to show you the upper part of the turret, which is in the attic. You expressed an interest it on your first visit but it would have been difficult to sneak you past Aunt Lettie to go up to the attic. We can do that now if you like or perhaps you would rather eat."

"Let's tap the wine and eat. I feel like I need a pickup."

When we returned to the kitchen, Annette said, "Paul, why don't you open the wine and pull the casserole out of the oven while I change my clothes." She was still wearing her Sturbridge outfit.

When I had the casserole on top of the stove, and the bottle open and poured, I sat down at the table. I was tempted to sip my wine instead of wait for Annette to reappear—no, not sip, the temptation was to quaff the whole glass and pour another one. Instead, I avoided the temptation by going over to look out the window. I was so deep in my brooding thoughts that I was not aware Annette had returned until she clinked on one of the wineglasses with a spoon. Standing next to the table, she was fully attired in a nun's habit and wearing her mischievous smile. Some joke! I thought—about as funny as when President Kennedy was shot. In fact, I felt—like I had just been shot in the stomach with a shotgun. Annette was not just showing me how she looked when she was a nun. After seeing her ascetic bedroom, I was pretty sure I was looking at Sister Annette. Even though she was smiling, in that outfit, she was an imposing figure—authoritative and intimidating. Her attire was completely white except for a black veil draped over the small cap or a coif, visible only as a white band across her forehead, and a black cord around her waist.

"Paul, you're not saying anything." The nun was still smiling but now her face looked composed.

I held up my glass and said, "Congratulations!"

"Paul, by the dejected look on your face, I would say you're not sharing my happiness."

"I don't know what my face looks like, but I do know how I feel, and it's not happiness—wretched, absolutely wretched best describes it."

"But, why, Paul, don't you see? This is a solution to my problem."

Her statement did not contain any information about why I should be happy or what problem this costume solved, but what it did do is close out any hope I might have held that this theatrical display was merely to show me her costume from a previous life. No indeed, Sister Annette was standing before me. I said, "Annette, let's eat and get quite drunk. Then I want you tell me what I'm supposed to be so happy about."

"Paul, I'm sorry I upset you. I'll go take it off while you get drunk, then I'll catch up to you."

Within a few minutes she was back looking like her old self in jeans and a loose blouse. She took a couple sips of wine and said, "Paul, straight out and clear, why were you upset over seeing me in my nun's habit?"

I did not answer for quite awhile. Then I said, "Because you didn't just put it on for the fun of it, you've reenlisted." I chugged my wine like I was drinking beer.

"What makes you think so?"

"Look. I don't know why you're playing this guessing game, but the fact is, you couldn't spare a single evening for me in over two weeks; and when you do find time for me, you offer to let me kiss your cheek; and now finally, I get to see your room only to discover its been stripped down like you're already living in a convent."

"Why are you yelling at me?"

"Because, I love you and I don't want to lose you."

"Yelling at me will prevent that?"

"I didn't realize I was yelling. I guess I feel desperate. What you seem to be telling me is that it's already over between us. It's already too late to even talk about it."

"Paul, it will never be too late for you to tell me you love me. It's just that your loving me doesn't solve my problem, and you shouldn't have to be involved with my problems just because you love me."

"That isn't true. I want to be involved in your problems. The least you could have done is to tell me what your problems are and why returning to the sisterhood is the best way to solve it—if that's what you've done. After all, if you reenlist, it affects both of us dramatically."

"We better get some food on the table. This is not a simple story."

"Give me the bottom line," I said.

"OK, you know that promise I made to Aunt Lettie about not selling the house—to keep it like it is? Well, I should not have made that promise. Reenlisting, as you put it, is the only way I can keep that promise."

I had my mouth open about to respond when she held up her hand and said, "Stop. Paul, that was the bottom line. People, who are built like me, have to eat on time. We don't have any body reserve to live on during a famine; and what's more, if I drink that second glass of wine on an empty stomach, I will be too drunk and foolish to tell you what my plan is, so forget about all this now and help me. You could put the casserole on the table; set out some plates, utensils and water; and put some bread on a plate while I make a salad."

15

As we put dinner on the table, my mind kept flashing back to the vision of Annette in her nun's habit—that combined with her sterile bedroom and the kiss on the check had me in pretty low spirits. Annette bowed her head and moved her lips without speaking, then made a sign of the cross. She had not done this previously before we ate; once we started, I asked if it was all right for me to talk now.

She laughed and said, "When I held up my hand earlier, it was to remind you that I had agreed to give you only the bottom line on what I was struggling with; but after I told you, you continued to press me with questions. I didn't mean for us to stop talking forever, I just didn't want to be confronted with any more mind numbing discussion that would derail dinner."

Annette was in a far better mood than I was. I knew it would be the grownup thing for me to try harder to be agreeable, so I forced a smile and said, "It's just as well you stopped us from talking because that's what would have come out, a cascade of mind numbing questions."

"Nothing else? Nothing simple? Whatever happened to sex? You used to think about that all the time—'till you saw my bedroom."

"As a matter of fact, after you changed out of your nun's clothes, my feelings of abandonment and despair have subsided enough for flashes of horniness to come through." It was a lie. My libido was so deeply buried I worried that it would never surface again.

"Feelings of abandonment and despair, Paul? Because of me? It never occurred to me that I might have that much influence over a man. Your flashes of horniness I'm beginning to catch on to, but then, I had Aunt Lettie coaching me on that. She used to tell me I would have a lot of power if I would deploy my resources better. Is that true, Paul? How much power would I gain over you if I appeared without a bra and unfastened the top two buttons on my blouse? That was the kind of recommendation Aunt Lettie would offer me when I told her you were coming over."

"I wish I had known your aunt earlier; she must have been filled with valuable wisdom; but I think she underestimated you. You already hold absolute power over me. But, any time you want to try the blouse experiment, I'm game." Immediately I envisioned Annette with no bra and the top two buttons of her blouse unfastened. I guess I was not as badly off as I thought.

She sensed I was becoming aroused, and suddenly she said, "Stand up, Paul." But before I could, I had to rearrange things under the table. "See, Aunt Lettie's experiment has great potential; but how long would my power over you last if I invited three or four other nuns to live with me; and whenever you came to visit, we were all wearing religious clothes?"

Before I recovered from her question enough to attempt an answer, Annette said, "Never mind, Paul, you're already answering the question." Looking down she said, "Going, going, gone, and there you have it; my power would last 30 seconds."

I did not have to look down to know my barometer had gone limp. I said, "That was a cute trick, Annette, but how much I care about you extends beyond how long I can keep a hard-on while you pour cold water on it."

"I guess I was just trying to mix the heavy news with humor; I know you care about me, Paul. Go ahead and ask whatever you want to."

"OK, I gather that what you're planning, Annette, is to go back into the nun business and turn this farm into a mini-convent. What I'd like to know is, if you personally like this plan or if you concocted it to satisfy Aunt Lettie's life-after-death wish? Also, I'd like to know if the project is too far along for us to look at alternatives, you know, like finding a way to include me in your life—unless you'd rather have me just butt out."

She looked at me for awhile without saying anything. Was she trying to summon the courage to tell me to leave or what? Her eyes became teary, but then she got a grip on herself and said, "It's not a done deal, Paul, I've written a few letters and made some phone calls. I am receiving favorable feedback but it has been only two weeks. For this to happen, decisions would have to be approved at higher levels than the people I've been communicating with. This could take a long time—too long in fact."

"Would you still own the property or are you giving it to the Catholic Church?"

"Aunt Lettie's will specifically bars me from giving it to a church."

"So what then? I didn't think nuns were allowed to own property."

"They can inherit and own property but they can't profit from it. I suppose if I return to the religious life I will have to place the farm in a trust or under someone else's control."

"Annette, I still don't know why you're doing this."

"It's the only way I know to preserve Auntie's precious house and farm. What I'm hoping to do is have four or five nuns living here, working to help the rural poor, especially children and the elderly, and maybe disabled people, too—you know, assisting them to live independently at home. It would also enable me to teach crafts and even keep Aunt Lettie's sheep. What was going to happen to the sheep concerned Aunt Lettie right up to the end. Whatever money the convent made from our activities would go to the church; on the other hand, I'm hoping the church will agree to lease Aunt Lettie's house and provide us with living expenses. Using her house this way would have to be approved."

As I listened, I had no way of knowing how far-fetched Annette's plan was. I could not get a reading on whether she really wanted to do this or if she was acting out of desperation to satisfy Aunt Lettie. I worried that Annette's limited experience with life may be dragging her back to something she was familiar with—back to something she was trying to escape. I also felt that, even if Annette's plan complied with the terms of her aunt's will, it violated its spirit. From previous conversations with Annette, Aunt Lettie didn't have much use for Catholicism even though she was reared a Catholic. I did not ask Annette how her aunt would feel about having a flock of nuns traipsing over her precious ground. I felt I had to guard against sounding too protective of Annette even though I did feel protective of her. The worst part of all of this was that Annette's plan, so far, did not leave any place for me. After a long pause, I said, "Annette, this may be a very good plan. You are probably better able to judge it than I am; but what I'm concerned about is if you're doing this for God, Aunt Lettie or yourself—or is it that you simply can not find an alternative?"

Annette arose from her chair and went over to look in the fireplace, which did not have a fire. Without turning to look at me, she asked, "Should I be able to answer that question?"

"I don't know. That's just the way I'm looking at it."

After struggling further, she said, "If I say I'm doing it for all three, you'll want to know if the proportions are equal."

"I suppose I would have asked that next; so who does come out on the short end?"

"I should have faced this earlier. Up to now, I just sort of thought all three issues were satisfied and let it go at that; but now that you're here, the whole thing has become more complicated."

"In what way?" I asked, hoping my status might enter the discussion.

"Paul, do you remember when I told you I was rethinking my feelings about religion?"

"Yes. You said you had completely dismantled your beliefs and were trying to rebuild a system based on your own independent thinking."

"Yes, I guess that's sort of what I said. Anyway, I thought I had made some progress. I had even gone so far as to consider that on a worldwide basis organized religion may do more harm than good—but when Aunt Lettie died, I was thrown into a turmoil. Just look at the contradiction I'm trying to create."

"You mean because you've found a need for the organizational structure of religion in order to carry out your plan?"

"Yes. I have been telling myself I'd just be making use of one of the good aspects of religion, the organizational capacity; but now I'm beginning to realize that that is what makes structured religions so dangerous. Could I live with the hypocrisy?" She paused, then said, "Paul, this is really too much, isn't it?"

Before I could respond, she continued, "Anyway, that's why I made up my room the way I did—to see if I could bed down with it the way I did as a novice. And, it's why I dressed in my nun's habit—to see how I would feel in it— and to see how you would react."

"And, what have you concluded?"

"By your reaction, I would have to conclude that my room and clothing either erased my sex appeal or castrated you." Annette smiled; she became more relaxed and returned to the table to finish her dinner. I stopped asking questions for awhile so we could concentrate on eating. When it looked like we were both finished, I said, "And the face kissing experiment, Annette? What was that about?"

She laughed and said, "All part of testing whether we could continue to be friends if I went back in the nun business."

"What did you decide there?"

Annette held up a finger for me to wait as she drained her glass. Then she said, "We're out of wine—you drank most of it." She got up and went to the basement.

I was putting the dishes into the sink when she returned with a bottle of brandy—an unopened bottle. When she handed it to me to open, I asked her what happened to the one we were working on. She said, "Gee, Paul, that was over two weeks ago. I've done a lot of hard, late night thinking since then."

I poured the brandy into the wineglasses and after she took a sip. She said, "This is more fun than drinking alone."

"I know. Why didn't you let me in on your parties?"

"Because if I told you what I was thinking about, I thought you would argue with me and think I was dumb. I didn't know you would listen to me."

"Does this mean we can be friends and do face kissing if you go back to religion?"

"I think so; at least for now. Anyway, I haven't re-enlisted yet."

"Earlier you mentioned, Annette, that your convent project had some kind of time constraint. What was that about?"

"A little while before Aunt Lettie died—the first time—she made out her will and set up a trust with the bank so when she died for real I would inherit the property. The trust fund was established to pay the taxes and the utilities, as well as to provide money for maintenance of the property. The fund was supposed to have enough money in it so the bank could invest part of it and from the earnings sustain the fund. Aunt Lettie was so secretive about her financial matters that what little I knew about her business was based mostly on vague hints—that's why I wasn't able to give you specific answers about how the farm was supported and whether or not I owned the property because technically I didn't own it until after her final death.

"It wasn't long after Aunt Lettie set up the trust that her failing memory started to become serious. She would misremember which relative or friend had said what, or talk about some event and be off by more than a decade from when it actually occurred. She reached a point where she was no longer able to figure things out, things she used to deal with quite well. If I tried to help her, she became angry. She refused to admit that her mind was slipping and tried to cover it up.

"When Aunt Lettie slept, she kept her purse on the table next to the bed. I thought it was a peculiar habit the way she continued to keep things in it. She hadn't left the house for more than a year and didn't need a handbag. Anyway, one night she fell asleep with her purse on the bed and her checkbook lying next to it. I picked them up to put them on the table, and when I glanced at the open checkbook saw that it was a mess. I paged through it and found so many pages scribbled over or torn out there would be no way to balance her account."

"How did money get into her checking account?"

"That much I knew. Shortly after I came to live with her, Auntie made a few adjustments in her life. She put my name on her checking and savings accounts so I could move money from savings to checking or make cash withdrawals for her. She also quit driving and signed her car over to me so she wouldn't have to face getting her drivers license renewed. But, for me to have a car was kind of a traumatic experience for both of us. I didn't know how to drive. Worse yet, she insisted on being the one to teach me. She was very tense about it. If I didn't do it quite right, she would yell at me and make me feel dumb."

"Aunt Lettie teaching you to drive would have been something to see. Is that when you acquired a gray fender for your beige-colored car?"

"You noticed that, huh? The new fender was a result of one of Aunt Lettie's prescribed driving exercises. She insisted that I learn her method of driving up close enough to the box to reach the mail without getting out of the car. If

I didn't get close enough on the first approach, she would have me seesaw back and forth until I could reach it. One day I knocked the mailbox down and crumpled the car fender. The box was mounted on a steel post and that wasn't at all forgiving to my fender."

"It's a wonder you didn't get clobbered by an oncoming car—I assume you were on the wrong side of the road while you practiced this feat."

"Yes, but fortunately there isn't much traffic on this road. Anyway, back to your original question about how Aunt Lettie knew when to transfer money from savings to checking. Until last year, I think she relied on the balance in her checkbook; but when her accounting went to pot, she depended on overdrawn notices from the bank."

"Didn't they charge her for overdrawing her account?"

"Yes, but that didn't seem to bother her enough to ask me for help. Anyway when Aunt Lettie died, I inherited a big box of her incoming mail reaching back for more than a year. It was a good thing she hadn't thrown it away; some of it turned out to be pretty important. So, if you're still wondering why I've been too busy to come out and play during the last couple of weeks. A large part of it was because I was trying to wrap my dyslexic mind around Auntie's old correspondence to find out what bills she's paid verses what she still owes."

"That and planning the rest of your life," I added, not wanting her to miss how badly she hurt my feelings by not inviting me to her planning sessions.

"Yes, that too. Let's see now—I keep getting sidetracked. Originally you asked about time constraints on opening up a nun business here on the farm. Well, one of the things I discovered in Auntie's discard box was a letter from the town tax assessor, who was bothered about the unpaid property taxes."

"Wasn't the bank paying the taxes from the trust fund?"

"I thought so and so did Aunt Lettie. But Mr. Tipper at the bank didn't know about the back taxes at the time he set up the trust. He had prepared a budget that provided for current taxes; but he didn't allow for back taxes. One of the letters I found in Aunt Lettie's box was from Mr. Tipper, inquiring about the copy of a letter to Aunt Lettie that he had received from the Town of Union's first selectman. The original letter, addressed to Aunt Lettie, advised her that the town would auction off her property if she didn't pay her taxes promptly."

"I don't suppose Aunt Lettie left a copy of her response to the first selectman."

"I don't think she even read the letter. The envelope had been opened, but the letter was stuck inside. She didn't have much patience anymore. My guess is that when she couldn't get it out of the envelope right away, she just tossed it in the discard box. The letter from Mr. Tipper, which hadn't been opened at all, explained to her that her trust fund didn't cover payment of back taxes."

"What was the date of that letter?"

"Six months ago."

This must have been overwhelming for Annette, who had little to no experience with finance. I asked her if she was pretty good at balancing checkbooks and she said, "I balance my own but that's quite simple. I bet you're surprised I have a checkbook."

I admitted that I was surprised, so Annette digressed enough to explain to me that two and a half years ago she received her first paycheck. "I was pretty excited about it and showed it to Aunt Lettie. Except for lapses in memory her mind was still good then. She told me to take my check to the bank and open a checking account, then every payday to deposit part of my check in the bank but save out enough cash to go shopping—my paltry wardrobe bothered her. After a year of receiving monthly statements, I became pretty good at balancing my own checkbook. I even went so far as to open a savings account, but that didn't grow very well. I guess you know how much skis and winter clothes cost—and summer clothes, too. I didn't have much of a wardrobe then; I guess I still don't, beyond jeans and sweatshirts."

"You didn't have to pay for sheep food and people food from your earnings, did you?"

"No. Aunt Lettie gave me a check for things like that."

"Is there enough money in Aunt Lettie's savings account to pay the back taxes?"

"No. That's what has me unsettled. I don't know where to get the money to pay the taxes. Between Aunt Lettie's savings and checking accounts, I barely found $5,000. The taxes owed are closer to $10,000. That's why I was hoping to lease the house to the Catholic Church. If they would pay the first year's lease and deposit the money in the trust fund at the bank, Mr. Tipper would be able to pay the back taxes without disturbing his long term budget."

I thought it was excessively hopeful for Annette to believe her plan could be put in place fast enough to keep her property off the auction block. Not only that, it calls for Annette to re-associate herself with the church, which I feel runs contrary to the person she has become. But, of course, my largest objection is that the only place Annette seems to have reserved for me is as a face-kissing, outhouse friend of a community of nuns. Is she not saying that when she speaks as though we will be continuing our relationship?

Whatever it is, there has to be a better way to save the farm than her plan. How would the old Paul Hurst have handled this? I would have waded into Annette's dumb plan with a sledgehammer. Once it was flattened, I would work out a viable solution. But Annette's innocence, desperation and selflessness—even at her own peril—were not traits to swing a sledgehammer at.

"So, what do you think, Paul?" Annette said in a positive tone of voice. "Your engine seems to have stalled."

"Yes, well, I guess I was pretty deep in thought," I mumbled. "It is an interesting thing that you have come up with."

Annette first looked down at the table, then looked up with a scowl and said, "Paul, that was an evasive and condescending comment. Is that all you have to offer? I thought you were my friend. Is that what friends do—tell each other what they want to hear?"

"I don't know; I never had a real friend before—at least not one like you that I care so much about."

"So, if that's it, if you're afraid of hurting my feelings, it tells me you don't think much of my plan. Or, are you afraid if I go back to being a nun you won't be able to get me into bed anymore?"

Saving our relationship was beginning to look like a larger fantasy than Annette's holy farm, but I was not ready to give up yet. "OK, first of all, don't belittle my interest in developing a long term loving relationship with you, including sex. In addition to that, I think you're moving too fast and in the wrong direction—a direction that if successful will lead to unhappiness for both of us." I paused for a moment to see how she would react.

Annette said, "Go on. I'm listening." The sharp edge to her voice could have meant any number of things, but I did not stop to analyze it. I told her, "You need to buy some time with the town office. One thing you might do is explain to the first selectman that Aunt Lettie died a little over two weeks ago and that you have inherited the property. You have only now found his unopened letter and become aware of the back taxes. Assure them that you will pay the taxes, but that you need an extension of time to assess the estate's financial resources."

"What if they insist on knowing where the money will come from if it isn't in Aunt Lettie's estate? They won't be impressed with my job at Sturbridge Village as a source for payment."

"I don't think they'll ask where the money will come from since you'll already have told them you need time to put your aunt's finances in order. Explain about her memory problem, how she didn't read her mail; and that's why she didn't pay her taxes."

"Paul, if I were the tax collector, I would want more than this general kind of assurance that the estate has the money."

"I really don't think they'll be that hard-nosed at this stage if you show honorable intentions."

"They don't know me, Paul. On the other hand, maybe that's a good thing if my plan to get the money from the Church is as bad as you think it is. Anyway, I just don't want to be stuck for an answer if they say 'show me the money.'"

"OK. Just offhand, I have two possible alternatives that wouldn't take a lot of time for you to deal with: one, find the source of the money that has been feeding Aunt Lettie's savings account over the years. It probably is a stock or bond mutual fund that pays regular dividends or interest directly into the account. You may be able to tap into the fund and use some of the principle to pay the bills. The second alternative is tell them that you're going to marry me next month and that I will pay the taxes. I could give you a letter of assurance to carry with you in case they want to see something in writing."

Annette sat very straight in her chair with a panicky look on her face. Finally she said in an uncertain voice, "Paul, are you proposing to me or are you trying to be funny?"

"I'm very serious."

"So, what you are saying is that if I can't find the $10,000, you will marry me and come up with it? But, if I do find the money, forget it? If you do have to marry me, the money is sort of a reverse dowry, isn't it? Or are you trying to buy me? I've always had doubts about my self-worth. How about $20,000, Paul, would you go that high?"

I sat quietly for a moment then said, "I guess it's getting late." I got up and swept Uncle Matt's gun/book off the counter top where I had left it; I had already reached the door when Annette said, "It isn't that late."

I took my hand off the doorknob and stood for a second longer uncertain whether or not to go. Maybe it was stupid of me to propose to her at this time and under these circumstances, but her response was overkill. I was deeply hurt. When I turned to look at her, she had tears in her eyes. She said, "Please, Paul, don't go." I continued to stand by the door while the sour events of the day flashed through my mind. "Come sit down, Paul. I need to have you explain to me what you said. I didn't understand most of it— mutual funds, stocks, bonds, marriage—all dumped together on one plate. These are foreign subjects to me. If you want me to know what you were talking about you have to tell me slowly and carefully and give me time to associate them with things familiar to me."

As I pulled my chair back and sat down, she apologized for her sarcasm, explaining that she was frustrated and frightened by not knowing what I was talking about and especially by my casual offer to marry her as part of a business arrangement. She said, "It made me feel like I just got off a boat from the old country and was supposed to marry someone within a certain length of time so I would get to stay in this country."

I said, "I see what you mean. I'm sorry about the way I dropped it on you. I've thought about us getting married so much I just assumed you had, too. Aside from the financial issue I do want to marry you, Annette."

"Is that what you want to deal with first, your proposal then talk about saving the farm?"

"Yes." I took her hands and held them and said, "Annette, I love you. Will you please marry me?" After I said it, I felt it sounded so corny I was surprised she did not laugh but she did not; she seemed to take it seriously.

After a moment, she said, "Paul, you were right, I have thought about marrying you, especially what I would say if you asked me. I'm very fond of you, Paul, and you have never let me down. I have such a strong physical attraction to you that all you have to do is touch me and I have to struggle not to submit. If it weren't for all my hang-ups, my behavior with you would be scandalous. At night, when I'm lying in bed thinking of you—and blocking out all other thoughts—the things I would like to do with you come to me like I'm some kind of wild animal. Sometimes I have to open my eyes and look up at that crucifix on my wall to keep from masturbating. In total I think this means I love you. I know I would readily marry you except for—"

She stopped talking and lapsed into deep thought that left me hanging. I said, "What, Annette? Whatever it is, we can fix it."

"History, Paul. Can we fix history? I have known so few happy marriages I almost think it's better just to live together and save the cost of a divorce. Certainly, my parent's marriage was a dismal failure and friends from the convent, who left to get married, seldom stayed together for long. I'm sure a lot of them had the same problems I have about guilt; but also quite a few of them wanted to have children. As it turned out for some, they weren't able to have children and that became a problem; or if they did have kids, the kids were often the problem—and infidelity, Paul, you wouldn't believe it."

"Oh, I believe it, Annette, but your sample isn't a very good cross section of the country. I know of a lot of successful marriages; and from the statistics which I don't remember exactly, I think successes run better than 50 percent."

"Yes, except those statistics include marriages that have failed—marriages that might better have ended in divorce. I saw enough like that when I was working with senior citizens."

"Annette, we're talking about us"—but then I realized I was arguing a lost cause, so I said, "I guess what you're still telling me Annette is *no*. I feel very badly about it; but for us to discuss marriage in terms of the probability of success, it doesn't sound like we have a very strong case for it."

"Paul, it's not you; I just have things to work out first. I hope you won't run off mad. Whether I turn Aunt Lettie's farm into some kind of service community run by nuns or blunder along here by myself, I hope you will stick with me. Either way I need your love and your help, and who knows what's possible for us once I resolve some of my hang-ups."

I nodded but I did not think I could talk in a normal voice, so I said nothing. It was probably just as well because I was not thinking clearly. Annette waited for me to respond. I went over to her; and when she stood up, I put my hands on her shoulders; and without drawing her close kissed her on the cheek and left. Halfway home I realized I had left the world atlas on the table but it was not something I needed badly enough to go back for.

16

I did not call Annette. I should have. I had behaved badly. I should have called her as soon as I got home; but how could a phone call reopen a door Annette had closed so tightly? Am I supposed to hope something of Annette will be left for me after she gives herself back to God? Face it, Paul, it's over, I thought.

I stayed away from the office as much as possible. I had been told several times that my mood was showing, but one day I had to retrieve some notes from my desk. Beth Turbot was at her desk pounding furiously at her keyboard. That is how she typed, one finger on each hand, fast and loud like a woodpecker. She added to the noise aggravation she generated by producing copy as fast as the rest of us do with ten fingers. The first couple of months I worked next to her the noise jangled my brain. Her response to my snide comments was, "Get used to it or work at home." To protect my sanity from noise versus loneliness I did some of each.

Today, I tried to sneak past Beth and get my notes while she was still smacking the keys; but before I could find what I was looking for, the clatter stopped. Without looking up, I knew her evil eye was on me. I ignored her and continued to search my file drawer until she said in a loud whisper, "Well, asshole, looks like you made as big a mess of Annette's life as you did your own."

Without looking up, I asked, "You take over for Aunt Lettie as Annette's confidant?"

"I helped put you two misfits together; I feel some responsibility for the relationship."

"I was wondering if Annette turned in her column yesterday. I guess she did—and gave you an earful of my bad behavior at the same time."

"You're probably both too young to be in love, you don't know what to do with it."

"She tell you about the nun farm?"

"We went out for a two-hour lunch yesterday. I think she told me everything."

"You didn't take that little girl out for one of your two-hour martini lunches!"

"How else would I find out what's going on? Other than a long soulful face, I haven't gotten anything out of you."

By now my resentment of Beth's intrusion into my private business was beginning to wear off; I turned to look at her as I asked, "So what's the prognosis, doctor?"

"I only heard Annette's version; but after seeing how sick you look, I'd guess you both have the same disease; untreated it can lead to prolonged misery and eventually the death of the relationship."

"What's your recommendation?"

"Stop taking cold showers and go over there and make your case."

"For god's sake, Beth, are you recommending sex in our weakened condition?"

"Of course, it's one of the things that worries her about marriage. You two apparently haven't taken the time or trouble to work the kinks out of your relationship—or even to put some kinkiness into it if that's what it needs."

"I guess if she told you about what happens in the bedroom, she told you about the nun farm and her overdue taxes, too."

"The martini method is thorough, that's why I'm such a good reporter."

"You're also a pain in the ass, Beth, but don't stop now. I'll need more help if I'm going to defeat God's plan."

"If you can't figure out how to keep three or four nuns from taking the farm, it's no wonder we lost the Vietnam War."

"Same problem, the enemy is among us."

"You're talking about Annette, Paul?"

"Who else? And what's more she doesn't know which side she's on. You're going to have to tell her, Beth."

"Why me, why don't you tell her yourself; or did you lose your balls in the last war?"

"Every time you kick me in the groin, I know my balls are still there. Anyway, one of the things that bothered Annette most about being in a convent was the strict obedience that was demanded. I can't start telling her what to do as a way of making her think she's better off with me than she is under a mother superior."

"Gentle help is what she needs, Paul; but especially she needs to talk about how she feels. You blew it when you walked out leaving her in the midst of indecision and in desperate need of financial advice." Then holding up her hand to keep me from interrupting her, Beth continued, "Annette told me about the lesson in finance you gave her. I gather it consisted of a single, run-on sentence that started with stocks, bonds and mutual funds and ended in a marriage proposal. When she didn't fall all over you with gratitude, you picked up your ego and went home. You even left her a gun in case she wanted to shoot herself."

"I never had a mother, you know."

"What I'm telling you, Paul, aren't things little boys learn from their mothers. Young men are supposed to have affairs with older women and learn something about life before they blunder out into the world to inflict their clumsy maleness on young women."

"Where were you when I needed you?"

"Yeah, I know. Well, let's hope it's not too late to save what's left of your life."

I promised Beth I would try harder, and after I found the notes I had come into the office for, I left for home. Along the way I stopped and bought a dozen roses. My answering machine had a message on it from Annette, who wanted me to call her. My guess was that Beth had called Annette as soon as I left for home. When I returned her call, she was not far from the phone. She sounded like nothing was wrong between us and wanted me to come out as soon as I could. She said she had Aunt Lettie's ashes and wanted me to help her decide what to do with them.

As I pulled into the yard, I noticed the sun was shining on a beautiful summer day. The sheep were grazing on the lawn between the house and the barn. I thought they might run off when I opened the car door; but as I eased it open, they stood their ground, watching me and chewing. I approached a couple of steps and the white one walked toward me the same distance, stopped and stamped her foot. Was that supposed to scare me or tell me I had come close enough? By then Annette was standing at the back door watching the show. She called out, "He's all right, Lily. That's Paul. You remember him. He's going with us." Lily looked back at Ebony, then back at me, both standing their ground and watching as Annette walked over to me. She was wearing a small green knapsack. I hugged her and tried to give her one of those religious pecks on the check but she turned her face toward me and caught my kiss on her lips. We lingered for a moment before she broke off to tell me, "We're all through with that cheek-kissing thing."

"I'm very glad to hear that." I returned to the car and took the roses out.

She exclaimed, "For me, Paul! They're so beautiful. This is the first time anyone has ever given me flowers. In fact, it's the first time I have ever seen a dozen roses." As she counted them, she discovered the card. "Oh, Paul, it says, 'I love you with all my heart. I'm sorry I behaved so badly.'"

I said, "Yah, I know. That's what I wrote and that's what I feel."

She laughed and said, "Beth let me know that I'm as much to blame for our rift as you are. She says that when we are together I should take my clothes off more often."

"She told me I should stop taking cold showers. All good advice."

"Yes, but first I better put these in a vase. Then I'll come right back and we'll put Aunt Lettie to rest."

When Annette returned, she handed me a small spade as she led the way down the same path we had taken on our ski hike last winter. I fell in behind her; Lily followed twenty feet behind me and Ebony brought up the rear. I assumed Aunt Lettie's ashes were in the knapsack. From time to time, I looked back to see if the sheep were still with us and chuckled to myself over this strange funeral procession. When we arrived at a tiny brook, Annette turned and went upstream a short distance to a tiny waterfall. Two years earlier Annette's sawyer, Hill Dillard, had removed a large tree near the stream. That opened the forest canopy enough to allow sunlight to fall on the water and on a surrounding area where patches of grass were now established. While Annette and I discussed the suitability of the site for Aunt Lettie's final resting place; the sheep dropped out of formation to graze.

Annette and I agreed on a spot; but when I started to dig, I discovered that tree roots laced the ground. Annette said not to worry about them; we do not need a big hole. She took off her knap sack and removed the small box of ashes. She said, "We aren't going to bury the box. Auntie wouldn't want any impediment to her fast return to the soil."

As soon as I had a small hole in among the tree roots, eight inches deep and maybe the same in diameter, Annette asked, "That's enough, isn't it?"

I said, "I guess so, but I'm really not very experienced at this."

Annette went down on her hands and knees, looked into the hole and said, "Yes, that ought to do it." She opened the box, unfastened the plastic bag and poured Aunt Lettie's ashes into the hole.

When she stood up, I asked, "Is that it?"

"I don't know. I guess so."

"Shall I just cover the hole with soil?"

Annette stood there looking at the hole as if she had not heard me. When my words broke through her ponderous thoughts, she said, "Oh, I'm sorry, Paul, I was trying to think of something to say. I've been trying to think of something all week, but I haven't come up with anything. Auntie gave me such specific instructions on what not to say that there isn't anything left. My brain keeps short-circuiting to various prayers I have heard at funerals, but Aunt Lettie gave me strict orders: 'No prayers.'"

"What else did she say, other than what you told me earlier, about not letting any of her ashes blow in the direction of Uncle Matt's grave?"

"She said I shouldn't keep her ashes around the house. 'Get them into the woods out in back where they can quickly become part of the forest.' How about it, Paul? Anything you want to say?"

I looked down and addressing the hole with her ashes, said, "Aunt Lettie, I have never had an aunt of my own. I hope that in some way you have been willing to think of me as family. The evening you shared with me as an elegant ghost, as well as the day we said goodbye to each other, was very meaningful to me. I also appreciate the role you played in bringing Annette and me closer together. I regard seriously the request you made, while you were dying, for me to take care of Annette and to even move in with her. I promise to do my best on both counts, but I may need your help. I hope you can stand by for a while and, if possible, assist me in carrying out your last request."

Annette said, "That was very nice, Paul, thank you. I'm sure that what you said were things she would have wanted to hear." She had tears in her eyes as she spoke. I reached for her and she pressed herself against me. I held her while she cried softly. The sheep watched, slowly chewing their cuds.

I added a shovel of soil to the hole and topped it off with a piece of sod while Annette fished around in her knapsack. When I stood back to survey my work, she stepped forward with a small kiln-fired clay plaque—an 8 x 10-inch tombstone—and pushed the base of it into the ground at the back of the grave. Etched into it was the message:

Aunt Lettie
We will always love you
1914-1996

"That's really beautiful, Annette, and you're right on the year, too; she would have wanted you to recognize the first time she died."

"That was a difficult choice for me. I know she enjoyed some of her last two years, particularly the period she was coaching me on how to court a man. And it is clear, too, that she liked you—that's why I put *we* on it."

"I had hoped that the *we* included me."

The sheep started for home, so we gathered the shovel and knapsack and followed them. At the end of the trail, where it curves around the side of the barn and into the yard, the sheep stopped. There was an extra car in the yard. Three nuns, in religious habits like the one Annette wore the night our relationship nearly fell apart, were at the back door of the house. Annette said, "Oh shit, they weren't supposed to come until tomorrow."

The attention of the nuns was on getting someone to answer the door, so they did not see us. With Annette's car and my car in the yard, they had reason to believe someone was home. The sheep sized up the situation, then made a dash for the barn. Annette went over and hooked the latch.

I said, "They haven't seen us yet. Let's duck back around the barn and into the woods." But, just then they turned to go back to their car and spotted us.

Annette said, "Too late." She waved and they waved back committing us to meet with Mother Theresa, Sister Kathleen and Sister Helen. When Annette introduced me, it was as her friend, Paul Hurst. She called the large one Mother Theresa then explained that her name was spelled with an 'h' as in Saint Theresa, unlike the famous Mother T-e-r-e-s-a of India. Mother Theresa's habit flowed down over her body in the shape of a bell and her strong alto voice rang as clear as a bell—beautiful, yet with a hint of authority. Mother Theresa apologized for arriving a day early and explained, "It was such a beautiful day we decided to drive around in the area to develop a feel for what it is like here. We had some time left before dark; so to make sure we could find your place tomorrow, we drove down your road—and here we are. I hope our dropping in like this isn't an inconvenience."

Annette said, "No, it isn't a problem; but you almost missed us. We have just returned from a hike in the woods. Aunt Lettie had requested that her remains be cremated and returned to the soil. Paul joined me in saying good-bye to her."

Mother Theresa introduced her two companions, who smiled and nodded, as they said they were pleased to meet me. Sister Helen asked if I was the Paul Hurst who wrote for the *Chronicle*. When I acknowledged that I was, Mother Theresa wanted to know if the *Chronicle* routinely covers funeral ceremonies as small as this. Did I sense disapproval in her tone? I wondered if cremation ran contrary to Catholic doctrine or maybe it was these private little burials that bothered her. In either case, Annette would have known—she did not have to bring up the burial issue—it was intentional. I simply said, "I'm here as a friend of Annette and of Aunt Lettie."

The other two nuns were calm and did not appear to react to what Annette said we had done. Sister Helen, probably in her early 50s and Sister Kathleen in her 20s, were both attractive women. Annette seemed to know all three of them. I did not feel that I had anything positive to contribute to this gathering, so I said to Annette, "I should be going; I'll call you later."

Before Annette could respond, Sister Helen said, "Oh no, Mr. Hurst, we are the uninvited guests." Sister Kathleen nodded emphatic agreement. Mother Theresa did not register her opinion before Annette said, "Please, all four of you stay, and do come in. I'm glad you're here, Paul. This visit involves you as much as anyone."

The course of Annette's conversation regarding our relationship seemed remarkably open. I could not imagine why she wanted me here at all; she knew how negative I felt about her plan and that I could easily scuttle it even accidentally. Why does she trust me not to? On the other hand, maybe that was what she wanted me to do, subconsciously at least.

Once we were in the kitchen and the sisters were through marveling at the room, Annette offered them wine or tea. Everyone waited for Mother Theresa to respond. When she suggested wine, Sisters Sister Kathleen and Sister Helen agreed. I was relieved by their choice; my attitude needed readjustment. Annette asked me to open the bottle, while she answered an earlier question Sister Helen had asked about the loom. That led to additional questions about spinning and weaving. I pulled the cork, took the glasses from the cupboard, and poured the wine. While Annette delivered mini lectures from her Old Sturbridge Village repertoire, I served the drinks. I was amused at the amount of pleasure I was taking from playing host—just as though I lived there.

Mother Theresa's eyes began to wander away from the loom and spinning wheel. After a short time she said, "As long as we're here, Annette, could you show us the rest of the house? That is, if you don't mind; it would save us from having to bother you tomorrow."

"It's less orderly now than it would be tomorrow . . ." Before Annette could finish her sentence, Mother Theresa rolled over Annette's reluctance with, "I'm sure it's fine." Annette led the way. I stayed back to re-cork the wine bottle, thinking, too, if they did not miss me I could pass up the tour and have another glass of wine. But, just as I was feeling glad Annette had bought the 1.5 liter bottle, and I was about to take advantage of it, I heard her ask in a loud voice, "Where's Paul?"

I called back, "I'm bringing up the rear, Annette, so I can watch for stragglers." Annette showed them the dining room and living room, then went upstairs to Aunt Lettie's bedroom bypassing her own little torture chamber in back of the fireplace. I could not hear what she was saying about the rooms, but I could see they were more organized and tidy than when I had last seen them.

As the women left Aunt Lettie's room for Uncle Matt's, I stepped back so they could pass. Then I fell in behind.

Once the religious women were gathered in the bedroom, I drew in close behind them so I could hear what Annette would have to say about her controversial uncle and his room. Before Annette could speak, Mother Theresa marveled at the great number of books Uncle Matt had collected. She said, "Many of them look old; they must be quite valuable. Did he read a lot?" As Mother Theresa spoke, she picked up the large World Atlas lying on the desk. Annette looked stressed and tried to say something; but before she could speak, Mother Theresa had rested the heavy book on her abdomen and opened it. When Uncle Matt's Colt .45 flopped out on to the desk, she said, "Oh!"

and dropped the book. "My word, Annette, did you know that was in there?"

Annette was slow to answer, which gave me time to say, "It belonged to Uncle Matt. Annette gave it to me to dispose of, but I forgot to haul it away the last time I was here. I apologize for causing you to be startled by it."

"I should think that between the two of you, at least one would have managed to put it in a safer place than on an open desk."

Defensively, without thinking, I snapped back, "Quite right, Mother Theresa, and I would think that at least one of the three of you would have managed to have this visit occur on the day it was scheduled. By then the gun would have been gone. I had planned to take it with me when I left this afternoon."

Mother Theresa gave me a long cold stare and said, "Nobody has ever talked to me that way before."

I said, "Perhaps they should have."

Mother Theresa turned to Annette and said, "Shall we continue our tour?" Annette led the way to the guest room while I put the gun back in the book. When they were out of sight I slipped downstairs with the package and locked it in the trunk of my car. I stood outside for awhile sucking fresh air into my lungs as I wondered whether or not to go back inside and continue my charade to its losing finish or just go home and forget about it. Before I decided what to do, the sheep started to call, so I went to the barn to feed them. Lord knows I wouldn't want hungry sheep to interfere with the tour.

When the sheep saw me instead of Annette, they stopped baaing to study me. They knew me well enough not to be afraid, even though they had never seen me without Annette, but they did seem to want an explanation. At first

I felt a little foolish telling the sheep where Annette was and what she was doing; but they seemed interested so I went on at some length even getting into the issue of how I felt about Annette and what I would prefer to do instead of have Annette continue in her present direction. Ebony said *baa*, which of course was how I felt about Annette's plan; so I gave them their grain and hay. Then I closed the barn door and turned to go back to my car. That was when I saw Sister Kathleen, the youngest one of the triad, standing by the cars looking around the yard. She waved and called, "We've been looking for you."

Talking to the sheep had elevated my spirits. I laughed and with a smile said, "Don't forget, I've got the gun now. I don't have to be afraid of you guys anymore."

"I couldn't see that you ever were; but I'm glad to hear you say it. Now maybe you will come back in the house."

"How many of you want me to come back in the house?"

"All of us."

"Even Mother Theresa?"

Sister Kathleen, hiding her amusement reasonably well said, "Yes."

"Does that mean she has forgiven me?"

"Probably not, I expect she'll have to pray first."

"From among these people so enthusiastic for my return, how is it you were the one sent to bring me back?"

"I wasn't sent. I volunteered. Being the youngest and least important to the purpose of our visit, I was the most reasonable one to go."

"Was it really that simple?"

"We lead simple lives. Why do you ask? What complicated scheme do you imagine?"

"Oh, nothing of that sort. I'm just trying to understand the world Annette came from and is considering returning to. But, tell me, if you are of so little importance, why were you invited to join this group in the first place?"

"I asked to come. If Sister Annette's plan is approved, I would like to be part of it. I'm a nurse. I work long hours in an understaffed hospital and live in a convent with older women and rigid rules. I would love to live out here with Annette and hopefully other young, religious women serving the elderly and rural poor."

"Do you think that's going to happen?"

"Do you hope it won't?" she snapped back.

"How did you know?"

"You are not hanging around here because of Aunt Lettie—or those sheep," she said, jabbing her thumb in the direction of the barn and looking at me like she had told a nasty sheep herder joke. Her amusement, though, was probably an expression of satisfaction over how cleverly she exposed my feelings for Annette.

"So, what will you do with your new found information?" I asked.

"Nothing. If Mother Theresa and Sister Helen haven't noticed how you and Annette feel about each other, it's not my business to bring it up. I'd like to see Annette's plan quickly approved so I can move in; but I can't imagine why Annette would even consider rejoining the order; her current situation looks just fine to me," she said as she made a broad sweep of one hand to include the forest, barn and house. With the other hand she gestured toward me. "But, I don't need to know."

Sister Kathleen's irreverence was a little like Annette's when she was in that kind of mood, but otherwise she was quite different. Her voice was sharper and more challenging, reminding me of a female assistant prosecutor I dated occasionally before I met Annette. Sister Kathleen was taller than Annette, handsome but not feminine-pretty.

I suppose Sister Kathleen thought she was ringing the truth out of me with her cleaver interrogation unless it was already clear to her that I did not support Annette's plan and had no interest in hiding anything to protect it. I asked Sister Kathleen if she thought her colleagues would be aware of how close Annette and I are to each other. She said, "I would be surprised if they didn't make note of how easily you found the wineglasses and graciously fell into the role of host. On the other hand, they may not have noticed how you and Annette looked at each other and how protective you were toward each other."

"How do you mean?"

"You know, like you're in love and trying to protect each other. You would know what I'm talking about if you had seen the flow of expressions across Annette's face while you and Mother Theresa were engaged in that gun fight. How I interpreted them was, when the gun fell out and Mother Theresa confronted Annette with, 'My word, Annette! Did you know that was in there?' Annette's look appeared startled and upset. She fumbled for a response; but when you explained that the gun had belonged to Uncle Matt; and then, you took the blame for not removing it, Annette looked relieved, like your apology settled the issue in a gentlemanly way with neither of you being badly damaged. But then, when Mother Theresa renewed her attack with, 'I should think that between the two of you, at least one would have managed to put it in a safer place than on an open desk,' Annette's expression of relief turned to pain. Before she could mount a defense, though, you came back with 'Quite right, Mother Theresa, and I would think that at least one out of the three of you would have managed for this visit to occur on the day it was scheduled. By then the gun would have been gone. I had planned to take it with me when I left this afternoon.'"

"Holy shit," I said without thinking. "You memorized it."

"Yeah, I wanted to get it right for my diary."

"And, for some of the other girls back at the convent?"

"Perhaps, one or two," she said, pinching back a smile."

"I was too focused on the target to see how Annette was reacting." I replied.

"Apparently seeing that you were able take care of yourself, she was now free to enjoy the exchange. Even when Sister Theresa said, 'Nobody has ever talked to me like that before,' Annette looked to you as though she expected an appropriate response. I thought you had already had your say to Mother Theresa and wouldn't bother to answer. That's when you said, 'Perhaps they should have.' I guess you wanted to make sure she was dead in the water. I couldn't see how the others were responding because I had bowed my head and started a silent Our Father to help us through this."

While my conversation with Sister Kathleen was going on, we were walking slowly toward the house. By the time we reached the back door, I realized I had not decided yet whether to rejoin the party or go home. Nothing really had changed. I still did not know why they wanted me back or what position I should take if they started asking me questions. The problem was worse now because, after I went outside, Annette may have told them things she would rather I didn't contradict.

When Sister Kathleen reached the door, she looked back in surprise that I had not joined her in the last few steps. "Aren't you coming?"

"No, I don't think this is my business and you haven't given me any reason to rejoin the party."

"No, I guess I didn't. Well, actually they didn't give me a reason to convey to you. How it happened was, as the tour progressed without you, Annette became so engaged in showing us things and answering questions that she didn't notice you were missing; but when she did, she seemed bothered and asked, 'Where's Paul?' Sister Helen responded, 'He hasn't been with us for quite a while.' Annette seemed alarmed and rushed back to the kitchen and we followed her. When she saw you weren't there, she looked out the window and said, 'His car is still here, he must be feeding the sheep, it's their dinnertime and they were calling but have stopped now. When he's through out there, he will probably get in his car and leave."

"Sister Helen said, 'I hope he doesn't do that.' I said, 'Maybe we should stop him before he runs off.' Mother Theresa said, 'Yes, we should assure him that we want him to come back.' That's when I volunteered to find you. So, you see nothing sinister is involved in the invitation."

Sister Kathleen's assurance did not sway me. She offered nothing that would cause me to believe Mother Theresa would not ask how I feel about Annette's plan or about Annette personally, especially now that she has seen us together. I could imagine she was surprised enough that I was the only one invited to Aunt Lettie's funeral, not to mention the show of affection and concern Sister Kathleen claimed that Annette and I revealed. I realize, though, that it would appear unfriendly of me to leave without saying good-bye. Worse yet, they may have thought I had been wounded in the exchange with Mother Theresa. I opened the door for Sister Kathleen and we went in.

17

When Sister Kathleen and I joined the others in the kitchen, Annette and Mother Theresa were at the table intensely involved in conversation. Sister Helen stood near the window where she would have seen me return from the barn and join Sister Kathleen but she would not have seen where we were standing at the back door while I hesitated about coming in.

Annette broke off the conversation when we entered to say, "Oh, Paul, I'm glad you're back. I was afraid you would head on home after you fed the sheep."

"You could tell they were fed, huh? I didn't know if they would be willing to accept food from me."

Annette replied, "They've seen you enough, Paul, to know you're family. Thanks for silencing them."

"You're welcome. I won't interrupt you for long I just stopped to say good-bye before I leave for home."

Mother Theresa said in a surprisingly friendly tone, "Please don't go, Paul. I have questions you may be able to help me with. If it's missing a meal that worries you, I would like to take you all to Little Eddy's for dinner tonight. This business trip is covered by my expense account."

Annette smiled and asked, "Have you ever been to Little Eddy's?"

Mother Theresa said, "No, but we drove by it in our travels today and I know it isn't far from here."

I looked at Annette to see how she felt about going. She said, "It's OK with me, Paul, but you're still my invited guest so it's your call."

I agreed to go; and once we were assembled in the driveway, I suggested we take two cars, "Annette and I can go in my car and lead the way." I wanted to be alone with Annette so I could find out what she had told them about us and how she wanted me to handle it.

But, Mother Theresa neatly thwarted that with, "Oh, nonsense, Paul, my car is large enough for all of us. You can sit in front and help me drive in case you're afraid nuns haven't progressed that far yet."

I said, "The only statistics I have is from Annette who knocked over Aunt Lettie's mailbox shortly after she first moved here." By then it was too late for additional input on the sitting arrangement; the other two nuns had maneuvered Annette in the middle of the back seat with one of them on each side. So, I held the driver side door open while Mother Theresa positioned herself behind the wheel.

Mother Theresa stopped at the end of the driveway, to ask which way she should turn. I told her, "Left, but watch out for the mail box."

"I think I do like you after all. By the way are you planning to marry Annette?"

"I'm hoping to. What did she tell you?"

"Sister Annette told me that you asked her to marry you, but that she told you she didn't want to be married. Clearly, you are close friends, though. Would it be presumptuous of me to think there is something beyond friendship here?"

"I have no reservations about assuring you that I love Annette, but I can't speak for her. The fact that Annette is still talking with you about turning Aunt Lettie's farm into a religious outpost, leads me to believe I may be losing this competition for Annette's hand."

"I like your honesty, even when you're confronted with a delicate, personal question, so let me tell you what our position is—we don't want to lose Annette—we hope we are winning. So there is no need for us to pussyfoot around on that or on related issues."

The three in the back seat were engaged in a separate conversation. Since Mother Theresa seemed to feel free to have this personal exchange with me, I asked, "Are you so short on nuns you can't afford to let me have one, especially since she has already left the convent and at a minimum is kindly disposed toward me."

"You probably know that the number of nuns has declined markedly in the last 20 years; we can't afford to lose any more, particularly one that is already trained and of the quality that Annette represents. Besides, she only thinks she has resigned."

"What do you mean? Didn't she write a letter of resignation?"

"Yes, but her resignation hasn't been accepted yet."

"Does she know that?"

"Probably not since she thinks she would have to apply to be re-instated if her convent plan is approved. So, if you two are having relations, be aware you're violating a nun."

"Why hasn't she been told?"

"Initially, she took a leave of absence, which was approved, and then she submitted a letter of resignation. As far as we are concerned she is still on leave."

"No disrespect, Mother Theresa, but you didn't tell me why she hasn't been told."

"You're right, Paul. I didn't." I saw her look in the rearview mirror, presumably to see if our conversation was being monitored before she said, "Her resignation hasn't been disapproved either."

"Is this what Catholics refer to as limbo? Why hasn't any action been taken?"

"Sometimes it takes quite a while; two or three years are not unusual."

Mother Theresa had lowered her voice as soon as we started this conversation. Since she apparently didn't want us to be heard in the back seat, I followed her lead. The next thing I asked was, "Do you know why some resignations take longer than others?"

She calmly replied, "Usually it's because of some problem, like not having made a convincing case."

"Mother Theresa, are you dodging my question?"

"Yes, but only because it's too complicated to go into at this time. It is enough to say that the letter Sister Annette wrote was not very convincing. It didn't address a major issue that was involved."

I strongly suspected the issue had to do with the picnic that Annette and Father Thomas had at the abandoned farm. I sensed that Mother Theresa knew something about it so I asked her, "Are you sure anyone wants to have the Father Thomas issue addressed?" Mother Theresa didn't respond. She looked neither to the right nor to the left. Finally, she asked in her bell tone, "Aren't we almost there?"

Annette said, "We went by Little Eddy's a half mile back. We can turn around in the next driveway if you wish."

NEITHER THE TIME NOR THE PLACE

When we walked in the door, it was comforting to see that some things in the world do not change. Melba was still waiting tables and had suffered no weight loss, Little Eddy was tending bar and the juke box was playing an old song. I led us to a booth and stood back to let the women sort out where they wanted to sit. The three smaller ones slid in on one side, and Mother Theresa suggested I go in the other side first. I thought it was considerate because it positioned me directly across from Annette. As soon as we were settled, Melba came to our table. Annette and I both said "Hi, Melba." Without responding, she surveyed the dramatically attired group. Then, looking from Annette to me, said, "Well—it looks like you two are going to have to behave yourselves tonight."

Sister Kathleen was the first to laugh. "Are you warning us, Melba that we're in bad company tonight?"

"Sister, let me tell you about the last time they were here, and you can judge for yourself. These two had a laughing fit that wouldn't shut off. Little Eddy told me later that he lost a lot of money that night when the customers quit drinking to try to find out what set these two off. The worst part of it was none of us ever did find out."

Annette looked at me with a big smile and said. "Hah! Wouldn't this be a great time to tell that story?"

I said, "Yes, but don't start until we've had something drink."

"Paul, you know full well we aren't going to talk about that," she warned, shaking her finger at me. Then she said, "I'll have a beer, Melba."

I said, "Make it two."

Sister Kathleen said, "Three." Mother Theresa asked what they had in wine.

"We have a choice, red or white," Melba said with a smile.

Theresa and Sister Helen ordered white and Melba left. When she returned with our drinks, she said, "Little Eddy told me the drinks for this table are on the house."

I asked, "Even for the two troublemakers?"

"Yes, I specifically asked Little Eddy that question and he said, 'Especially for the two troublemakers. We haven't had a good laugh around here since the last time they were here.'"

Mother Theresa saw Little Eddy looking in our direction, so she raised her glass in a salute of thanks. Sister Helen said that was nice of him, and Melba replied, "That's nothing, Little Eddy even goes to Mass on Christmas Eve whether he needs to or not. Have you decided what to order or should I give you a few more minutes?"

Some of us said we're ready, so Melba started taking orders. When she had four of them, Mother Theresa, said, "Sorry to hold you up, I guess I'm so hungry it all looks good. What do you recommend?"

Melba laughed and replied, "Customers either think all the food here is good or all of it is bad, depends on your background. I'll bring you the meat loaf. That way you'll have more time to talk than you'd have with the steak."

After Melba departed, Sister Kathleen said, "I love rural philosophers."

Sister Helen poked a thumb toward Sister Kathleen and said, "She's from New York."

Sister Kathleen waved her off with one hand and said to Annette, "OK, you two, you've had a couple sips of beer, now it's story time. What were you laughing at the last time you were here?"

NEITHER THE TIME NOR THE PLACE

Annette's story, about believing she was pregnant, became vivid in my mind—how she was denied a leave of absence and considered "letting the muffin rise in their ecclesiastical midst." The three nuns were smiling and waiting for one of us to respond. I, too, smiled but it was over how unlikely it was that Annette would tell the story. Annette was not laughing nor even smiling."

She leaned over and whispered, "I hope you know, Paul, that you are a rat."

I leaned toward Mother Theresa and whispered "The story is sort of a takeoff on a name I dropped on the way here—you know, when you locked up and drove right by Little Eddy's."

Mother Theresa stopped smiling, too. She leaned toward me and, with one hand cupped over her mouth, whispered in a voice loud enough for everyone at the table to hear, "Annette is right, Paul, you really are what she called you. I won't ask you to leave the table but I think you know this is not the time nor place to discuss any of that business. God forgive you, though, if you're able to draw humor out of that issue."

Annette with a serious expression but still trying to keep the mood light said, "Yes, Paul, you can stay but you can't have any dessert." She told Mother Theresa "If he raises that issue again, step on his foot. I can't reach him from here."

"OK," she said, "Either that or I'll make him say three Hail Mary's before I let him out to go to the men's room."

Sister Kathleen, squirming on the edge of her seat, said, "All this secrecy sounds intriguing; when will I be old enough to hear the story?"

Mother Theresa said, "When Sister Annette is old enough to tell it."

In spite of the lighthearted banter, the fact is our amusement was based on Annette's most traumatic experience in life. I was still curious to know, though, what happened to Father Thomas and what he was really like. I felt Mother Theresa knew more about him than Annette realized. Not only that, but Mother Theresa was probably the one holding Annette's resignation captive. The threat of having to say three Hail Mary's when I had to go to the restroom was probably just some kind of religious humor, but the mere thought of having to do it was enough to make me have to go. When Annette picked up the conversation and started talking about the Lynns, I was relieved. I guess she was trying to provide an example of local problems among the rural poor. She told the story well including assistance she had given them that I was completely unaware of. When she told about the clogged chimney and the frozen waterline she made me sound like a hero.

Mother Theresa asked me how I felt about Annette setting up a care program at Aunt Lettie's farm. I was taken by surprise that she was interested in my opinion. After a brief hesitation, I said, "I'm not the right person to ask. All I can tell you is that the community would be very lucky to have Annette helping out; and if other women with additional skills joined her, that too could be good. Annette has a gentle way with stubborn, irascible people and a bagful of useful skills. She even knows how to balance a checkbook.

But then I went on to say, "I'm not sure, though, that the extensive forests in the area harbor enough clients to justify such a program, and some of these folks are hard core Yankees too proud to accept help. Even with the Lynns, who Annette was able to help considerably, she had to work around Mr. Lynn's Yankee ways, and in the end usually had to accept some kind of payment, like fish from his pond or venison from deer he killed. But, like I say, she was good with them and infinitely patient."

As though Sister Kathleen was not following what I said, she turned to Annette and, with little girl surprise asked, "Where did you learn to balance a checkbook? I wouldn't know where to begin." I thought she intentionally changed the subject to shut me up. By the time Annette finished answering Sister Kathleen, Melba arrived with our orders. The three of us beer drinkers ordered another round; the wine drinkers had had enough. In the midst of this activity, Mother Theresa whispered to me, "Your comments were interesting. I'm sorry we were diverted. Perhaps we can talk later." When Melba withdrew, Mother Theresa quietly blessed the food. By now the other customers had become used to us and were not paying much attention to our table. I ate quietly, not because I felt subdued, but because the conversation was mostly about events and people at the convent where Annette had once lived and where the other three resided. Mother Theresa said that Sister Carol, the woman Annette had worked with on the inner-city project, was not well and was considering retirement. Mother Theresa expanded on what she had mentioned earlier about the personnel shortage. She said that a high percentage of religious women at the convent consist of retired sisters or sisters about to retire. "It is a particular concern for us, Paul, since nuns don't have Social Security benefits or Medicare."

Until now I had not thought much about how nuns are supported. Annette had told me earlier that the incomes of religious woman, who are teachers, nurses, or whatever, are turned over to the church. I had seen convent bread, jelly and cheese sold in local stores; I assumed the living and dying expenses of nuns were paid for by these activities, supplemented by the large cornucopia of the Catholic Church.

I wondered why Theresa was raising these financial issues at the dinner table, but then, adding to my surprise, Sister Helen came to life. She had her fingertips on the financial condition of religious communities all over the Northeast; most of them I had never heard of. As she spoke, she became more confident and started using words like cost effectiveness, cash flow, and deficit spending. I wondered why Theresa and Sister Helen addressed me with these financial issues. Were they hoping I would write an article on the financial plight of religious communities, or was this their way of pointing out to Annette that her proposal has a problem—that its success will depend on her preparing a supplement to her proposal showing how her project will be self-supporting?

Melba came to take our dessert order. Everyone ordered something except me. Melba said, "I know, you want an extra spoon so you can eat half of your wife's fudge Sunday."

I said, "You're getting to know us pretty well, Melba."

"Yes, enough to know I should add a little extra to this serving."

When Melba was gone, Annette said, "Paul, when we were here earlier, did you tell Melba we were married or did you put her up to asking that question tonight?"

"Innocent on both counts," I replied.

Sister Kathleen said with amusement, "Maybe Melba has a crush on you, Paul, and was checking to see if you're available."

In no uncertain terms Annette said, "I'll straighten her out on that score next time we come in here." It was not clear to me if she planned to assure Melba we are not married or whether Annette would warn her that I belonged to her and was not available.

The rest of the dinner conversation was pleasant and without pitfalls but my mind was divided between listening to what was being said and trying to understand what this visit was about in the first place. Three things in particular puzzled me. First of all, Annette did not seem to care if her plan was adopted or not; yet at times, for example when she was talking about the Lynns and their problems, I felt she was enthusiastically selling her proposal. The second issue was Annette's resignation. It was my belief that Mother Theresa was the one holding it up but I did not understand why. She acted like she knew why Father Thomas was transferred, but she seemed to want Annette to document her experience with him in her resignation. Finally, there was Sister Helen saying, "Show me the money." At least that is what I felt she was saying and that Annette's proposal would have to defend its cost effectiveness before it could be approved. Or, have I placed too much importance on what was said tonight; maybe they just wanted to check out the housing and the ambience of the surrounding area. The discovery of a man on the premises opened an unexpected area of inquiry, so they extended their visit to include me.

Sister Helen, Annette and Sister Kathleen went to the ladies' room, while Mother Theresa was waiting for Melba to return with the bill and her credit card. Since Theresa continued to block my exit to the men's room, I felt I may as well ask the forbidden question again, "What happened to Father Thomas?"

This time, in the absence of the other nuns, Mother Theresa looked at me very seriously and said, "Annette was right, you know, you are a rat—so was Father Thomas. In answer to your question; however, he was transferred to Cincinnati shortly before Sister Annette took leave to be with her dying aunt."

"After Cincinnati where did they send him?"

"Cleveland." Then anticipating my next question she added, "He spent four months there, then transferred to California where I lost track of him. Two months ago he turned up at a meeting in Bridgeport, Connecticut, but he avoided me. That's all I know regarding his whereabouts. Now it's my turn, to ask a question," she said. "Why do you want to know what happened to Father Thomas?"

I was stuck for an answer. Since it was Annette's secret, I could not say anything about Father T and was sorry I said anything about him in the first place. I told Mother Theresa Annette had mentioned that he participated in a program with her and had suddenly disappeared. When I brought up his name I was just curious and thought you might know what happened to him.

"I think you know Aunt Lettie was only part of the reason Sister Annette left the convent; and since her aunt didn't die until three years later, it was hardly an emergency. Sister Annette's resignation had something to do with Father Thomas, which you apparently know something about. I don't know the specifics, but whatever they are, they would not provide her with sufficient reason to resign. Until she spells it out more clearly, her resignation will not be finalized and we will expect her to return from leave."

"She would be happier with me," I said.

"She'd be living in sin." Mother Theresa replied, then worked her way out of the booth to let me use the men's room.

I met Sister Kathleen, who was on her way back. As we passed she said, "I'm glad to see you're still able to walk."

I laughed and said, "Barely," thinking she was referring to my full bladder, but then, I wondered if she thought Mother Theresa may have mauled me.

Everyone was quiet on the way home, either we were all in deep in thought or tired. When we pulled into the yard, Lily released one *baa*, a pleasant greeting from a contented animal. I silently congratulated myself for being able to provide a satisfactory meal for sheep and for my progress in learning their language. Annette invited everyone in, but Mother Theresa thanked her for receiving them so graciously on short notice and said it would be long past their bedtime before they were home. We all exchanged pleasantries; and as they drove away, Annette urged me to come in.

I said, "It's been a long hard day for you, are you sure you want to bother with me?"

"You are one of the few things I am sure I want to bother with. I'm tired, though, so you can do most of the talking. I am anxious to hear what you think happened today."

I suggested that a cup of tea might perk us up and invited her to relax while I put the water on. Annette sat at the table and watched while I set the cups out, put a tea bag in each, then poured in the water. When I placed a small pitcher with milk on the table, she said, "No wonder our visitors knew almost immediately that you were not just a friend of Aunt Lettie's here for the funeral. As soon as you served the wine, they probably thought you already live here. I'll bet that all through the house tour they were watching for a room with men's clothing and a shaving kit."

"Did you show them your room back of the fireplace?"

"No. I didn't want them to know I was engaged in that stupid exercise."

"Then they didn't see your clothes either. They probably decided that our clothes were hanging in the same room—a room you didn't show them."

She gave me a tired smile and said, "I suppose."

"You don't care, do you?"

Still wearing her tired smile she shook her head *no*. Then as an afterthought she said, "I guess it shows, huh?"

"But what if your plan is approved?"

She looked at her cup, then at me and shrugged. After a pause she said, "Paul, don't ask me any questions. I'm too tired to try to answer them. You talk. You're not all beat out like I am. You're still able to think and talk coherently. If you run out of material, just keep on talking. It doesn't matter if you say anything. If I fall asleep, put me in bed."

If I were allowed to ask questions, I would have asked her which bed? Or I might have inquired what would we have for breakfast. Instead, I did what she said—I talked. I started at what I thought was the beginning—when the gun fell out of the book and offended Mother Theresa. "After I talked back to Mother Theresa, I decided I should go home rather than be an additional liability to your cause, or at least what I thought was your cause."

"That whole episode over the gun was awkward for me. What all did you do after you left?"

"I put the dreaded gun in my car and was about to go when I became aware that the sheep were calling and had been for quite awhile. I realized it was time to feed them and it would be hard for you to interrupt what you were doing, so I decided to see if they would let me feed them. I thought I could at least help that much. When I went into the barn, they quieted down and apparently accepted me immediately, at least they started pushing their grain boxes around with their noses. I gave them each a scoop of grain as I had seen you do and they wolfed it down in nothing flat, so I added hay to their feeder. They quietly watched me as they munched, so I explained to them what you were doing in the house. I was surprised how attentive they were; I found it relaxing to talk to them and to listen to their contented munching. When I finished, what turned out to be a lengthy explanation, Lily said, "Baa." Not long after that, I left the barn and headed back to my car. That's when Sister Kathleen intercepted me."

"Otherwise you would have gone home?"

"I think so."

"But you weren't sure? Did you think you might like to come back in and rip up my proposal?"

"I had discussed that with the sheep but we decided that probably wouldn't win me any points. The only reason I had for going back in the house would have been to say good-bye to you and your guests rather than run off looking like a sour ass. I guess you knew that when I gave in to Sister Kathleen and returned, it was only to say good-bye."

"Yes, but I'm glad you stayed, Paul."

"I wasn't any help."

"You were more help than you would know, but I'm not going to tell you how until you tell me what you think happened today."

"Are you sure you want to know?"

"I won't know until you tell me."

"OK. About the only thing I can say with any assurance, is that Sister Kathleen is very supportive of your plan. She would like to live here and would like to be a part of your program. Although I would guess she may be able to influence the others, she told me she doesn't have any decision making power. As far as Sister Helen is concerned, you know as well as I do that she's worried your community would not be self-supporting. My guess is she won't take a position until she sees serious financial estimates of income and expenses. Mother Theresa, now, is harder to read. When she talked with me alone, her focus was on getting you back in the nun business, preferably under her roof rather than in an outpost in the wilderness. She told me your resignation has never been approved and that you still belong to them."

From a position with her elbows on the table and her chin in her hands, Annette popped straight up in her chair and exclaimed, "What on earth do they think they're doing? I told them I quit. Do they think they can hold me against my will?

"Oh beyond that, Annette. Mother Theresa warned me that if I'm sleeping with you, I should know that I am violating a nun."

"She told you that, Paul! My God, there's no end to that woman's gall."

Once Annette calmed down, she said, "So tell me, Paul, Mother Theresa's game aside, what do you think will happen to my proposal?"

"Annette, I don't know anything about the decision making process in religious communities."

"I know you didn't before tonight, but you learned a lot from their visit, a lot more than I did; and you understand some of this stuff better than I do. Just give me your best guess—I'll let you know if I think you're out of the bleachers."

"Do you mean *ballpark*?"

"Probably, except you're mostly a spectator—well—on the other hand, maybe you have become a player; but I can't judge how much weight they will give you in evaluating my case. Anyway, Paul, what do you think?"

"I think they'll be undecided about your proposal and put off dealing with it the same way they did with your resignation. In the mean time, Mother Theresa will press you to come home where she can protect you from sin and put you back to work. I think she's the one who's holding up your resignation."

"Why would she do that, and why do you think that?"

"When you three went to the rest room and left me with Mother Theresa, she didn't show any interest in letting me out, so I asked her again what happened to Father Thomas."

"Oh for God's sake, Paul, you didn't. "

"She told me Father Thomas was first transferred to Cincinnati; and from there he went through a series of transfers to other places. She lost track of him after three moves until she recently encountered him at a meeting in Bridgeport."

"Could you tell if Mother Theresa thought I had something to do with Father Thomas before he was transferred?"

"Yes, but I don't think she really knew what. It was more like she was hoping I would tell her. She let me know, though, that your resignation didn't go through, because you didn't provide adequate reason for resigning. She knew it had to do with Father Thomas; but since you didn't include any of that in your letter, she regarded your application incomplete. I think she was telling me that whatever Father T did to you wasn't your fault; and if feelings of failure or guilt contributed to your attempted resignation, your reasons are insufficient. Mother Theresa didn't say so, but I think that once she established that Father Thomas was being shuffled from one parish to another, she realized he was a sexual predator. She may have been hoping to use your letter to document his bad behavior to higher authority."

I did not want to say anymore until Annette had time to digest what I had already told her. After a short time, she said, "Is that it, Paul? Did you tell me everything you heard and thought about tonight?"

"Yes, as best I can remember."

"I bet you'd like to know what I think about it."

"Yes, but I presume that what I just told you had a lot of emotion laden information. I can wait until you've had time to think about it."

"Yeah, well, I'll probably think about this sometime; but mostly it doesn't make any difference."

"What do you mean?"

Annette looked down at her hands and said in a barely audible voice, "I decided against turning Aunt Lettie's farm into a convent." When she looked up, she was wearing a small, uncertain smile.

I was so dumbfounded it must have registered on my face because Annette, still smiling, nodded three times, apparently to assure me it was true.

When I was able to find words, I asked, "At what point in today's scattered winds, was that decision uncovered?"

"The first glimpse I had of it was when you were saying good-bye to Aunt Lettie."

"Annette! That was almost at the beginning of our day."

"I know. I should have mentioned it sooner; but on the way back from Aunt Lettie's graveside ceremony, I was still mulling my decision and at the same time thinking about what you said. I was recalling, too, what you and she had talked about before she died, you know, about asking you to take care of me and move in with me, and how you told her you would do your best to take care of me, but that you might need her help. Your message sort of brought things together for me. It made me feel warm and cozy that the two people I love the most conspired to save me from myself. So, indirectly, Paul, Aunt Lettie did help you; she provided you with words for her eulogy and they are what helped bring me around. I didn't tell you sooner because I had a lot of other issues to come to terms with. As we trudged home behind the sheep, things you tried to tell me earlier were drawn into my thoughts. I began to realize how much you worried about me and how stubborn and stupid I was to think about returning to my former life. But before I could tell you, we were back at the house and there was my former life knocking at the back door. Even though I had pretty well made up my mind by then not to go forward with my proposal, I couldn't just tell them to go away. After all they and the religious life were a part of me for 23 years and they were here to try to do me a favor. But, as the day moved along, my resolve to make a clean break became strengthened and now I can tell you with certainty it's over."

She reached for my hands across the table and did not say any more. I held them for awhile. Then we went upstairs to bed.

Epilogue

by Annette Devon Hurst

While I was poking around in the attic, I found a large manuscript that Paul had not unpacked after he moved in with me. Since he had not told me about it, I was surprised to discover he was writing a book; I was even more surprised to discover that it was about us.

After reading all 250 pages of Paul's secret manuscript, I did not know what to do with it. Later I decided to save it and give it to Oliver when he is old enough; he is only four now. I felt, though, that the story was not finished. Important things happened between us after Paul stopped writing—things Oliver will want to know about. I decided to record these things in a letter to Oliver while they are still fresh in my mind. My plan was to put the letter with the manuscript and give them to him when we are both old enough—that would be when he is 40 and I am pushing 80; by then maybe I will not be embarrassed to let him read about things his mother and dad did before he was born.

You may wonder how it is that someone with dyslexia happened to expand a letter to her son into a whole book chapter. I blame Beth Turbot for that. Remember she is the reporter whose desk was next to Paul's at *The Chronicle*.

Yes, the same woman who initially helped us get together, and then later put us back together when our relationship started to fall apart. Well, one day while I was working on the letter, Beth asked me how come I spend so much time at the computer. I made the dumb mistake of telling her about Paul's manuscript and about the letter I was writing to Oliver. Immediately, Beth demanded to see the manuscript; like a fool, I let her read it. When she was finished, she again asked me what I was going to do with it. I repeated what I had told her earlier about saving it for Oliver. "Like hell!" She said. "You're going to finish this and publish it as a book."

"Publish it, hah! Not likely. I don't know anything about getting a book published; besides who would want to read my scrambled chicken tracks?"

Beth assured me that when she is finished editing the manuscript, I will recognize how important it is and want to publish it. Well, I lost track of how many red pencils and bad words Beth used correcting my chapter. She also would not let me call it a chapter; she insisted it is an epilogue and told me that is what I have to call it in the published book. Readers, though, should remember that when I started writing this chapter it was a letter to Oliver. I skipped things, especially if they were of an embarrassing nature. Beth soon discovered what I was doing and insisted I redo those parts and maintain the same level of treatment on sexual matters that Paul did. She argued that understanding the intimate interaction of this couple is crucial to understanding the story.

I told her she was just feeding her own voyeurism. She said, "Yes, that's what women do who haven't had all their joy juices squeezed out of them by the Catholic Church."

If these pages survive the disagreements Beth and I had over this project and a book is published, do not blame Beth for the bumpy nature of the dialog. Some bumps are too stubborn to be ironed out even by a conscientious editor like Beth.

Anyway, picking up the story where Paul left off, which was shortly after Mother Theresa and her inspection team departed, Paul and I went upstairs to bed. Uncle Matt's bedroom was the one most ready to receive guests, so that's where we slept that night. Later we fixed up the guest room for us and used Uncle Matt's room as a study. Paul knew not to take advantage of me that night after the taxing day we had had: first burying Aunt Lettie's ashes and then meeting with Mother Theresa and the others. But it was awfully nice to lie next to him, to feel wanted and protected from my mixed-up life. The next morning, however, we did make love and it was wonderful but not perfect because we had to rush off to our jobs. Also, I was not very comfortable being naked in Uncle Matt's room.

The following night we spent at Paul's—in the dollhouse. He arrived home before I did and had everything nicely arranged—dinner and all. I can not describe what happened that night, not the way Paul would have, except to say that I had the most beautiful experience I have ever had in my life—twice it happened, once in the evening and again in the morning. And what was so great about it was that from that time on we seldom had any disagreement about time and place. My previous sensitivity to trivia was usually overwhelmed by the anticipation of ecstasy.

Both of us felt we had a wonderful marriage even though we were quite different from each other. We learned to use these differences to our mutual advantage instead of trying to change each other. This degree of compatibility did not come about suddenly; but it must not have taken very long to develop since we recognized and talked about this aspect of our relationship even before we were married.

You may remember Paul wrote about some of these glitches that we had to work out, like our intimacy problem and how I resisted marrying him even though I loved him because I was concerned that I might never achieve sexual gratification and both of us would be left unsatisfied. Well, like I said, that issue did go away; but there was still another thing that was harder to define than sex, and more difficult to overcome. I suppose I was silly to worry about it, especially the way things turned out. I did not want to feel dependent on a husband. I wanted to know that I could survive outside of a convent and that I was not substituting Paul for a mother superior. I do not believe Paul described the issue well; and I understand that because I probably did not comprehend it either until I tried to write about it. I felt Paul was excessively self-assured and often too quick to take over. This may have been an acquired trait left over from when he was a sergeant in the Army.

At times Paul was impatient with my attempts to be independent. He felt he should do the things he could do easier and faster than I; but other things that he was not especially good at he felt were better left to me. I worried that I might turn more and more of my life over to him instead of learning things a reasonably independent person should know. Well, it was not too long before he caught me in a big one. He was especially polite about drawing my attention to it because the previous day we had had a heated argument over his take-charge attitude. In approaching the subject on this occasion, he played it like it was something that had just occurred to him. He innocently asked, "What did you ever do about the town's threat to auction off Aunt Lettie's property for overdue taxes?"

I turned red. I know I did because I felt warm all over as I confessed that I had not done anything about it. I was sure he knew the answer to his question before he asked it. He, of course, wanted to know if I had pursued his suggestion to go to the town hall and tell them about Aunt Lettie's recent death and ask for an extension of time. I think he knew how intimidating it would have been for me to go before the town officials to plead my case. The next thing he said was, "Why don't we look through Aunt Lettie's papers and see what's there—that is, of course, if you don't mind me poking around in your business?"

"Heck no," I said, "I don't mind." Actually it was a great relief to me that he was willing to become involved. It was not only the property taxes, but also the hospital bills, ambulance people, the crematorium. I do not remember now who all was screaming for money, but my paycheck from Sturbridge did not allow me to promise anybody anything.

When I held the box of papers upside down and let the contents fall on the dining room table, Paul looked at the pile briefly. Then with deliberate calm he tossed the advertisements and requests for donations back in the box. What was left, less than ten percent, he started to read and sort into piles. After about four hours, he rose from his chair, stretched his back and said, "Annette, I think it's going to be all right."

"Aunt Lettie was rich after all?"

"Not exactly. It's more like she left you cab fare home from a near tragedy." Paul picked up a brown envelope across which I had scrawled the words "Aunt Lettie's

Will." He asked if I had looked through this envelope recently.

"Not really, about a year ago Aunt Lettie had me read her will; and when I was through, she had me put it back in the envelope. Why, was there something else in it?" Paul took out a letter and read:

> Dear Annette:
> When I die, you will have immediate expenses. What is left of my estate may not be readily turned into cash, so I left a small pile of money in the safe for you to live on until other resources become available.
> Love, Aunt Lettie
> P.S. Marry Paul as soon as you can and let him deal with this shit.

I said, "Paul, you turd, you added that P.S." He always laughed when I used vulgar language—he never got over his image of me as a saintly nun, except maybe when we were in bed; even then I suspect he retained enough of that image to still enjoy defying Mother Theresa's admonishment about "violating a nun." Anyway, he handed me the letter, and sure enough, the P.S. was in Aunt Lettie's handwriting, her last bit of advice to me on how to deal with men. I said, "OK, Paul, but since you're already dealing with this problem, I don't have to marry you. So—what are YOU going to do next?"

"Annette, if you think I should deal with this on my own, remember I don't know where this safe is. Even if I find it, I'll have to blow it open since I don't know the combination. At any rate the solution to your problem apparently is in there."

I told him we could share this part of his project, that first we could start with him helping me remove the picture from the wall behind him. Once the safe was uncovered, I had him hold the picture while I found the hidden numbers for the combination written on the back. I wrote them on a slip of paper and gave the paper to Paul so he could open the safe. Inside was a stack of hundred-dollar bills wrapped in bundles, adding up to $20,000. Not much else was in there except for the deed to the property, Aunt Lettie's wedding and engagement rings, and some gaudy jewelry. After I removed the money, I tried to show the jewelry to Paul, but he was busy trying to find the numbers for the combination of the safe on the back of the picture. He was having trouble finding them among the many numbers written upside down, sideways and at variable distances from the edge and from each other. He did not know that they were the numbers closest to the corners. When he did look at the jewelry, like me, he had no idea what it was worth, so we locked it back in the safe and returned to the kitchen.

Paul was in an unusually good mood. I had not realized how much strain my financial problems had put on him. No, I take that back. I remember that I nearly drove him mad when I almost returned to religious life to resolve my financial problems—God, I was dumb about that!

Back in the kitchen Paul asked me what I was going to do next. I told him, "As soon as the town offices open, WE are going to take our new-found money over and pay our tax bill. Then I'm going to help you move your stuff over here. It's what Aunt Lettie wanted you to do, you know. I feel more comfortable asking you to move in now that I see how gentlemanly you were about rescuing me from disaster."

Paul went to the town hall with me, like I wanted him to, and broke trail for us by introducing himself to the tax collector. Then he introduced me and explained to her that I was Lettie Hyde's niece, that Aunt Lettie had died and I had come to pay the back taxes.

I explained that Paul was my fiancé. The woman was nice; she expressed sympathy about my aunt's passing. Then she offered congratulations about our engagement. She was quite surprised when we paid the taxes in cash. Paul had suggested we put the money in my checking account, then pay with a check; but I was anxious to get the job done quickly, so I carried the money over in a brown paper bag. Next the tax collector asked questions about where to send subsequent tax bills, who owns the property now and other things that Paul paid more attention to than I did. Sharing responsibility had become comfortable.

The tax collector introduced us to the first selectman, his secretary and the town clerk. On the way home Paul said, "There, that wasn't so bad was it?" Like I said, Paul knew all along that I had been timid about dealing with the town and my tax problem.

The next thing Paul wanted to know was if we really are engaged. I told him, "Of course, we just haven't set a date." Then he wanted to know if he should buy me an engagement ring and I told him no, not until we set a date, that I was not ready to think about marriage until we had the finances settled. I also said I want to make sure I can afford you. Besides, if I want to wear an engagement ring, I'll get Auntie's ring out of the safe. He must have known I was teasing but he did not say much the rest of the way home. For some things his serious nature got in the way of his sense of humor.

Paul still had a lot of paperwork to take care of after our visit to the town hall. My contribution was mainly to listen to his explanation of what each piece of paper was about, then sign my name to it. He was deliberate in making sure I knew what I was signing. He even made sure I understood about the mutual funds and stocks that provided the small flow of money into Aunt Lettie's savings account. For a lot of the papers, Paul said to simply cross off Aunt Lettie's name; she had already added mine as a co-owner. Many of these he put in envelopes with a copy of Aunt Lettie's death certificate and mailed them off.

Time went by. I was working full time at The Village and Paul was busy with his job. When he was not on assignment or working at *The Chronicle,* he liked working in the new office we created from Uncle Matt's bedroom. I also used it. After I saw what Paul's computer could do compared to my ancient box, we bought me a new one and he helped me learn how to do all kinds of things. First I learned to run the spell and grammar checker, which enabled me to identify scrambled words and sentences.

One night Paul got out a bottle of Uncle Matt's brandy and set it on the table. "Good news or bad?" I asked.

"Actually it's not news, it's more like a discussion." He poured us each a generous amount; and after we marveled at the wonderful flavor and how it felt going down, he said, "I forgot to mention something to you that Mother Theresa told me in the restaurant that night—what nine months ago. It was when the rest of you nuns went off to the ladies' room," he grinned to let me know he enjoyed the fact that I was still a nun at that time. He went on to say, "I started thinking about it the other day; it has to do with your future."

"Oh, God," I muttered to Him or Paul, or whomever was listening.

"No, don't fret, Annette, it's not that bad," Paul said. "What Mother Theresa told me is that you need only two or three more courses to finish your B.A. degree."

"So?"

"Well, I just thought you might like to finish your degree. Maybe when spring semester starts, The Village could get along without you while you knock off these courses and get your degree."

"I laughed and said, 'Paul, you've forgotten, that's not how I do it. I don't 'knock off courses' I take them one at a time and hope they don't knock me off."

"So, how many courses do you need?"

"I don't know. It depends on what I major in and whether I graduate from UConn or Eastern. I've taken courses at each and I don't have any idea how many are transferable, from one school to the other. Also, I think I remember a requirement about having to declare a major or complete the degree program within a certain length of time or the courses can't be used toward a degree. But, I also know exceptions can be made." Paul had trouble understanding that I was so near to a degree in terms of credits but had not bothered to declare a major or even an alma mater. He had trouble believing that I didn't care about having a degree. We had a long boring discussion about what I really like doing or thinking about. I told him I could not see that having a degree would affect any of these things. Then he talked about making sure I had an adequate income—just in case. That was even more mystifying. In the end, the conversation was pretty much a waste of good brandy because of the way he spoiled the party. Why I bother to mention it here is because that "just in case" thing that he brought up came back to haunt me later and would not go away until finally I realized that during my whole adult life, I had not thought much about planning for the future. It had always been planned for me, but now that I was no longer sheltered under the wings of the convent, maybe Paul had a point. Not just maybe, as it turned out, he did have a point. It had to do with my independence that I had made such a fuss about.

Somewhere along the line, Paul stopped asking me to set a date for us to get married. I think I may have been relieved—if I thought about it at all. I probably assumed that to live with me and have sex regularly was all he really wanted in the first place. I was content to have this worry-free courtship or prolonged engagement, whatever it was, go on forever. It was not until some time later that I focused on the fact that Paul was not as worry free as I was.

Anyway, after I became pregnant—no false alarm this time—Paul began to talk about marriage again. He felt our baby should have a last name and be born legitimate. I finally agreed with him, so we got married. It was a simple ceremony out in the backyard. Beth Turbot and Hill Dillard stood up with us. By this time, Hill and Paul had become good friends; Hill and I, of course, had been friends for several years. I was still working full-time at the Village then, so I invited friends from there but I did not invite any of my former convent associates. Paul did not want to invite any of his former colleagues from *The Chronicle*. He had quit his job and said he had lost touch with those people, except for Beth. The endurance of that relationship was with my blessing and Paul's mixed feelings; it was driven mainly by Beth's continued intrusion into our affairs.

NEITHER THE TIME NOR THE PLACE

Not long after we were married, I discovered Paul had a second reason for wanting to set a wedding date, I mean besides my pregnancy. He had kept that reason from me as long as he could; but I suspected something was wrong even before he left *The Chronicle*. I think it may have gone back to that *just in case* phrase he used the night we talked about my education. What he gave me as the reason for quitting his job, though, was that he wanted to do some freelance writing.

Paul stayed close to home most of the time now. Hill Dillard helped him build a small room in the attic at the top of the turret where he could look off into the distance. Hill was a Vietnam veteran, too. Occasionally when I went to see how the project was progressing, they were not working. They were just sitting on a couple of boxes talking. As soon as they saw me, they awkwardly changed the subject; but I knew they were talking about the war—serious talk, not funny stories. When the construction was finished, Paul took his laptop computer up there. He worked on an old desk he had found in the attic that he had moved into the turret. He sold several articles to newspapers and magazines but he did not seem excited about it. His heart really wasn't in it. The picture of his army buddies found its way up to his desk along with other things that accumulated there. Paul seemed to divide his time between writing, staring at that picture and looking out over the treetops toward the beaver pond. But I am not sure he saw the same view from the window as I did. He never mentioned things like hawks, eagles, deer, or even the beaver family working on their dam. The beaver pond could not be seen well at that range, so I put Aunt Lettie's binoculars on his desk. When he did not appear to be using them, I explained that I had put them there so he could see what the beavers were doing. He acted interested, but two weeks later the binoculars had not moved from where I had placed them.

There is no time I can point to and say this is when Paul started to withdraw. I could not tell if he was losing interest in things because he was worried about something or if he had a physical problem. When I asked him about it, he always said he was fine or that he had a small headache. I do not think they were small headaches, though, judging by the number of painkillers he took. Then one night after we finished dinner, he stood up to leave the table but sort of faltered and had to brace himself by grabbing the chair. He said, "Annette, I can't see." He tried not to show concern. He said it was more like I had turned the lights out when he was still in the room; but he could not hide the slight quaver in his voice. He tried never to show fear; but after this, I realized he played little games to disguise it, dumb jokes or diverting my attention to something else. He had always been good with words and names of people, but now he sometimes fumbled or used the wrong word. He would ask, for example, where I put the towels when he meant to ask for bath soap.

He quit driving his car. The only time he went anywhere was with me. He always asked me to drive him if he had a place where he had to go. When it was time to renew his car registration, he put my name on the title as coowner. As a teenager still living at home with my mother I swore that I would never become a nag; well so much for good intentions. By now my perpetual theme was for him to see a doctor. He would say, "O.K.," but he did not go.

Meanwhile, I started having prenatal check-ups. During one of my visits to Dr. Blick, she gave me the results from my amniocentesis. She had said it was important to have this test since I was over 35 and somewhat at risk of having a baby with Down's syndrome or spina bifida. She told me the baby was fine and that I would have a healthy baby boy. Perhaps I should have taken my good news and gone home, but instead, almost uncontrollably started to talk about Paul's symptoms. She assured me my concerns were not trivial and that I should take him to a neurologist as soon as possible.

I told Paul about my conversation with Dr. Blick and what she said about his seeing a neurologist. This time when he said, "OK," as he always had previously, I told him, "Fine, I'll make an appointment for you."

He did not reply immediately. When he did, he said, "I already saw a doctor."

"When you were discharged from the Army?" I asked.

"Yeah," he smiled, "but a couple times after that, too. The last time was after you told me we were going to have a baby."

"And what did the doctor say?"

After another pause, he said, "Not good."

Without waiting for the specifics, my face became numb. Paul told me later that it had turned completely white. I remember, too, that he held me, that I was totally disabled with panic and fear, and sobbed out of control. That was not like me. Bad news and disappointment I was used to. I never let them interfere with my composure. Whenever someone needed my support, I was always there for them. Paul had not even told me what the bad news was, so why did I come apart? Why indeed? Dr. Blick had told me some of the things his symptoms might be indicative of, none of them good. My first sign of recovery was when I was able to ask Paul, if that was why he quit his job?

He said, "Yes, I wanted to spend more time with you; but I guess I didn't, did I? I hid away in the attic instead. I didn't think there was any point in tormenting you with my problem sooner than I had to. I'm not sure even now that talking about it will help either of us."

"Paul, I have already plunged to the bottom of my emotional pit. Whatever the bad news, I'm prepared to deal with it and to help you through it. What caused me to come apart was, when you told me your doctor said the news was not good. I thought he was saying you have a terminal illness. That is what he was saying, isn't it?"

"Yes. I guess I may as well tell you the whole story now. He paused for a moment then said, "That night I told you about Vietnam, about the grenade going off and blowing pieces of Nhu's skull into my head and face; well, what I didn't tell you was that a piece of shrapnel also hit me in the head and lodged in my brain. The doctors decided that because of its location it would be more dangerous to remove it than it would be to leave it where it was. Well, for all these years it hasn't been a problem, so when I fell in love with you, I thought it would be OK to get married. A few months after I moved in with you, I started having headaches and blurred vision so I visited a doctor, who sent me to a neurologist, Dr. Marsh. He ran me through a series of tests and x-rays and after showing them to other specialists in Boston, he told me that the piece of shrapnel in my brain has moved from where it was originally and that what I have been experiencing is a series of mini-strokes. And like the Army doctors told me, Dr. Marsh said, its location makes it too dangerous to be removed; but he also said its movement makes it too dangerous to leave it where it is. He suggested I get my affairs in order; and at the same time, decide which course of action I wish to pursue; wait and see or risk the operation. So, when you asked me if I was talking about a terminal disease, yes, I guess that's the proper name for it."

Neither of us said anything for a while; we alternated between looking down at our hands and back at each other, struggling to hold ourselves together. Paul spoke first; he took my hands in his and said, "It's easier having you know about this than to continue trying to hide the obvious."

"You should have told me earlier."

"Yes, but when? Should I have told you at the time you announced we are going to have a baby?"

"You should have told me as soon as you started to worry about your headaches; and then when you visited a doctor, you should have updated me at each stage of his diagnosis, after the X-rays, and after his consultations with other doctors. The bomb you just dropped on me now wouldn't have been such a shock if we had worked through this together; and it would have been easier on you, too."

"I didn't want you to worry unnecessarily."

"If I have to raise our child alone, is that how you want me to do it, not tell him anything that might worry him?" Paul did not answer me. I finally realized that in the midst of all our pain, I was mad at him, mad at him because he was dying. I could not stop feeling angry. I said, "You knew you were seriously ill when I told you I was pregnant. And you knew, too, while we were deciding to get married. Paul, did you think I wouldn't marry you if I knew you were ill? It wouldn't have made any difference. It just would have been nice if we were using the same information to make that decision. As it stands now, I don't know why you married me. Was it because I was pregnant and you thought it would be the right thing to do?"

His response was slow in coming and slow in delivery, "You had already said you weren't ready to marry me a dozen times before that. The prospect of going blind, being unable to walk, or to lose my memory or my mind—or any of the other things Dr. Marsh said might be in store for me didn't make me any more attractive. And, I wasn't looking for pity or someone to take care of me either."

In as mild a manner as I could summon, I asked, "When were you planning to tell me?" After it was out, I wished I had not said it because it still sounded argumentative.

Paul sat quietly for a moment, then said, "I wasn't going to tell you until I couldn't hide it any longer."

"Well, I guess that's where we are now, so can we talk about it? I mean like what to do. Should we seek additional opinions on an operation versus whatever—I mean maybe the thing will stop moving and quit causing strokes. Did they say all those things are going to happen to you, or they might happen? You're not making any of that up, are you?—Oh, shit, Paul, shit, shit, shit. I'm not very good at this. I thought I was. I used to be. It's different when it's someone you love. I guess that's why you didn't tell me; you knew I wouldn't handle it well."

"The reason I didn't tell you at first is because, from what's left of my life, I wanted to squeeze out as much good as I could. Now, however, my hope has shifted; I want to hang on until our baby is born. I would like to see him before I die."

"Paul, I want to assure you again, that with or without child, I would have married you. I want to be with you as long as God will let us."

Paul's condition progressed more rapidly than he had hoped it would. He began to recognize that he would not be able to hold out for the birth of his baby. His doctor told him that he may experience periods of drowsiness, which was already true. He was sleeping 12 to 14 hours a day. His balance, too, was unsteady; he now used a walker to get around. Along with these changes, conversation became more difficult as words he wanted to use escaped him.

About this time another change occurred in our lives. Beth Turbot decided to retire and move in with us. She had been thinking about retiring for several years but felt she did not have a reason. She gave up her apartment and took over Aunt Lettie's room. So, once again, I had a mother superior. Beth had decided it was too much for me to attend to Paul's needs, grow a baby in my belly and keep up a house. "Don't think it's going to get any easier," she told me. Not only did Beth take over the cooking and running the house, she found time to banter with Paul. I think they argued every subject available. It did not matter to Beth that Paul had to struggle for words; she just took advantage of his stalled engine to interrupt him. I never saw people enjoy getting mad at each other like those two did. However, their sport continued for less than a month, at which time Paul was no longer able to do it. When we talked in private, though, he was still able to refer to her with any number of epithets. One in particular that I liked was "that blessing disguised as a pain-in-the-ass." I thought of her often in those terms during the year she took care of Oliver and the house and then later, too, while I finished my degree and pursued a career as a social worker. But, that isn't part of Paul's story, so let's get back on track.

Paul continued to lose ground physically. But, when I wanted to move him down to my former room in back of the kitchen, he said, "Not unless you come with me." I think he was afraid to sleep alone, afraid he might have a seizure or something. He told me it was because when he woke up in the night he liked to feel my big belly against him. So we set up a double bed and both of us slept downstairs. The room barely had space for anything more than the bed, but its ground floor location allowed Paul to get to the table with his walker, go outdoors to the car or visit the sheep. He liked talking with the sheep, and they seemed never to tire of listening to him.

Those last few months were pleasant for us in spite of Paul's deteriorating condition. I quit work; and Paul abandoned his attic office, leaving his Vietnam buddies up there. I presume his fixation on the picture arose from guilt over being left alive while the rest of his platoon was dead. I suspect he had started to communicate with them again when he felt he would be joining them. I was glad to have him back; I needed him more than they did.

Once Paul had confessed his illness to me and came out of the attic, we began to talk quite a lot. Our conversations were slow paced and I had to supply a lot of words he could not find, or words he got wrong, but we did get to know one another. I felt his ego was at peace and there was no male role to defend. We rarely discussed what I should do when he died or the pace at which he was declining. I think he believed I was in denial about what was happening. On one occasion, though, the issue of Aunt Lettie's resting place came up. It was in another context, but suddenly he said, "Maybe that's where you should put me."

I said, "It's too soon to think about that," but of course I had thought some about funeral arrangements.

"No." He said. "It's not too soon. How do you feel about it?"

"I don't want either of us to be cremated, and I don't think the law allows burials outside of cemeteries. Besides, if you die before me, I want to be able to visit your grave and know you are there, that you haven't been washed away by the rain or washed down stream by the spring flooding. When I visit you, I expect you to hear me. I know, too, that Beth will want to be able to go there so she can get the last word in."

Paul laughed and said, "At least I know not to depend on you to let her know how wrong she is about her liberal opinions. I guess I'll have to set her straight before I go. Anyway, regarding the box versus ashes, whatever you want to do it is OK with me."

While we were on this subject, I said, "Paul, I noticed Uncle Matt's gun has returned to the atlas. I thought you were going to get rid of it."

"Yes, well, I must have changed my mind."

"Why?"

He looked embarrassed and said, "No real reason I suppose; I just like having it around."

"Paul, if you have any thoughts about using it on yourself, forget it. I want you to promise me right now you will never do that. It would be too hard on me and it would be too difficult for your son to know that his father committed suicide. Besides it's too macho, on the one hand, and too cowardly on the other."

Paul did not respond for quite awhile—long enough for me to know that the thought of using it had passed through his mind. Finally, he said, "OK."

Two weeks later Dr. Marsh told us that Paul may not last until our baby reaches full term. Like I said earlier, I am sure Paul already knew this; but now it became official. I had been driving Paul to his appointments. Paul had asked Dr. Marsh to share his opinions with both of us. Dr. Marsh explained to me that Paul had a subdural hematoma from blood seeping out of tiny blood vessels damaged by movement of the shrapnel. He said the symptoms are similar to what one might expect from a brain tumor and that at any time Paul could have a seizure, lapse into a coma and die. Paul asked if the risky operation they had talked about earlier was still available. Dr. Marsh said it was, but it was no less risky. He said not only is the location difficult, but that patients with this kind of hematoma respond poorly to surgery, anesthesia, and nervous system depressing drugs. Later he sent us a letter reviewing Paul's situation. I recently found it in Paul's desk with other notes he had stashed away, which was a good thing because it helped me remember what Dr. Marsh told us that day. It also reminded me what he said when I asked about the odds of Paul surviving surgery versus waiting it out. He said, "Some surgeons will give you a number; but if I tell you there is only a 10 percent chance of Paul surviving the operation, I really don't know if it's 5 or 20 percent. I can tell you this, though; it's not 50-50. But, if your next question is, How do those odds compare with Paul still being alive when your baby is born? I'd have to admit I don't know that either."

Unlike me, Paul was always decisive. It would have taken me forever to make a decision based on that information; but he told me on the way home, "If I don't go for the operation, at a minimum I will be spending my last days in a hospice. I have already become too much of a burden to be taken care of at home. At the rate I am deteriorating, the operation is the only chance I'll have to see our son. If you are OK with it, I'm going to risk it." The way I have been relating what Paul said here and earlier is not how the words came out of him, but I don't see any point in trying to duplicate his struggle with words. His thinking, though, was always clear, just slow to relate.

* * *

The crowd that gathered for Paul's memorial service in the backyard was large. Beth coordinated it. I wasn't much help what with being so pregnant and emotionally spent. Beth had called a few key people to let them know Paul had died and to tell them about the memorial service and I guess they spread the word; more than 200 people came. Beth rented a big canopy in case of rain, and a crew of men came to put it up. She also arranged to have loud speakers and outdoor toilets. I never would have thought to have these things available in view of the small crowd I had envisioned. People came with chairs, card tables, food and everything, even a keg of beer and boxes of soft drinks donated by local merchants. I did not know if Paul was that popular or if Beth was simply a good organizer and arm twister.

There was no regular service. People spoke, recited poetry, played musical instruments, sang solos or sang in small groups of two or three. The only role I played in organizing the program was to ask Barbara Filmore to sing *Amazing Grace*. She and Gordon, you remember, owned the little house that Paul rented, the one we referred to as the dollhouse. Mrs. Filmore sang in the church, on the corner, close enough to where Paul lived so he could hear her sing. He said she had a fine voice and that he enjoyed listening to her though his open windows in the summer.

Several colleagues from *The Chronicle* told lighthearted stories about Paul. Beth topped them by relating some of the humorous knockdown-drag-outs she and Paul had over the years. The last speaker was Hill Dillard. He was shy at first about speaking before an audience; but once he was started, he described Paul's military service including how he was wounded, the awards he had won and how much he hurt over the loss of his platoon. Hill was very effective and brought everyone to tears, including himself. The ceremony part ended with the sound of taps in the distance and a three-gun salute; the party and reminiscences continued long into the night.

The End

Comments and Acknowledgments

During book signings I am frequently asked how much of my novels are true. In The Fugitive at Greyledge and Charred Remains, the story lines are pure fiction and all characters of significance are either fictional or are composites of two or more people I have known. In the present novel, however, substantial aspects of some characters are real. All names however have been changed.

Sister Annette, the female protagonist in *Neither the Time nor the Place* is purely fictional. Development of her character and of her background, though, led me through considerable research in unfamiliar territory. Initially I had not intended to become as involved in her back-ground as I did; but when I entered "nuns" into my computer the first document to appear was a doctoral dissertation by Jacqueline "Fran" Fisher entitled *Making A Transition between Elective Asceticism and Secular Life: A Life-Narrative Study of Former Roman Catholic Nuns*. Dr. Fisher's thesis introduced me to fascinating issues that became part of Annette's life. I also found that Carole G. Rogers's book *Poverty, Chastity and Change* provided me with a diversity of information to consider. Later, when I needed answers to specific questions, I talked with Sister Mary Peter and the late Sister Mary Aquinas at a local convent. I very much appreciate the time and valuable assistance they gave me.

In my novel Mother Theresa and Sisters Kathleen and Helen are purely fictional characters. Harriet and Nathan Lynn, however, were real people—friends of my wife and me over a period of eight years. What they were like and how they lived is as well represented as I can remember. Mrs. Lynn wrote to us a couple of times after they moved to South Carolina; one letter was to tell us that Nathan had died. He was 89. Harriet died two years later at the age of 86. Her sister wrote to tell us when she passed.

The Vietnam experiences of Paul are based on personal stories told to me by a late friend and neighbor. He like many other veterans had latent injuries that put his life on borrowed time. Paul's backyard memorial service was similar to that of my neighbor's; the rest of Paul's life is fictional.

The court hearing of Todd Bowen is based on a trial my wife, Mary, and I attended in Virginia in 1997. Unlike the character in my book the real murderer did not plead guilty but went to trial where he was found guilty by the jury and sentenced to life in prison without parole. The evidence used in that trial was comparable to the evidence presented at Todd's evidentiary hearing in my novel. Todd's appearance and personal bearing were similar to those of the accused in the Virginia trial and much of his character was provided by testimony from witnesses. During an intermission at the trial, my wife, and I talked with the real victim's great aunt and uncle, who in my novel became Melissa's Aunt Zetta and Uncle Ben. The things they told us about their niece and events at the farm were comparable to what was said during the conversation that took place in Paul's car at the Witter Farm.

All the other characters in *Neither the Time Nor the Place* are fictional.

As with my two previous novels I am grateful to Roberta J. Buland for editing my manuscript, this time especially so since she has worked for five years in a convent and was prepared to warn me if my interpretation of nuns was incorrect.

Karen Castaldi painted the cover picture. I feel she captured my vision of where Annette lived.

My wife Mary and my daughter Karen read various stages of the manuscript and provided important advice.

Other Novels by Jack Schultz

The Fugitive at Greyledge

Charlotte Henderson, owner of an old plantation in Virginia during the mid-1950s, allows an AWOL soldier to hideout in the former slave quarters, then she maneuvers him into working the farm. Jude Bartholomew, the young soldier, discovers that Charlotte has problems of her own—perhaps life-threatening. He tries to help her, but he may have been better off to have stayed at Ft. Knox and face a court martial than to fall in love with Charlotte and become entangled in her problems.

Charred Remains
(A stand alone sequel to *Fugitive*)

Four charred bodies of the Klansmen who assaulted Charlotte Henderson are found in the burned-out ruins of her mansion. Sheriff Batley arrests Jude Bartholomew for the killings and for setting the fire to destroy the evidence. He claims that the young sharecropper and Miss Charlotte are lovers and that the killings were not committed in an attempt to rescue Miss Charlotte but out of revenge. Charlotte claims the sheriff is a Klansman himself and set the fire to conceal his role in a Klan activity gone sour.

Robin Jaynes, the young attorney Charlotte hires to defend Jude finds it unthinkable that Miss Charlotte, a beautiful, older woman—a sophisticated and successful author—would have an affair with a young and simple farm hand. But she soon discovers the defendant is not so simple; she, too, finds him attractive. The entangled lives of Jude, Robin and Charlotte leave a trail of jealousy and suspense from Virginia to a small college town in New England.